RHYS STOOD THERE, WATCHING HER.

She crossed her arms over her chest, trying to hide herself. But she could tell from the smoldering glow of his eyes, he'd seen.

The burn of embarrassment mingled with the fire those intense eyes created inside her. She so wanted this man.

His gaze left her covered chest, and he held her eyes with his.

She shifted slightly under the hunger she saw there.

"Sorry," he said, his voice huskier than usual. "I thought I heard you calling me."

She stared at him. Well, her body had been calling him, but she didn't think her voice had. "I . . . No."

He nodded sharply. "Then I will leave you to your bath."

They stared at each other for a moment longer; then Rhys bowed slightly and left, pulling the door shut behind him.

This was impossible. It had taken every bit of her rational mind to not invite him to join her in the tub. What was wrong with her? She'd always been so practical, so reserved. Now she was acting like a wanton.

Novels by Kathy Love

Fangs for the Memories

Fangs But No Fangs

I Only Have Fangs for You

My Sister Is a Werewolf

Getting What You Want

Wanting What You Get

Wanting Something More

FANGS
FOR THE
MEMORIES

KATHY LOVE

BRAVA

KENSINGTON PUBLISHING CORP.

http://www.kensingtonbooks.com

BRAVA BOOKS are published by

Kensington Publishing Corp.
850 Third Avenue
New York, NY 10022

All Kensington titles, imprints and distributed lines are
available at special quantity discounts for bulk pur-
chases for sales promotion, premiums, fund-raising, ed-
ucational or institutional use.

Special book excerpts or customized printings can also
be created to fit specific needs. For details, write or
phone the office of the Kensington Special Sales Man-
ager: Kensington Publishing Corp., 850 Third Avenue,
New York, NY 10022. Attn. Special Sales Department.
Phone: 1-800-221-2647.

Brava and the B logo Reg. U.S. Pat. & TM Off.

ISBN-13: 978-0-7582-1132-3
ISBN-10: 0-7582-1132-5

First Trade Paperback Printing: September 2005
First Mass Market Paperback Printing: September 2007
10 9 8 7 6 5 4 3 2 1

Printed in the United States of America

For Kristen

Acknowledgments

Time for my long list of thank yous . . .

I want to first thank my editor, Kate Duffy,
who has once again taken a big chance on me.
Thank you so much, Kate!

Thank you to the Tarts.
I'll do better next time.
Really.

Thank you, Mom and Dad.
You help me more than you will ever know.

Thank you, Bill and Mary Ellen.

Thank you, Teresa, Gary and Megan.

Special thanks to Lisa, Julie and Treena—
for listening, plotting, sympathizing,
and telling me to get this darn thing done.

And another special thanks to Cindy,
Toni, Beth, Cat and Julie
for lots of encouraging e-mails and chats.

And all my love to Emily and Todd.
Especially to Em, you are a very patient two-year-old.
Mommy loves you.

Chapter 1

"Hey, baby, you lookin' for a little holiday cheer?"

Rhys paused on the sidewalk in front of a run-down bar and glanced over at two women leaning against the side of the building. They both smoked cigarettes, the smoke escaping their red lips, mingling with the steam of their breath in the icy night air. Their shabby winter coats were opened wide to reveal their thin bodies clad in skimpy, clinging dresses. One shivered, but still managed to shoot him a desperately inviting look.

And he thought he was having a shitty Christmas Eve.

"I'm looking for a drink," he told them, gesturing to the bar's door with a slight jerk of his head.

"Oh, come on, honey," the one who had voiced the invitation coaxed, "I've got some mistletoe right here." She threw down her cigarette, shoved away from the wall and waved a plastic sprig toward him.

It was imitation holly, but Rhys didn't see much point in mentioning that fact. "Sorry, no."

"Well, after you've had yer drink, gorgeous, I'll be waitin' for ya." She smiled, reaching out to trail the fake greenery down the lapel of his coat.

Rhys didn't respond and stepped past her to push open a windowless door sporting a tattered wreath. Before slipping into the smoky darkness of the bar, he stopped and looked back at the two prostitutes.

Even though they were young, if his senses were correct only in their late teens, they looked old, haggard. The reverse of him—with his youthful body and ancient existence.

On impulse, he reached into his pocket for his wallet.

The one closest to him watched his movement, the tip of her tongue running hungrily over the unnatural red of her lips. The one still against the wall stepped closer, her eyes also fastened to his movement, avarice burning in her dark eyes.

No, not the reverse, he realized. Not at all. They were truly just the same. Hunger ruling them, making them do things they never believed they would. The only difference was their bitterness was etched into their skin, where his was deceptively hidden, eating at his insides.

Rhys's hand stilled for a moment, but then he did pull out his money. He supposed he deserved to pay for feeling sympathy for these two. It must be that it was the season. He wouldn't let his hard-learned lessons slip his mind again.

He withdrew two bills. "Find a warm place to stay tonight."

The one near him snatched the money from his hand. Her eyes widened as she noted the denomination. "Thanks, mister." She immediately walked back to her coworker. "Come on, girlfriend. Let's go party!"

The two clacked away on worn high heels. Now that their need was satisfied, Rhys was forgotten.

Again, just like his kind, he thought tiredly. Getting what they crave, then moving on.

He entered the bar, and the door slammed shut behind him. He was immediately enfolded in a hazy, surreal glow of blue and red neon. He slid onto a stool at the end of the bar and ordered a scotch, neat.

"You want to run a tab, mister?"

Rhys nodded and took a deep swallow of the fiery liquor. Setting the glass down, he twisted, his back to the bar, to survey the room. The small place was quite busy. On Christmas Eve, no less.

He twisted back to his drink, staring into the amber liquid. He appeared oblivious to the rest of the room, but if anything, he was more aware of what was going on around him than when he'd been glancing around.

The two men a few stools away were regulars here. They drank whiskey and water and smoked filterless cigarettes. The one closest to him was complaining that his wife had left him. Of course, he didn't mention that he'd beaten her for years before she'd finally worked up the nerve to go.

The woman at the end of the bar wore cheap perfume and an abundance of AquaNet. She was waiting for someone—a lover. Rhys could practically taste the craving radiating from her. Although Rhys couldn't quite tell if the lust was for the man or for the drugs he would also provide.

The four men playing pool were friends and deep in their cups, celebrating. Not the holiday season but the fact that the one with the boyish face, which disguised a soul that was extremely dark, had just been released from prison. Out on good behavior, and looking to undo all that proper conduct.

These were the types that were in seedy bars on Christmas Eve—people without families or love or lives. The lost, the hungry, the violent.

And then there was him. So full of hunger, it almost crippled him.

He polished off the remainder of his drink and signaled to the bartender for a refill.

Drinking numbed him. Alcohol didn't affect him as it did normal people, but it did insulate him. It anesthetized his feelings and made him capable of living in his own skin. But ultimately, the liquor never did what he wanted it to do. It never killed that raging hunger— the hunger that constantly ate away at him. No, only one thing appeased that, and even then, it was nothing but a quick fix. A brief reprieve from the gnawing in his soul.

He nearly snorted out loud. His soul? Yeah, right, he'd lost that a long time ago.

The bartender returned with another drink. Rhys took a long swallow, closing his eyes to savor the smoky flavor, when a prickling danced over the back of his neck.

He shifted on the barstool, searching for the being that managed to so abruptly shift the foul hopelessness of the room.

She stood in the doorway, looking every inch of her five feet out of place. A tiny woman with pixielike, dark hair and huge eyes. Even in the distorting neon glow of the room, Rhys could tell they were green—a true green.

An innocent fey creature lost in a harsh, cold land. Rhys raised an eyebrow at his thoughts. There must be something in the air tonight; he was never so fanciful. Besides, he thought bitterly, *he* was the only otherworldly creature here.

He took another deep swallow of his drink, still watching her over the rim of his glass. The small woman glanced around, nervousness clear on her face. Then, to his surprise, she straightened her shoulders and headed to the bar.

She climbed onto the stool next to his and waited for the bartender to come take her order. Still, when he did, she took a moment to consider what she wanted.

Again she surprised Rhys by asking for a tequila shot, although there was a faint rise at the end of her request as though she wasn't quite sure if a tequila shot was a real drink.

Rhys pretended to focus on his scotch, but he continued to center his attention on her. Not only was she nervous, but she was miserable, filled with hurt and anger and . . . despair. But all those strong emotions couldn't overshadow her natural scent. She smelled fresh and sweet like flowers warmed by sunshine. He couldn't remember the last time he had smelled a mortal that untainted, that pure. Not an adult mortal anyway.

All too quickly, her fresh scent was overwhelmed by another smell, which couldn't be masked by the strong odor of stale beer and cigarette smoke. It swirled around each of the people like spun sugar—enticing, yet sickening to Rhys because of its sweet intensity.

He swallowed and concentrated on the woman's wholesomeness. He could suppress his reaction to the other scent, the smell of blood. He did all the time, but it was harder than usual tonight. It always was once he'd made up his mind that he would feed.

But he'd do that later—picking from the worst of the lot. It wouldn't be difficult tonight—many of the patrons here were so bad they were completely lost. Lost to redemption—just like him.

And then there was this woman. Why was she here? She certainly didn't belong here, but he didn't need preternatural abilities to tell that. She was dressed in a green wool skirt with matching blazer. The white blouse she wore underneath was simple and plain. Her leather pumps were sensible.

The outfit was modest and practical, but she looked far from dowdy. The skirt displayed her well-shaped calves and gave brief flashes of a little thigh. But it was her face that captivated Rhys. Not a classically beautiful face, but she had sweetness to her features, full lips, a small pert nose and those huge eyes. Her eyes alone were enough to hold him spellbound.

He frowned. No mortal in his two hundred years had held so much interest for him. He supposed it must be the fact that she was so obviously out of place that intrigued him. Or maybe because she reminded him of the place where he'd once come from—where people were good and kind and loved one another.

The bartender returned to her with the shot, a slice of lime in another shot glass and a shaker of salt.

The pixie stared at the objects with obvious confusion. She glanced around, her eyes stopping on him for a moment. She immediately looked away.

After another moment, she took the lime from the glass. She frowned at the segment, then started to squeeze it into the shot of liquor.

A masculine hand clasped hers, stopping her.

"Hi there," the boyish-faced ex-convict said. "Want me to show you how to do that?"

The pixie hesitated again, and Rhys sensed her wariness. Smart girl. But then she straightened and nodded. "Yes. Please."

The ex-convict raised a hand and called to the bartender for a shot for himself.

Rhys watched as the ex-convict demonstrated the proper way to do the shot. Lick, salt, lick, shot, then lime. The pixie mimicked him, except she sputtered and coughed around her slice of lime.

"Not bad," the man told her, once she'd stopped gagging. His eyes roamed over her, and Rhys could tell that the comment was as much about the woman herself as her drinking style.

The ex-convict's eyes lingered on her legs, and that suggestion of lovely thigh. Lust mixed with violence quivered just under the surface of his friendly good looks.

Rhys suppressed a wave of irritation—aimed as much toward the woman as the convict. Why was she here? She should be with her family in front of a twinkling Christmas tree, singing carols. Hell, what he wouldn't give to be with his family one more time.

The ex-convict snapped his fingers and requested two more shots.

Rhys shifted on his seat. He should step in. Instead he sipped his own drink. He remembered the prostitutes. He'd done his good deed for this year. With a few days to spare, even.

"Hey, Joey, you gonna spend the night scammin' on chicks, or are you going to hang with your boys?"

Joey gave the pixie a sheepish look. He was as deceptive and dangerous as any of Rhys's kind. "Sorry, I've got money on this game."

The woman nodded. "That's fine. Thanks for the instruction."

Joey's smile deepened; arousal laced with a cruelty flashed in his eyes. "No problem. And who knows, maybe you can show me a trick or two yourself sometime?"

"Okay," she agreed, completely missing the innuendo in his words.

Joey returned to his buddies, and Rhys made up his mind that the ex-convict would be his Christmas dinner.

The bartender arrived with the two shots Joey had ordered, placing them before the pixie.

She opened her mouth as if she was going to tell him to take the drinks back, but instead she sighed and then, almost reluctantly, licked the expanse of skin between her forefinger and thumb. She dashed a liberal amount of salt to the wetted area.

Rhys watched as her small, pink tongue reappeared and lapped over her skin, and for the first time in a long time, desire unrelated to *the hunger* shot through him.

She swallowed the shot, managing to down all the golden liquid with only a violent shudder as she reached for the lime.

Out of the corner of her eye, she noticed him staring at her. With the lime still in her mouth, she turned to frown at him. Her eyes showed only the briefest flash of wariness before she glared at him.

"What are you looking at?" she demanded, after she had plucked the citrus fruit out of her mouth.

His eyes moved from her lips, glistening with juice, and he shook his head. He returned his attention to his drink, although his body was still fixating on how that mouth would feel sucking on him.

What the hell had gotten into him tonight?

Jane Mary Harrison could not believe she had just yelled at a complete stranger. She'd never been that rude in her entire life. But then, she'd never been in a big city either. Or in a bar. Or done tequila shots. Oh, the difference a day makes.

And what a day she'd had. She'd been in New York City only one day, and in that time, she'd lost the job she'd just gotten, which in turn caused her to lose the apartment she had lined up. When she was leaving the realtor's office, some man had stolen her purse, and she'd had to spend nearly six hours in a police station with all sorts of frightening people, waiting to place a report with a very uninterested officer. If she was going to start doing tequila shots, this seemed like the time.

Today was supposed to be the beginning of her new, adventuresome and fun life. So far, it had been long on adventure, and very, very short on fun.

But she was determined to have a little fun tonight. It was Christmas Eve, for heavens sake. And, thankfully, she'd had the foresight to put traveler's checks in her suitcase, so she wasn't destitute—yet.

She looked at the one full and three empty shot glasses in front of her. Was she going to have to spend her precious money on four shots? Three of which she didn't order.

She sighed. Ah, well. At least Joey had been nice—the nicest person she'd met so far in the Big Apple. She glanced at him, leaning over the pool table, lining up a shot. He was sort of cute, too. And he'd flirted with her—at least, she thought he'd flirted.

Her eyes darted briefly to the man sitting beside her. He wasn't flirting with her. In fact, he'd done nothing but cast her cool looks since she entered the bar. And she would never describe him as cute. She'd be willing to bet that cute wasn't even used to describe him as a child. No, he was stunningly, dauntingly beautiful. She couldn't recall ever seeing anyone that—perfect.

He had long hair that just brushed his broad shoulders. She'd never been that crazy about long hair, but on this man, it looked amazing. Glossy and thick in shades of sable threaded with burnished gold.

In profile, she could see the cut of his jawline, the wide, sculpted shape of his lips and slight arrogant flare of his nose. But it had been his peculiar eyes like whiskey in flickering firelight that had taken her breath away. They were so beautiful, so intense—almost predatory.

He was gorgeous.

She cast him another furtive look. In his black turtleneck sweater and black trousers, he didn't seem to fit in here any more than she did, although not for the same reasons. He looked too affluent for a place like this. Too cultured. But under all that beauty and urbaneness, she still sensed something dangerous about him— that feral quality that lurked in his strange eyes.

She snorted quietly. The stress of today must be addling her mind. She was sure the only thing this man would be dangerous to was the female heart. With those looks, he was the definition of a heartbreaker.

She regarded the full shot glass in front of her. Her throat still burned, but she was starting to feel a nice, soothing heat in her limbs. Who would think such a small amount of that stuff could make her feel so much more relaxed. And after the day she'd had, she needed to relax.

She reached for the salt shaker.

The third shot went down so smoothly, she grinned with pride. For a nondrinker, she was a pro.

She lined the glasses up in front of her and tried to decide what to do next. She didn't want to go back to her hotel. But she didn't exactly feel comfortable here.

Plus, she kept having this uncontrollable urge to look at the man beside her. She shifted on her stool, peeking at him quickly. Maybe she should apologize to him.

"Oh, baby"—Joey suddenly reappeared at her side, startling her—"you drank my shot."

She looked at the empty glasses guiltily. "I did. I'm sorry."

"Well, I guess we just have to order another round."

"Don't you think you've had enough?" a deep, husky voice said from beside her.

She blinked up at the beautiful stranger. He leaned toward her, those peculiar eyes burning into hers.

"Why don't you mind your own business, buddy," Joey said, irritated. Then his voice became soft, cajoling, as he asked her, "You aren't going to let this jerk ruin our fun, are you, baby?"

Jane tore her gaze from the beautiful stranger to look at Joey. "No," she said, although she knew her response sounded more than a little unsure.

Suddenly loud music began to play, and Jane noticed a blond woman adding money to a jukebox in the corner. Between the two men looming over her, the sudden thumping beat of the music and the alcohol coursing through her, her head began to spin.

"Can I get two tequilas down here," Joey called to the bartender.

Jane stood, her legs unstable. The beautiful stranger caught her arm and steadied her. His hand was strong and felt good, even through her blazer. Her head swam.

"Are you okay?" he asked.

She nodded, taking a deep breath. "I think I just need a little fresh air."

He started to stand, when Joey caught her other arm. "Baby, let me take you outside."

Jane looked at the beautiful stranger. His hand still held her arm, his strength clear even in the gentle hold. His eyes blazed with something she couldn't quite read, but she did know that she needed to get away from his touch. It was doing crazy things to her insides.

She tugged her arm free from him and allowed Joey to lead her to the door.

Right before she stepped outside, she glanced over her shoulder. The beautiful stranger watched her with those predatory eyes.

Chapter 2

The chill of the winter air on her face and in her lungs immediately made Jane feel less light-headed. She closed her eyes and lifted her head toward the sky. After another couple deep breaths, she felt almost normal.

"That better?" Joey asked, standing close to her.

She opened her eyes and smiled at him gratefully. "Yes. I don't usually drink."

He left her side and peered down the alley that ran along the side of the bar. "There's some stairs down this way. Why don't we sit for a few?"

Jane wandered over to him, following his gaze. The alley was a long, dark tunnel except for one dim light-bulb in the center illuminating a set of concrete stairs. Trash cans stood beside the stairs, open, spilling over with garbage.

"I think maybe I should just head back to my hotel," she decided.

"Hotel?"

She nodded. "Yes, just got here yesterday afternoon."

He gave her a disbelieving look. "That's crazy. I just got here yesterday, too. I used to live here, but I've been away."

She smiled.

"Come on. Come sit for a few minutes."

She hesitated, but his smile was so charming, she finally agreed.

The cement steps were cold and mottled with stains of God knew what. Jane opted to lean against the wall. Joey didn't seem to have the same qualms about the stairs.

They were quiet for a few seconds.

"So where did you live before you came back here?" Jane asked.

"A place in Jersey."

"Oh, I've never been to New Jersey."

He stood up, shoved his hands into his jeans pockets and kicked an empty can down the alley. The metallic sound echoed off the concrete walls surrounding them. "I can't say I was too fond of it. My life there was really— confining."

Jane could understand that. "I grew up in Maine, which is a beautiful state, but the town I grew up in was too small, too suffocating. People got labeled at a young age, and they could never escape that label. Never."

Joey walked toward her, and for the first time, she realized he was rather big. His boyish face gave the impression he would be thin, lanky, but he was actually quite broad and muscular.

"Now, you see, I get that. I've been labeled myself." He stepped closer, stopping only inches from her. "You know, baby, you are really a pretty lady."

"No," she denied, her skin heating even in the cold.

Even though she didn't know Joey, the flattery was nice. She'd never had a man say that to her.

"I haven't seen a lady as pretty as you for a long time."

Again the flattery made her chest swell. She didn't quite believe him, but the words were nice to hear.

He stepped a little closer—still not touching her but making it clear he wanted to.

She liked his compliments, but she wasn't willing to kiss him. She didn't know him. And she just wasn't the type of woman to do such a thing.

Then again she was in New York City to start a new life. To find some excitement.

Was she really considering kissing a stranger? No. Then the beautiful stranger popped into her head. Would she kiss him?

What was she thinking? She must be drunk. She giggled.

"What?" Joey asked, leaning a hand on the wall so that if Jane moved she'd brush against him.

She sobered. She didn't want to give him the impression she was interested. She shifted down the wall a bit.

"I was just thinking what a crazy day I've had." Maybe if she kept talking, he'd get the idea.

"Oh, yeah?" He moved toward her again.

She swallowed. Maybe she should just leave. Something in his eyes suddenly made her nervous.

"What happened?" he asked, and she decided it was possible she was just being paranoid. She told him about her job and apartment and then her hours in the police station.

"Man, I hate police stations. I've spent way too much time there myself."

"Really?"

He nodded. He stepped closer, and his hand came up to hold her waist, then slid down to cup her derriere.

She jumped, and he chuckled. "Skittish, eh?"

She swallowed. She was in way over her head. She didn't know how to handle alcohol or men or life in the city. All she knew how to deal with was grieving families and funeral arrangements. *And not one of the funeral mourners had ever touched her bottom!*

"I think I may have given you the wrong idea. I think I should go back inside."

He didn't remove his hand. "Oh, no, baby, you have been giving me all kinds of good ideas."

His fingers pulled at the hem of her skirt.

Panic stole her breath, but she forced herself to breathe, to stay calm.

"You—you know I really do have to get inside. That guy beside me at the bar—he's my boyfriend. I—I was just trying to make him jealous." She was grasping at straws, but it was all she could think of at the time.

Relief trickled through her as his fingers paused. But then he shrugged. "Baby, if he was worried about you, he wouldn't have let you leave with me."

His mouth came down roughly on hers.

She struggled, pushing at his chest, and he broke off the kiss, but used his free hand to grip her neck in a choking lock, shoving her hard against the wall.

Her mouth gaped open, but no sound came out and no air in. She was going to die.

Just then his hold relaxed slightly, and she managed to struggle in a hitched breath.

"Now, listen, baby." His voice was hard and his boyish features contoured. "I ain't had a woman in three years.

So I don't care if it's all nice and friendly or if it's rough. Cuz either way, I plan to fuck you."

Black spots started to appear before her eyes. She couldn't pass out. She didn't think that would stop this guy.

The hand at her hemline moved to the front of her skirt and pulled it upward.

She had to keep him talking. Buy a little time.

"Thr-three years is a long time." Her voice didn't even sound like her own, breathy and shaking.

He grunted. "Ain't too many women in the pen."

It took her terrified brain a moment to grasp what he meant. This guy had been in prison! Fear shot through her. He might have done this before. He might have killed.

But she rallied her willpower, forcing herself to stay as calm as possible. "What—what did you serve time for?"

"This and that. All just labels. Unfairly given," he assured her with a grin, his boyish smile now sinister.

She swallowed, struggling for another shallow breath. "That is terrible."

"Well, I'm thinking what you've got under this skirt will go a long way to making me feel a whole lot better." He had her skirt up around her waist, and again black spots flashed in front of her eyes. She was going to pass out. She closed her eyes and fought for air.

All of a sudden, Joey's bruising grip was gone, and she was able to pull in a deep, lung-filling breath.

She opened her eyes. Joey wasn't there, but she didn't look around to see where he was. She ran, not seeing, just knowing she had to get back to the street, to the bar. Suddenly, she slammed into something solid, immovable.

Arms closed around her, and she screamed.

"Shh," a deep, husky voice said. "It's okay."

She blinked up to see the beautiful stranger holding her. She sank against him, allowing him to support most of her weight. Relief churned with nausea in her stomach.

Suddenly he swung her up into his arms, turned and walked out of the alley. Once on the street, he stopped, but he still held her.

"Are you okay?"

Jane nodded, but didn't speak. Her heart still pounded painfully in her chest while her breath came in ragged bursts.

He continued to hold her against his broad chest. His arms feeling so solid, so safe.

Finally, she calmed and realized that she must be getting heavy. "I'm okay to stand."

He seemed almost reluctant to let her go, but he did lower her to her feet. Although he kept an arm at her waist as if he thought she might faint.

She wouldn't—she didn't think.

"Thank you. I—I can't even think about what would have happened if you hadn't stopped him."

He nodded slightly, but didn't say anything. He stared down at her, those amber eyes unreadable. After a few moments, he shrugged out of the expensive leather jacket he wore. "Here, put this on."

She shook her head. "I have my blazer. I'm fine."

He shoved it toward her. "I'll be fine, too. Put it on."

His gruff kindness touched her. And she'd thought that boyish Joey was the nicer of the two.

She accepted the coat, pulling it on, and was shrouded in cold leather. She shivered. Strange that it would be so cold given that it had just been on his large body.

"Do you live around here?" he asked.

"Yes, I'm at a hotel a few blocks from here."

He nodded. "I'll walk you there."

She smiled gratefully, but then the smile slipped as she cast a wary look down the alley.

As if reading her thoughts, the stranger said, "He's long gone. The coward."

She glanced into the dark tunnel once more, then gestured down the street. "It's this way."

Before Rhys fell into step beside the little mortal, he concentrated. The ex-convict coward was still in the alley-way, unconscious. He lifted his head and breathed in deeply to commit the coward's scent to memory, so if the man should rouse and run, Rhys would be able to find him. He meant to make a meal of that one as much for the pixie as for himself.

But the pixie's sweet, brilliant scent kept overwhelming the coward's tainted stink. He'd never known any mortal's scent to be as strong and alluring as hers.

Then her voice as well as her smell distracted him. "Is everything okay?"

He inhaled once more, fairly certain he would be able to track the ex-con if he fled. He turned to her.

She stared up at him, her pale skin lustrous in the streetlight. Her eyes wide, concern clear in their green depths.

Again the sweetness of her amazing scent filled the air. This mortal was truly good. Unbelievable.

He cleared his throat and answered her more gruffly than he intended. "Yes. You said your hotel was this way?" He pointed in the same direction she just had.

She nodded.

They headed down the cracked concrete.

Maybe it had been her genuine goodness that had allowed Rhys to sense that the pixie was in trouble. He'd still been sitting at the bar when all of a sudden the whole room had been flooded with her smell. But it wasn't the same scent as when she'd first arrived. It had been flowery and warm—but there had been a sharp undertone to it. Then all her emotions were clear to him. Desperation, terror, pain.

That had never happened to him before. He'd never been able to read the emotions of a mortal not near him. In fact, the only one he could connect with across any distance was his brother, Sebastian. And he was a vampire, too.

He glanced at her again. With his black coat wrapped around her, the pixie did look a bit like a child dressed up as a vampire for Halloween. But she wasn't. And he should have no connection with her.

But he had.

"I had been just about to apologize to you when that guy showed up again."

Rhys frowned, confused by her sudden announcement. "Apologize?"

She nodded, not looking at him, but watching the sidewalk in front of them. "For being so rude to you."

"Rude?"

She glanced up at him. "I yelled at you."

She did?

"I asked you what you were looking at," she clarified.

He shook his head, and felt a wry smile tugging at the corner of his mouth. "That wasn't yelling. In this city, that was just a typical greeting."

The pixie laughed slightly, but it broke off into a strangled sob. She stopped, holding her hands over her face. Her shoulders shook.

Rhys stood beside her, listening to the heart-wrenching crying, feeling her awful distress. The pain of it in his own chest almost crushed him. He found he wanted to comfort her, but he didn't know how to do that. He hadn't consoled anyone in—so long. But cautiously, he touched her shoulder.

"Shh, it's okay."

She swiped at her face, obviously irritated with herself for falling apart. "I'm sorry." She forced a shaky smile at him. "This was supposed to be a new beginning. I sold everything I own, my house, the family business, everything, to start this great, new life. But after today, I'm thinking I made a big mistake."

He didn't know what to say. She was talking about life, and he didn't have one of those. "Maybe tomorrow will be better," he offered lamely.

She stared at him for a moment. Then a genuine laugh escaped her, even though she did hiccup slightly at the end of it. She rose up on her tiptoes and flung her arms around his neck. She pressed her warm, soft lips to his cheek.

If his heart were beating, it would have stopped. When was the last time he'd felt the warmth of a human's embrace, the tenderness of a kind touch. But it wasn't tenderness that he felt in return. Not even close. Raging, searing hot desire ripped through his icy body.

He wanted this woman. He wanted to sink into her heat. Devour her. Making her scream for him. And he wasn't talking about with his fangs. Although he couldn't imagine what it would be like to taste her as she orgasmed for him.

His cock spiked and his fangs unsheathed.

Roughly, he disengaged her arms from around his neck and set her away from him.

"I'm sorry," she said, although she couldn't quite keep the wounded look from her eyes.

He quickly ran his tongue along his teeth to make sure his fangs had receded. "No, I just . . . " What could he say? *I didn't want to either screw you or bite you or both right here on the sidewalk.* "I just don't want you to think I'm like that coward back there."

She smiled, then shook her head. "I'd never think you were like that guy. That man is a violent monster. You saved me."

Damn, if she knew the truth about him. She'd run so fast.

"We better keep walking." He had to get away from her. He had to put distance between them and sever this connection he felt with her. He didn't understand it, but he knew it was dangerous. Any association with a mortal could only bring them both pain. That's why he'd worked so hard to stay away from them, except the ones as empty as he was.

She looked around nervously and matched her steps to his rapid pace.

Her hotel was a nondescript building, square and run-down with tread-worn carpeting and shabby sofas in the small lobby.

She followed his gaze. "I was only supposed to be staying here a couple days. Now I might have to stay a little longer." When she saw his deepening frown, she added, "It shouldn't be longer than a week or so."

He nodded, but he hated to leave her here. Still, she was safer here than with him. He didn't think he could keep looking into those green eyes of hers and not touch her. His longing for her appeared to be growing by the second. And although it was lust, the feeling seemed to be laced with something else. A craving for warmth, and caring, and affection. All things that were dangerous for him to want.

"Okay, well, good luck," he said.

The slight curve of her lips was more a forlorn grimace than an actual smile. "Well, like you said, things will probably get better tomorrow."

She waved at him and started toward the rumbling, creaking elevator. She stopped.

He felt a wave of anticipation. Maybe she would return and touch him once more. There couldn't be any harm in that since he'd never see her again.

"I almost forgot." She shrugged out of his coat and held it out to him. "Your coat."

He stepped forward and took it from her.

"What is your name?"

The sudden question took him by surprise for a moment. "Rhys. Rhys Young." The irony wasn't lost on him.

She smiled. "Thank you, Rhys Young."

He nodded, but just as she stepped onto the rickety elevator, he called out, "Hey, what's your name?"

"Jane Harrison."

Suddenly the elevator's silver doors started to shut. Jane put out a hand to stop them; the ancient machine did not respond. He heard her good-bye before the doors muffled her voice completely.

"Good-bye, Jane Harrison." He wished he hadn't asked for her name. It would be so much easier to forget her if he didn't have a name.

Chapter 3

Jane closed her door, bolted the main lock as well as slipping the chain lock into place. Then she rushed around the double bed to the dingy windows, pulling back the coarse beige curtain. She caught a glimpse of Rhys just as he disappeared around the street corner.

She sighed and closed the curtains. Tonight had been a nightmare, yet she didn't feel nearly as shaken as she should. Her limbs were weak, and her heart seemed to be beating a little out of rhythm, but she wasn't sure whether that was residual fear or the overwhelming attraction she felt for Rhys.

This is stupid. She'd just been attacked, nearly raped. Possibly killed. And she was thinking about Rhys, although he had been her hero. And it was much nicer to think about him than what might have happened if he hadn't been there.

Maybe that was why she felt so attracted to him. Wasn't there a name for this kind of thing? Hero worship?

Of course, any woman in her right mind would be attracted to him. Beautiful men like Rhys didn't happen along every day. Still, she'd never been the type to become instantly enthralled with a man. Then again, her life had never really allowed room for crushes.

She unbuttoned her blazer and dropped it on the bed. She kicked off her pumps and padded into the bathroom. She needed a hot shower. Maybe that would make her feel more normal.

She turned on the water, then crossed to the mirror over the sink. Just as with everything else in the room, it was old and discolored. But Jane could see herself well enough.

Her lower lip appeared a little swollen from being kissed so roughly. Her complexion was paler than usual, but overall, she looked relatively unscathed.

She patted her ruffled hair and felt a twinge of pain on the back of her head. She gently fingered the spot and found a small lump there, probably where her head had hit the concrete wall when that jerk had choked her. Not bad, though. It certainly could have been a lot worse.

She started to unbutton her blouse and noticed redness around her throat. She pulled back her collar, examining it closer. Mostly just irritation, it probably wouldn't even bruise.

She finished undoing her shirt and tossed it out onto the bed with her blazer. The mark had probably been made by the chain of her necklace being ground into her skin as he'd throttled her.

She tested the shower's water temperature, when she stopped. She returned to the mirror, wiping the steam off the glass.

Her necklace was gone.

"Oh, no." She touched her neck as if the gold chain had to still be there, and she just couldn't see it. No, it was gone.

She sat down on the closed toilet seat. Tears filled her eyes. This was truly the last straw of an awful, awful day. The necklace held the wedding rings of her parents, and she wore it always—a small way to keep her parents close to her.

The chain must have broken when that man was strangling her. She ran out to look around the bed, hoping the chain had gotten stuck in her clothing. Nothing. No necklace. No rings.

She checked the bathroom mirror again, examining her neck. The marks definitely looked like abrasion created by a chain.

It had to have fallen off between here and the bar.

She debated for a minute. She should wait until morning, then go search. But if the rings fell off on the sidewalk, anyone could find them between now and then.

She couldn't wait. She didn't want to ever go near that bar again, but she had to. She had to find those rings.

She turned off the shower and hurried to throw back on her blouse and blazer. She added her heavy winter coat and sneakers.

She unlatched the chain lock, then paused. What if Joey was still hanging around the bar?

She rushed to the bathroom and dug through her toiletry bag. Finding a travel-size aerosol hair spray, she shoved the can in her coat pocket. It wasn't mace, but she'd bet it would work in a pinch.

* * *

Rhys walked into the dark alley. The coward was still there. Still unconscious. He hoped he could rouse him, because he wanted that asshole to experience the same fear Jane had. Except no one was going to save him.

Rhys found him exactly where he'd dropped him. He hadn't even changed positions. Rhys leaned over to capture the inert man by the jacket, when a flash on the ground caught his attention. He released the man and reached past his shoulder to pick up the sparkling item. It was a delicate gold chain. The clasp was broken, but two rings still dangled from the thin metal.

The gold was warm in his hand. He lifted it up to his nose, already knowing what he would discover. The necklace belonged to Jane. He could smell her, and he had no idea how or why, but the touch of the inanimate object warmed him, literally to the bone, as though she was hugging him.

He stared at the rings in his palm for a moment. Was she married? Had she been married? What would it be like to have someone that sweet, that lovely, in his life every day?

He ground his teeth. Stop! There was no point. No point wondering. But he shoved the necklace in his jacket pocket anyway.

He returned his attention to the lifeless man. He grasped him and lifted him fully off the ground. He shook him like a rag doll, and the man groaned to life.

Joey was disoriented for only a moment. Then he saw Rhys. His eyes bulged, and he opened his mouth to speak, or more likely scream.

Rhys shifted himself around and slammed the man hard against the concrete wall. The man moaned.

"How does it feel to get a taste of your own medicine, my friend?"

"Wh-what are you?"

Rhys smiled, knowing the wide curl of his lips would fully reveal his two long, very sharp canines. "I'm the one who is going to speed up your arrival in hell."

Rhys yanked Joey to him and sank his teeth deep into the ex-convict's neck. Blood coursed through Rhys, but he didn't taste it, didn't savor it. He thought about Jane's sweet scent and those innocent green eyes. He thought about the tenderness of her touch. And he thought about his desire for her.

The coward struggled for only a few seconds, then fell limp.

Rhys didn't kill the mortals he fed from. Even though he used only the dishonest and depraved as his food source, he didn't believe he, a beast himself, had the right to act as their judge and jury.

Tonight, he planned to let that belief slip his mind.

But at the last moment, when the man's heart would cease to beat, he pulled away. As full of rage as he was at this man, who dared to injure someone as true and kind as Jane, he couldn't kill him.

He dropped the coward to the ground and stepped back from him. Rhys wiped the back of his hand across his mouth, disgusted with the man, disgusted with himself.

"My, my, my. Isn't this a scene?"

The smooth, cultured voice startled Rhys. He spun around. Only a vampire could sneak up on another vampire.

"Hello, Rhys."

Rhys didn't speak for a moment. He couldn't. Shock mingled with the warmth of the blood in his veins.

"Christian?" He knew he was looking at his brother,

but he couldn't believe it. He hadn't seen his middle brother in—over a hundred years.

"Yes."

Rhys started to cross to him, to pull him into a fierce hug, but his brother's words stopped him.

"You still can't kill, can you? At least not a pathetic mortal."

Rhys frowned, letting his arms fall loosely to his sides. "What?"

Christian strolled to the once more unconscious man. He peered down at him with a slight grimace tugging at his lips, then turned back to Rhys.

"I just came to tell you, and I'm sure you will be pleased, Lilah is well and truly dead."

Rhys wasn't pleased. He hated Lilah, but he knew how her death would affect Christian. Christian had loved the vampiress with his whole existence. If vampires could truly love.

"Christian, I'm sorry."

His brother laughed humorlessly. "Are you? Are you really?"

"I know how you felt about her."

"Mmm." Christian nodded, moving to slowly pace around Rhys. "And you knew how I felt about her when you went to her bed, too. You knew how I felt about her when you allowed her to bring you over. I would imagine you even knew how I felt about her when you drained her, over and over, until she was nothing but a mad little vampiress—made insane by being brought to the point of death too many times."

It was on the tip of Rhys's tongue to point out it was hardly his fault that Lilah had a proclivity for a vampire's version of auto-eroticism. The observation would only serve to hurt Christian and make his brother further believe that Rhys had truly wanted Lilah. He'd wanted Lilah only once. After that, he knew her for what she was—a greedy, selfish, violent vampire.

He'd tried to make Christian realize that what he'd done, he'd done as retribution for the way she'd hurt his family, for cursing them. Lilah had needed to pay.

Christian had never believed him—about any of it. But Rhys felt the need to tell him again. To do otherwise would be like relenting that Christian was right.

"Christian, I never meant to hurt you. I meant to punish Lilah—for you, and Sebastian and especially for Elizabeth. For destroying our family."

"Yes, so you've told me."

"It's the truth."

"No, the truth is Elizabeth had consumption. She was too weak to cross over."

Rhys couldn't believe Christian still accepted Lilah's lie. Lilah had killed their baby sister out of spite, out of petty anger for not getting what she wanted—Rhys.

"You can keep believing what you want, Chris. But I am the one telling you the truth. I always have."

Christian finished circling around Rhys and stopped directly in front of him. "Well, I suppose it doesn't matter now. Lilah's gone."

Rhys nodded, hoping maybe now that she was gone, they could mend their badly severed relationship.

Christian started back down the alley toward the street.

Rhys took a few steps after him. "Do you think we will ever be able to end this?"

His brother turned, and cocked his head as if he was considering the question. "Yes, I think we can end it tonight." And with that Christian flew toward him, so quickly his movement was almost invisible.

Rhys didn't even have time to brace himself for the hit, before he found himself slammed against the side of the building. Bits of concrete rained to the ground around them.

Rhys dug at the hands at his throat, but Christian held him there with little difficulty.

Rhys knew that under regular circumstances he and Christian were about the same strength—created by the same vampire at nearly the same time. But tonight, Christian had anger on his side, blind fury that could make him extraordinarily strong for a brief time.

Rhys clawed at his brother's hands.

Christian stared at him, his eyes black, the entire irises and nearly all of the whites gone. Nothing but an empty blackness.

"I should have done this a hundred and eighty-five years ago." Christian's voice sounded deeper, harsher, like the growl of an animal.

As Rhys still struggled, his brother went for his throat, ripping into the flesh, taking half his throat in the first bite.

Despite the savageness of the attack, Rhys felt no pain. He continued to struggle—until Christian bit him again on the other side of his neck, and Rhys felt the blood and energy being sucked from him.

Christian didn't intend to simply teach him a lesson, to show his strength or humiliate Rhys.

No, Rhys thought as he began to fade into oblivion, his once much-loved brother intended to kill him.

* * *

Jane shifted from one foot to the other and chewed at the corner of her nail. She'd carefully searched the sidewalk and even the gutters, but she hadn't found the rings.

Now she was back at the bar, and her nerve was waning. She hadn't even worked up the nerve to get close to the bar's front entrance, much less the alleyway.

She tugged at her nail a moment longer, then dropped her hand to her side and straightened her shoulders. She had to look. She'd never forgive herself if she lost her parents' rings because she was scared. She'd come this far. But just to make herself feel better, she slipped her hand in her coat pocket and pulled out the cylinder of hair spray. With the small can held out in front of her, she approached the bar, scanning the ground as she went.

When she reached the entrance of the bar, she heard a sound. She froze and clutched the hair spray tighter.

There it was again. The sound of someone gagging—no, gasping.

Her heart clattered against her breastbone, and she held her breath. The sound came from the alleyway.

She considered turning and running, but her feet were paralyzed.

Another gasp, and the faint sound of a struggle.

She pulled in a slow, quiet breath, sure the person or persons in the alley would hear her.

Another wheezing gasp, which Jane was fairly certain didn't come from her, then silence.

Jane tilted her head, listening. Somehow the silence was now more unnerving than the scuffle and the strained breathing. Silence might mean whoever was in there struggling was now unconscious or—dead.

What if Joey was attacking another woman? She couldn't live with herself if she just stood by and listened while another woman was getting hurt.

But maybe it wasn't anything. Maybe she'd been hearing things. Her stressed, overactive imagination playing tricks on her.

She looked around. The street was deserted. And the bar was dark. She had no idea what time it was, but it had to be late.

Taking another steadying breath, she repositioned the hair spray in front of her. Cautiously, she crept to the alleyway. Clinging to the side of the building, she peeked around the corner.

The alley appeared empty. Nothing but blackness and that small, dim bulb burning over the back steps. Relief washed through her, and she sagged against the wall.

Then she saw it, just a faint movement, the shift of shadows, and a man's face appeared.

She peered harder. Not just any man's face. Rhys's face. His head hung to the side at an unnatural angle, and his eyes were closed.

The shadows shifted again, and she realized that there was another man in the alley. He looked toward her, but she couldn't quite make out his features, the light only illuminating his profile. But from his height and his width, he couldn't be Joey.

The shadowed man released Rhys. Rhys crumpled to the ground.

Jane stared at his downed form, sickness welling in

her belly. Rhys had to be all right. But she had a terrible feeling he wasn't.

"Well, silly mortal, this is what they call, 'being in the wrong place at the wrong time.'"

Jane blinked. The man who had been beside Rhys was now directly in front of her. Had she been focusing on Rhys so intently that she didn't notice the other man moving toward her?

"Wh—what did you do to Rhys?"

He took another step closer. The streetlight illuminated his face.

Despite her fear, Jane couldn't help but notice he was breathtakingly handsome with dark blond hair, streaked with gold, and pale eyes.

"So you know Rhys? Very interesting. I didn't think he mingled with mortals—at least not pretty, little, pure ones."

She shook her head slightly. Why did he keep referring to her as a mortal? Was this street lingo of some sort? Lingo meaning that she was mortal, thus capable of dying?

Before she could even think to move away from him, his hand snaked out and caught her wrist. She tugged and dug her heels into the pavement, but it was useless. He hauled her into the alley as easily as if she were held by a steel manacle.

"Let's go see what is wrong with Rhys," he said, almost cheerfully.

He dragged her up to Rhys's prone body. Rhys's head was still at an awkward angle, and now, Jane could see why. Thick blood glistened on his neck, and she could see his throat had literally been ripped open.

She put her free hand up to cover her mouth. Not that her trembling fingers could suppress her scream or the bile rising up the back of her throat.

The man, still clasping her, laughed.

She sank to her knees, both in horror and distress, but he jerked her back up and spun her to face him. Her shoulder throbbed, but she barely registered the pain.

"Unfortunately, now that you have seen my brother, well," he said with a regretful tilt of his head, "I can't let you go."

And just like that, the man's features changed. At first, Jane thought the distortion had to be a trick of the dim light. Or the terrible fear wracking her body.

Then he smiled, and she saw the light glint off his long, razor-sharp teeth. This had to be a nightmare, but she knew it was real. She didn't know what he was, but he was real. And he really meant to kill her.

She screamed again. And again, he laughed.

She began yanking frantically, trying to break his unyielding hold. That was when she realized she still held the small hair spray can in her captured hand.

As the monster's head lowered toward her, those vicious teeth coming closer, Jane grabbed the can with her other hand and sprayed a steam of Extra Firm Hold directly in his eyes.

He cried out, the sound eerie and keening like a wounded animal. He released her as his hands went to his face.

Jane didn't waste a moment. She turned and ran. But she never even made it to the street. Blackness encompassed her, and she dropped to the ground like a bug sprayed by Raid.

* * *

Sebastian stood over his wounded brother. Rhys looked as though he'd been gored by a wild animal. But Sebastian could tell by the bite marks that it had been a vampire attack. He couldn't detect the identity of the vamp, however. The vampire had used a masking hex to cover his or her tracks.

Sebastian knelt down, holding a palm over Rhys's chest. He'd already checked once, but he felt the need to check again. Just to be sure.

He felt faint waves of energy radiating from his motionless chest. Rhys would be okay, but it was a close call.

Sebastian wiped a hand over his face, still shaken. He'd been back at his nightclub, having a lovely dinner with a delightful mortal, who not only happened to enjoy a nice meal, but also loved being a meal as well, when he'd sensed Rhys's pain.

No, he hadn't just sensed the pain. He had experienced it. He pressed a hand to his neck. The throbbing was still there, but not as intense as it had been.

He and Rhys had always had a connection. Blood-related vampires often did—but he'd never received a contact that vivid before. And it was probably a good thing it had been that powerful. He'd sped to Rhys—and likely saved him.

He glanced at the male mortal near Rhys. He could tell Rhys had fed off him. But the feeding was not Rhys's usual style. He didn't usually drain them quite so much. The man would live, but he was going to be a hurting unit for a while.

Sebastian stood and walked over to the mortal woman

lying facedown in the middle of the alley. She was unconscious and unhurt. He could sense a memory hex around her. Probably the other vampire had cleared her memory, so she wouldn't recall what happened here tonight. But what shocked Sebastian as much as anything was the scent of Rhys all over this woman.

Rhys wouldn't normally interact with a wholesome mortal like this one. But Sebastian could smell not only Rhys's scent, but also his desire heavy on her skin.

What the hell happened in this alley tonight? And he thought he'd been having an exciting Christmas Eve.

He bent and scooped up the female, hefting her onto his shoulder. Then he returned to his brother and balanced him on the other shoulder.

It was times like this when being able to shift into shadows really came in handy. Wandering through the streets with a couple of unconscious people slung on your shoulders tended to raise a few eyebrows. Even in New York.

Christian stood on the roof of the bar, peering down at his baby brother as he lifted Rhys and the female mortal and dissolved into shadow.

Christian gritted his teeth. That may have been the only chance he'd ever have to kill his older brother, and that stupid mortal had ruined it. Rhys would never be caught off guard again, and Christian couldn't take him without the element of surprise.

He looked at the sky. The sun would be up soon. The sun that had killed Lilah.

No, Rhys killed Lilah. It had just taken him a hundred years to make it happen. For Lilah to finally give up—and end her own existence. She'd risen from their bed and walked out into the blazing noonday sun.

He didn't know how, but Christian would make Rhys pay. He'd been patient this long. He could be patient as long as it took.

Chapter 4

Rhys stretched. Damn, his muscles ached.

Had he been working with one of his horses yesterday? His groggy, sleep-filled mind could not seem to recall.

He supposed it did not really matter. He'd just stay in bed where it was nice and warm. With this nice and warm . . .

Rhys sat upright and looked down at the woman sharing his bed.

Ah, so this was why his body felt so tired. Although he did not recall bedding a woman last night. Had he been foxed? Had he and Christian gone on one of their wild sojourns to the gaming hells?

He frowned. Was this woman a lightskirt? He made it a practice to never bring whores back to his home. His sister, Elizabeth, was only seventeen. Plus, that was just bad show.

He turned his attention back to the woman beside him. She did not look like any of the whores he'd known. Her face was turned slightly away from him, but he could still tell she wore no rouge on her lips, nor any of the other paint they put so liberally all over their faces.

He tilted his head and cocked his eyebrow, studying her shiny dark hair, her tiny hands with smooth skin and tidy, short nails. A fresh, clean scent seemed to encompass her.

She was also far too clean to be a whore.

So who was she?

He hesitated for a moment, then lifted the covers. His breath caught in his throat.

The woman was naked except for three pale pink triangles, two of which barely covered her small, but nicely rounded breasts and the third covered between her legs. He could see the hint of dark curls through the translucent material.

Perhaps she was indeed a whore. And from the look and smell of her, he must have paid a very pretty penny for her.

Damn, Christian! His brother was supposed to make sure he did not do such decadent things.

Wait. The reason he must be so hazy on the previous night had to be because he had been out celebrating his upcoming nuptials. Or rather trying to forget them.

Betrothed to a savage American. He looked back at the lovely creature beside him. He certainly deserved a fine memory such as this to warm him at night when he was lying unsatisfied beside his beefy, American wife.

And this little tart was truly beautiful.

He reached out and touched her breast, teasing the shadow of her nipple through the thin material of her naughty little costume. Her nipple hardened instantly, poking greedily at his fingers.

He smiled. She was delightful.

He ducked his head and lapped the hard pebble, then suckled. He moved to the other nipple, drawing it deep into his mouth.

She twisted her head against the pillow, a whispery breath escaping her lips.

He sat back and admired his handiwork, loving the look of her pointy nipples and rosy areolas now visible through the moist material. This costume was quite a boon.

He looked back up at her face. She now faced him, and he was struck by the sweetness of her. Her full lips and rounded cheeks made her look almost angelic. How unfair that he couldn't just keep her. But he supposed he could, mistresses were common enough. He had just never considered he would have to take one. He had always assumed he would have a happy marriage like his parents. Of course, he could blame those same parents for his current predicament. An American! Damnation! But he would marry the woman out of respect for his parents. And respect to their memory.

Well, he could dwell on that or he could concentrate on—other things.

His gaze returned to his bed partner. Her face may look angelic, but her body was absolutely sinful. He reached out a hand to stroke her belly, amazed at her heat and the softness of her skin.

Again another whispered breath slipped past those kissable lips.

He grinned and ran his fingers lower. If her skin was this hot, he could only imagine what her quim would feel like. He touched her through the triangle, taking pleasure in the slide of the sheer material over her springy little curls.

This time she whimpered, and her thighs fell apart, begging him to touch her more intimately.

He crawled down between her spread thighs. The diaphanous material thinned to a narrow little strip that barely covered her sweet mound. A musky scent seemed to radiate from her, warm and delicious.

He gritted his teeth. God, could he remember ever feeling this aroused? This hungry for a woman?

He looked back up at her face, and something mingled with his desire, intensifying it, making him mad for her. He wanted to enter her, to thrust himself into her so deep that he could feel every inch of himself surrounded by her luscious heat.

Part of him was excited at the idea of taking this woman while she slept. But another part of him wanted to stare into her eyes as he filled her. He wanted to see her desire, her need in her wide green eyes.

He paused. Why did he think her eyes would be green when he could not even recall who she was? Strange. But the unanswered question did not distract him long.

She moved her leg and whimpered softly.

He smiled, focusing on the delights before him.

He traced the strip of the triangle where it narrowed between her thighs. Silky material and fine curls tickled his hand. Moisture scorched his fingertip, and he nudged the thin material away from her, admiring her pink, moist flesh. Gently he parted her and pressed his finger to the tiny nub waiting for him.

She gasped, her lips parting. Her eyes remained shut, but her legs fell wider apart, giving him full access to her heat. He accepted it, stroking her, circling her. Only leaving her to sink his finger into her startling tightness, but then he went right back to that tiny nub.

She moaned, wiggling her hips against his hand.

He gave her what her body begged for, touching her relentlessly, building the pace and the pressure until she cried out.

"Rhys! Oh, Rhys!"

Oh, yes, he was going to keep her.

Rhys was over her, touching her with his hands and his mouth. She exalted in the feel of him, so happy that he was there, bringing her back from the black, empty place where she'd been trapped, unable to struggle to the surface.

But this new place. Mmm, she liked this place, all sensation and arousal. All Rhys.

His lips on her breasts, tugging at her nipples, nipping her. Pleasure shot through her.

His hands were large and strong on her skin. He stroked her belly, her hips. She was drowning in need.

Then his finger found the spot where she most wanted to be touched. Touched by him. He rubbed and swirled. Until she exploded.

Jane gasped and panted, and finally once the ecstasy slowly subsided into long, slow waves of satisfaction, she opened her eyes.

"Oh, my," she breathed. She'd never, never had a dream like that.

"I agree," a rich, husky voice said.

Jane shot up and made a startled noise. Rhys knelt, fully naked, between her spread thighs.

"Good morning." He greeted her with a lopsided smile.

Jane backed away from him, mortified, until the headboard stopped her retreat. Then she scrambled off the bed and dashed through an open door that she prayed was the bathroom. Slamming the door, she leaned heavily against it.

What had she done? She tried to recall how she could have gotten here—with Rhys—but nothing was clear. The last clear memory she had was Rhys saving her in the alley. He walked her back to the hotel. She realized she lost her parents' wedding rings, and she went to look for them. And then . . .

Here. Having an orgasm. An orgasm Rhys gave her.

Even thinking about that made her knees feel weak.

What? Was she mad? Wasn't she worried about what else had happened between them—things she couldn't remember?

Had they had full intercourse? Again, her knees felt weak, and longing pooled deep in her belly.

Was she deranged? She shouldn't be feeling turned on by the prospects of a night with him that she couldn't remember. She should be freaking out.

Well, she was freaking out. But she feared it wasn't for the right reasons.

A light rap on the door caused her to jump.

"Are you all right in there?"

She took a deep breath. "Yes. I'll be out in a minute."

She closed her eyes. What did Rhys think of her? He must think she was a first-rate hussy.

Rhys sat on the edge of the bed. It would cost a few hundred pounds and likely a house in town to keep her as his mistress. But whatever the price he would keep her. She was first-rate.

He glanced at the nightstand, looking for his pocket watch. It was not there, but two gold rings and a necklace sat on the dark, polished wood.

He picked up the small ring, noting that the circle was so tiny it would only fit someone the stature of the little woman in the other room. He picked up the other ring. It was bigger, thicker, more masculine. He vaguely remembered these. Remembered that they had to do with the woman in the other room.

He twisted it over and over in his palm, trying to remember, when an inscription on the ring caught his eye.

To R—Yours forever, J.

His chest tightened. Was this ring intended for him? Slowly, he slid the gold band onto his finger. It was snug, but it fit.

He stared at the ring for several seconds before he crossed to the closed door and threw it open.

The woman squealed and tried to cover herself with her hands.

Rhys ignored her modesty, although he knew her reaction was real. Not even ten minutes ago, he would have thought the behavior was an expensive whore's trick to entice him. Now he knew different.

"Are we married?" he demanded, holding up the smaller of the two rings.

Chapter 5

Jane's first thought was to say, no! But then she realized she couldn't be sure. She didn't remember, and apparently, neither did he.

Did New York have those all-night chapels like Las Vegas? She'd never heard of them, but at this point, anything seemed possible.

"I—I don't think so."

She stared at him. He was still bare-chested, his torso defined with hard muscle. Thankfully, he had pulled on his trousers; otherwise she never would have been able to speak. Although the pants were unfastened, revealing a vee of flat stomach and light whorls of hair trailing downward.

She dragged her eyes upward to his face. That didn't help. He was a truly beautiful man. His hair was mussed from sleep, and his eyes were intent, studying her.

He frowned, even as a look of realization washed over his features. "You are Jane Harrison." He said it slowly, almost experimentally, as if he was dredging the name up from somewhere way in the back of his mind.

She nodded. *Please don't tell me he has forgotten even more than I have?* What happened to them? How had they both forgotten last night?

"Yes, I remember those amazing green eyes," he said resolutely. "You are my betrothed."

Jane stared at him. What was he talking about? And why did he suddenly have an English accent? She didn't remember him having an accent when he'd walked her back to her hotel.

"Jane Harrison from America?"

She nodded. She supposed that was true. But where did he think he was from?

"I should have realized." He stepped forward and touched her hair, letting the unruly strands slip through his fingers. "Your hair—that smart crop. Is that the fashion in America?"

She eyed him warily. "Yes?"

He studied her a moment longer, then gave a decisive nod. "I like it."

Before she could respond, he crouched in front of her, and she clapped her hands over her scant undies.

He noticed, his sculpted lips twisting into a slight smile. She supposed it was a little late to be modest now.

His smile disappeared into something akin to astonishment as he gently reached out and touched her calf.

Heat immediately ran through her. Her skin felt electrified where his fingers brushed over her, and she remembered those wonderful long fingers touching other parts of her body. She bit her lip to stifle a moan as he slowly ran his hand up to her knee and then back to her ankle.

He peered up at her, amazement clear on his face. "Americans shave their legs?"

"Only the women." Then she amended that. "Well, I guess a few men do, too."

He considered that for a moment, then finally nodded with understanding.

He stood. "I must find Christian and Sebastian. Hopefully they will recall what happened between us last night." He left the bathroom.

Oh, dear, was he implying that others might have been involved, too? She really, really hoped not. Although she did hope these men could explain how she got here and why Rhys was acting so strange.

"Christian!" Rhys bellowed as soon as he stepped out of the bedroom into the hall. "Sebastian!"

Jane didn't follow right away, relieved to see her blouse and skirt folded on a chair in the corner of the room. She stopped and pulled them on.

She heard Rhys shout again and chased after him.

In the hallway, Jane squealed with surprise as she nearly ran into a blond man who stepped out in front of her from one of the doorways lining the long hallway.

"What the hell is with all the yelling?" he asked in a raspy, sleep-filled voice.

Jane didn't answer, too amazed by the sight of him.

This man looked younger than Rhys, with shorter hair which stuck out in a wild mess. He had hazel eyes like Rhys, although his didn't seem to have that unusual amber glow. She could see, since he wore only black silk pajama bottoms, that he was leaner, too—not as wide or as tall as Rhys. But he did remind her of Rhys.

"Hey," he said, not seeming to notice that she was staring. "I'm Sebastian, Rhys's brother." He offered her a hand and a lopsided smile very similar to the one Rhys had given her this morning.

"I'm Jane." So this man *was* related to Rhys. They must come from one amazing gene pool.

"Is that my crazy brother yelling?"

Jane nodded, wondering exactly how crazy he was talking.

"Sebastian," Rhys said, striding down the hall toward them. His eyes dropped to where she and Sebastian still held hands. His eyes narrowed, and Jane pulled her hand out of Sebastian's hold, feeling guilty. Rhys probably thought she was easy as it was; she didn't want him to think she was moving on to his brother.

But instead of being suspicious of her, he turned his attention to Sebastian. "I would be careful, brother. I do not intend to share my woman."

Heat sizzled through Jane's belly at his possessiveness. But she immediately admonished herself. She shouldn't be enjoying this. She had no idea what was going on—and Rhys was clearly not acting normal.

"Especially since she is now, very likely anyway, my wife and thus your sister," Rhys added, smiling down at her as if he was quite pleased with that idea.

Not normal at all.

Sebastian turned to stare at Jane.

She gave him a weak smile.

Sebastian frowned back at his brother, and Jane changed her initial opinion. He could look as intense as Rhys. "Rhys, what the hell are you talking about?"

"This is Jane Harrison." Rhys came to stand beside her. "The lady to which I have been betrothed."

When Sebastian just stared at him. Rhys clarified, "From America."

When his brother still didn't speak, Rhys turned to her. "I am sorry. Sebastian is often considered the gre-

garious member of the family. But apparently today he
is—"

"Freaked out," Sebastian suggested.

Rhys shot his brother a puzzled look. "Freaked out?"
He said the words as if that phrase was totally unfamiliar
to him, but then he smiled at Jane apologetically. "I
should also add that while he is gregarious, Sebastian
often says things which are best just disregarded."

Sebastian didn't respond, although his facial expression said the same thing he'd already voiced. His brows
were drawn together, and his hazel eyes were opened
very wide. He looked—freaked out.

That had to be a good sign; if Rhys was truly insane,
then presumably Sebastian would not be unnerved by
this behavior. Right? She hoped so.

"Rhys," he finally said. "I think Jane would probably
like to have some . . . tea. Tea and—kippers. So I'll take
her to the kit—dining room and get her settled. Then I
will talk to you about all this—amazing news."

Rhys debated, then nodded. He touched Jane's
cheek, his fingers gentle, his thumb close to the fullness
of her lower lip. "Will you be all right? My brother is relatively harmless."

She nodded, fighting the urge to nuzzle her face
against his large hand. She was truly pathetic. Any sane
person would be running. Maybe she was the one who
was crazy.

He glanced at Sebastian. "Although, he does not
know how to dress in front of a lady"—then he cast a
wry look at himself and his own state of undress—"but
nor do I."

Sebastian still sported that same muddled, yet concerned look. "I'll make an effort to be more modest around your—Jane."

Rhys nodded as if he thought that was a good idea, but Jane noticed he didn't make the same pledge.

"I will let you and Sebastian get acquainted."

"The dining room is this way," Sebastian said, gesturing down the hallway.

Jane followed him, looking back over her shoulder once. Rhys still stood in the center of the hallway, watching her. A look laden with desire and something very like wonder made his amber eyes seem to glow.

Again her insides did a little flip.

This was ridiculous. She should not be reacting to Rhys this way. She didn't know him. She didn't remember how they'd ended up back together—and in bed.

Yes, he was the most beautiful man she'd ever seen, but she had to be sensible. And sensible women didn't have relationships with men who were possibly crazy. Although he hadn't seemed crazy when he'd saved her. Or when he'd walked her back to her hotel. And Jane knew crazy.

As if he'd been reading her mind, Sebastian said, "My brother isn't normally a nut."

He'd led her into a large room with dark wood paneling and two windows hidden behind burgundy velvet drapes. The light in the room came from two elaborate chandeliers dangling over a long, heavy, dark wood table surrounded by a dozen ornately carved chairs with burgundy velvet backs and cushions.

He closed the door behind them.

She turned from surveying the room. "I don't know your brother very well, but he did save my life last night, and although I can't remember much else, I know he wasn't insane." She couldn't say why she felt so strongly about that fact, except for maybe because she'd lived with someone not quite sane. Jane's father hadn't been certifiable, but he had been a little strange.

"He saved your life?"

"Yes, I didn't use very good judgment and trusted a man I shouldn't have. Fortunately Rhys realized this guy was not a nice person. He followed us and . . ." She took a deep breath. Again, she was so thankful that Rhys had been there. "He stopped the guy from doing something awful. Then he walked me back to the hotel where I am staying, and he left."

"But he must have come back? Or you went to find him?"

She shook her head. "That's the thing. I don't remember seeing him again. I did leave the hotel and head back toward the bar. But I never encountered Rhys. At least not that I can recall." She frowned, confused. "But I suppose I must have."

"Yes you *were* with him again. I mean, otherwise, you wouldn't be here now."

His words were obviously true, but there was something about the way he said them that struck her as strange. A certainty that almost implied he knew more than he was saying.

But then he smiled at her, a nice, encouraging smile, and she decided she was reading too much into his simple agreement to her own ponderings.

"Okay, well, let me show you to the kitchen," he said, leading her through the dining room to another door. "I think we have tea and sugar. There might even be bread and butter or jam or something."

Jane nodded, thinking that it was odd that he seemed so unsure of what was in his own kitchen. But then maybe he just didn't cook. Or eat at home.

"Help yourself to anything. I'll go talk to Rhys, and hopefully, I can get some answers out of him. Or at least figure out why he's acting so strange."

Jane nodded, but she didn't move. She just looked around the kitchen, suddenly overwhelmed by the weirdness of the situation—of the past two days.

"It will be okay, Jane."

She offered him a forced smile as he left the kitchen. She did appreciate his comforting words. It had to be pretty odd for him, too. He must be really shaken up about Rhys.

Sebastian grinned as soon as the kitchen door swung shut behind him.

Wasn't this turning into another interesting evening.

Rhys, his detached, surly and annoyingly gloomy brother, *had* saved a mortal life. Unbelievable!

Rhys adhered to one cardinal rule: *never get involved with mortals*. At least no mortals outside of the ones he used as his food source. And they were always the dregs of society.

Sebastian shuddered, just thinking about it. They didn't use the word *dregs* for no reason. Lowlifes tasted like the residue at the bottom of the barrel—vile and stale as if their life forces were decaying with each evil act they'd done.

But Jane had done no evil acts. Not a one. That fact was clear in her very scent—she was wholesome. The last type of mortal with whom Rhys would entangle himself. But he most definitely had. They had somehow gotten entangled with each other. Sebastian could smell that, too. Both of them reeked of unbridled lust.

Sebastian grinned again with amusement. Who knew his brother grim even had a sex drive. Sebastian had always believed Rhys's thoughts of sex had been cast aside to make more room for all his languishing. Apparently not. Rhys had just required the right lady.

But who was Jane? Sebastian's steps slowed, and his smile slipped. Great. Rhys had a romantic interest, but Jane's story certainly hadn't clarified what had happened in the alley last night.

He could deduce that the male mortal in the alley was the guy who had attacked Jane, which was why Rhys had gone dental on the guy. But he still didn't know who had attacked Rhys or why. And he had no idea why Rhys was acting so weird earlier. He thought Jane was his betrothed. And he'd even smiled a couple times. Rhys never smiled.

So much was still unexplained. Who was he kidding? Nothing made sense. He really hoped Rhys had snapped out of his lust-induced delirium and had some sort of explanation.

It didn't take long for Sebastian to find Rhys—in the library, a large room full of books and music, and Rhys's favorite room in the apartment.

Rhys sat in a chair, leaning back against the cushions, legs crossed, looking unusually relaxed. Two glasses of scotch were already poured and waiting on the table.

"There you are," Rhys greeted with a broad, warm smile. "I thought we might have a drink to celebrate."

Sebastian blinked. He couldn't recall the last time he had seen that smile, certainly not since Rhys crossed over. And Rhys celebrating? Brooding was about as celebratory as Rhys got.

"Is Jane settled with her tea?"

"Yes. She's fine."

"Good." Rhys stood and crossed to the giant stone fireplace that took up most of one of the walls. He picked up a fire poker from the hearth and stirred the smoldering ashes. Then he tossed a log onto the orange coals.

"She is lovely, is she not?"

"Jane? Yes." Sebastian studied his brother. Why was he talking so stiltedly? And when had his English accent gotten so pronounced? They'd both lost their accents almost totally over the decades.

Rhys returned to pick up his scotch. Then he crossed back to the fireplace, leaning an arm on the mantel. He took a sip of the golden liquid, then sighed. "I am quite pleased with the match, I must say. When Father had told me that he had arranged for me to wed an American, I had been more than a little outraged."

Sebastian remembered, even though the incident had happened nearly two hundred years ago. Was that why Rhys was talking and acting so strangely? Somehow he believed he was back in nineteenth century England?

"I was picturing a hulking woman who pushed a plow through the fields all day," Rhys told him, and it took a moment for Sebastian to realize what he was talking about.

"A woman with no social graces," Rhys continued. "A savage, in truth. But out of respect for Father and Mother, I would have married her."

Sebastian almost chuckled at that. Man, Rhys had really dodged a bullet on that one. Rhys's image of his American fiancée was dead on. Sebastian couldn't recall her name—Bertha, he seemed to think. And she *had* been a hulking, abrasive and very unattractive woman.

In fact, Sebastian wished he'd remembered ole Bertha earlier. When Rhys was lamenting being a vampire, which he did often, Sebastian could have reminded him that he could have lived and died in the arms of big Bertha.

Which brought him back to the mystery of who Jane was and what happened in that alley last night. Jane didn't know. And it was pretty darn obvious Rhys had no clue either as he was quite happily back in merry old England.

Sebastian concentrated on Rhys. He couldn't sense anything physically wrong with him—even his maimed neck had healed completely. So why was he acting this way? Rhys was too angsty to be insane. Insanity would normally be way too fun for him.

"Where are Christian and Elizabeth? I want them to meet Jane. They will love her."

Suddenly Rhys's current predicament didn't seem quite so amusing. He had somehow forgotten the past two centuries. And all the painful things that had happened in that time. Elizabeth's death. Christian's hatred toward them both—but especially Rhys.

The loss of his siblings had devastated Rhys, but he'd subsisted, not ever returning to the Rhys whom Sebastian had known in life, but he kept going. Somehow Sebastian didn't think Rhys could survive losing them all over again.

Wait, if he didn't remember Elizabeth's death, and

he didn't remember his rift with Christian, then he certainly didn't remember he was a vampire. He didn't have a clue that he was undead.

"Sebastian," Rhys asked sharply. "You are a thousand miles away. Did you hear me? Where are Elizabeth and Christian?"

"They are—at the country estate," Sebastian said quickly. What the hell was the name of that old place?

"At Rothmere?"

That was it. "Yes. Remember, Christian took Elizabeth there, because her friend was having a house party?"

Rhys frowned, obviously trying to recall. "Elizabeth is always attending this or that. I cannot keep track."

Sebastian took a swallow of his scotch. This was too weird. Who knew a vampire could even get amnesia, but that appeared to be exactly what Rhys had.

Rhys walked over and turned on the floor lamp beside a tan, overstuffed chair.

Sebastian watched him closely, expecting him to react to the whole concept of electric lights—an invention they didn't see until the late 1800s, nearly fifty years after their undeaths.

But Rhys didn't react. He sat down and refilled his glass. He held up the decanter to Sebastian.

"Please," Sebastian said. He was going to need a couple drinks to grasp what was going on here. It was on the tip of his tongue to remind Rhys what he was, but he hesitated. Rhys was calm, content—unlike he'd been in centuries. Perhaps it was better to let him remain blissfully oblivious for a while longer. At least until Sebastian understood more of what had happened to him.

"Jane is far more perfect than I could have hoped for." Rhys sighed and leaned back in the chair.

"Yes."

"I must admit, though, I do not seem to recall how she got here. Nor do I remember last night."

"You've forgotten a good bit more than just last night," Sebastian said wryly, but quickly covered his comment. "You and Christian were celebrating your upcoming wedding before he left with Elizabeth."

Rhys nodded, readily accepting that explanation. Christian had always been the wildest of the three brothers. He would be the one who would have convinced Rhys to make the party last well over a few days.

They drank silently for a few moments, and Sebastian tried to figure out what he should do about this. Maybe he should talk to some of the other vampires that frequented his nightclub. Maybe one of them had heard of this disorder. And he would definitely ask about any rogue vampires in the city—a vampire who was attacking other vampires.

"Upcoming wedding?" Rhys asked, suddenly. "Jane and I are not wed already?"

Sebastian shook his head. "No. Jane only got here last night."

"Good Lord, you mean to say, she got off the ship, and I herded her straight into my bed and compromised her? While I was drunk, no less?"

Sebastian blinked. This was just way too weird.

"She seemed agreeable to it."

Rhys shook his head, his eyes dark with self-reproach. "That is simply not how one treats their intended. And the wedding will obviously have to happen as soon as possible. I cannot have her reputation in tatters because I was a randy, soused caper-wit."

Randy, soused caper-wit? Did they really ever talk like that?

"Sebastian," Rhys said, drawing Sebastian's attention back from the oddities of the English language. "I intend to keep Jane. To find happiness with her."

At first, Sebastian found Rhys's wording strange. *Keep her.*

But his attention was immediately drawn back to Rhys as a wave of overwhelming need flooded the room. Then it was promptly replaced by a devastating, heartbreaking sense of loss that seemed to weight the air and crush Sebastian.

Sebastian blinked, forcing himself to focus on his brother, realizing the emotions came from him.

Rhys stared straight ahead, his eyes distant, almost as if lost in a trance.

Sebastian started to ask Rhys what was wrong. But before he could get the words out, images began to bombard his brain like a rapid-fire slide show. Visions of Elizabeth. And Christian. Other things from their pasts.

Sorrow nearly choked Sebastian—as the visions continued at a speed that offered only brief glimpses of lives now lost.

And just when Sebastian thought he couldn't handle any more, that his brain and emotions were going into overload, the grief evaporated away.

One final image flashed in Sebastian's mind. Jane. Then that image, too, vanished.

The air grew lighter—only the subtle scent of Rhys's desire for her drifting through the room.

Sebastian blinked. What the hell was that? The flashes had been similar to what happened to him when Rhys had been attacked. He was again feeling what Rhys was feeling.

He looked at his brother. Rhys's gaze no longer had that faraway look. He actually even smiled again, although there was a determined edge to the set of his mouth.

"I cannot explain it," he said, and for a moment, Sebastian thought that Rhys knew what had just occurred. "I realize I just met Jane, but I simply cannot let her go. I must have her."

Then suddenly, between Rhys's words and the images Sebastian had seen and the loss surrounding those visions, he understood what must be happening in Rhys's muddled head.

Rhys wanted Jane, but as a vampire, Rhys would never allow himself to grow attached to a mortal. He'd already lost too much in his vampire state. Been hurt too much.

But if he could go back—before the losses, before the vampirism—maybe then he could have Jane.

Sebastian knew his brother's connection to the little mortal had been very strong. That had been the main reason he'd brought her back here, and even put her in Rhys's bed. So Rhys would sense her near, and he could rest easier and heal. But Sebastian had no idea the extent Rhys wanted her.

Not until now.

He wanted her enough to forget what he'd been for almost two hundred years. Rhys was forcing himself to forget he was a vampire, simply going back in his head to before Lilah, to before they crossed over.

That had to be why he didn't seem fazed by this apartment or the modern conveniences. To question how those things could exist in the nineteenth century would ruin this fantasy world he had created.

But Sebastian decided to put his theory to the test.

He pointed at the lamp on the end table. "What is that?"

Rhys glanced at the light, then gave his brother a wry look. "It's a lamp," he said slowly, as if Sebastian was the one who'd lost his wits.

"And that?" He pointed to the state-of-the-art stereo system on one of the many shelves.

"A CD player."

"And that?" He gestured toward the wall.

"The thermostat. Listen, is there any point to this little game of twenty questions?"

"I'm just pointing out all the fine things you have to offer Jane," Sebastian told him. "Not many men in London at this particular period of time could offer his bride so much."

Rhys stared at him for a moment, then shook his head, clearly thinking Sebastian was mad.

Sebastian wasn't mad; he was brilliant. Rhys *was* suppressing only the bits of his past that he couldn't accept. The loss of all the things he loved. Elizabeth. Christian. His life.

But even as he was pleased with his own deductive reasoning, he was also stunned by the extent of his brother's pain. He knew Rhys had never been able to accept himself as a vampire—but Sebastian had never truly realized the agony and guilt he felt. But it did make sense. Rhys had always been the head of the family. And he'd lost the most when he lost Elizabeth and Christian.

Sebastian watched his brother for a moment, trying to decide what would be the best thing for him. Finally he decided. He couldn't give him back their sister or their brother, but he could help him with Jane. He could give him a chance to love this little mortal who had managed to touch his brother's heart. A heart that had been frozen for . . . Forever.

Chapter 6

Jane sat at the dining room table, sipping tea and trying to decide what to do. She considered leaving several times, but she couldn't do it. She couldn't leave without knowing that Rhys would be okay. Plus, she wanted to find out what had happened to her the night before, too.

She nibbled her toast, but she didn't have any appetite. She picked up her plate and carried it back into the small galley-style kitchen. Glossy, black granite counters lined one wall, and there was every appliance a cook could ask for, all in ultramodern brushed stainless steel. The room was ultramodern, but no one seemed to have ever used all the luxuries. The cupboards were practically bare. And the fridge had only a few items on its many racks.

She supposed that wasn't particularly strange—she couldn't picture either Rhys or Sebastian being big culinary aficionados. They were probably the type who grabbed a bite on the go.

One thing she did know for sure, these two brothers

were rich. Her judgment about Rhys when she'd first seen him in the bar had been accurate. His home screamed culture and sophistication. A far cry from where she'd grown up, in an ancient Victorian with half the old rooms used as a funeral parlor.

She wandered back into the dining room, which was so different from the kitchen. When she was in this room she felt as if she had somehow fallen into a time warp and sat in a grand dining hall in an ancient English manor.

One of the doors, which connected the dining room from the hallway, opened, and Sebastian strolled in. Considering his brother was acting more than a little weird, he looked very calm.

"First, you will be happy to know you aren't married to my brother," he told her.

Jane had already, more or less, made up her mind that they couldn't be married. But the relief she'd expected to feel at the confirmation wasn't as strong as she'd thought it would be.

But before she could wonder at her lack of reaction, Sebastian added, without any real concern in his voice, "He has amnesia and apparently thinks he's a viscount from nineteenth century England."

"What?"

"Yup." Sebastian came to sit at the table across from her. "He can't remember much of anything about his present life."

She frowned at his wording, but he quickly added, "I guess *present* isn't the right phrase—his real life."

Jane nodded. She'd seen television movies about amnesia, but those depictions were fictional. Or maybe they weren't. This sounded as fantastic as any movie she'd seen. "Is this how amnesia usually works?"

Sebastian shrugged. "Amnesia can manifest itself in many different ways."

Again Jane was struck by Sebastian's cavalier attitude toward Rhys's problem. A viscount from England? That seemed like a reason to worry to her. "Shouldn't he go to a doctor? What if this is something more?"

Sebastian looked a little ill at ease, but the expression disappeared almost before Jane saw it. "We have a family physician. I called him. I explained Rhys's behavior, and he told me it was amnesia."

"Without seeing him?"

"He said there was really nothing else it could be."

"But what if he has an injury to his head? Something that needs medical attention?" She couldn't believe a doctor would make a diagnosis like that over the phone.

"He is going to come see Rhys. Tomorrow. But he didn't think Rhys should leave the apartment, because— since he does believe he's from another time period, the current world, cars, skyscrapers, that sort of thing might freak him out. Apparently that could be devastating to Rhys."

Jane supposed that was reasonable. And these men certainly appeared to have enough money to get a doctor to make a house call.

"Well, it's good the doctor believes that he will be fine. Did he give you a time frame when you could expect Rhys's condition to improve?"

Sebastian shook his head. "No. He will get better, but it could be weeks, or months."

Her heart went out to Rhys. The poor confused man. That was a horrible way to live. Her father hadn't been completely delusional, but he had wanted so desperately to believe that Jane's mother was still alive that he'd act as though she was there. He'd talk to her. His behavior had broken her heart.

Rhys wasn't trying to get back people he'd lost, but this broke Jane's heart, too.

"I'm so sorry for him, Sebastian."

"I know you are." He smiled warmly.

Jane sighed and then started to rise. She should go. She knew that Rhys would eventually be okay, and she had no other reason to hang around. Dejection filled her, although she couldn't say why exactly.

"Jane." Sebastian reached out and caught her hand. His fingers enveloped her smaller ones. They didn't feel nearly as big as Rhys's, as strong. "Rhys needs to be watched all the time. The doctor said it was important to keep him under close supervision, because so many things could shock him."

Jane nodded, not understanding why he was telling her this.

"This apartment is actually located over a nightclub. The nightclub that Rhys and I own. And at night, we are usually down in the club. It is popular—and without Rhys to help me, I'm going to be very busy. I won't be able to watch him and run the club. So that's where you come in. Is it possible that you could stay and take care of Rhys?"

Jane's eyes widened. He wanted her to stay here— with them. With Rhys.

"Is—isn't there someone else you could get?" She couldn't take care of Rhys. She could barely look him in the eyes after this morning, much less watch his every move. Besides, there was something absurd about the idea of her watching a man like Rhys anyway. He was too potent, too powerful.

"Well, the thing is, he still believes he's engaged to you," Sebastian told her. "So you would be the perfect one to be with him. He wouldn't question it."

That did make sense, but why would Rhys continue to believe they had a relationship? She supposed it could be because he woke up with her spread-eagle in his bed. She was probably lucky he *had* assumed they had a relationship. He could have decided she was a prostitute or something.

"I—I don't know." She pulled her hand out of his hold. She didn't know these men. She couldn't very well move in with two strangers.

"I really need your help," Sebastian told her.

"How am I supposed to stop him from leaving the apartment if he really wants to?" Why was she asking this? Why was she even considering staying?

Sebastian's lips curled at one corner. "I think you can control him quite easily. He's fascinated with you."

His words didn't lessen the tightness in her chest. Although they did make her skin tingle again.

She was losing it.

"And I'd pay you, of course," he added. "You said you were in a hotel, right? The room here would be free."

She looked around. She did need a place to stay until she could get her finances in order. She had her few traveler's checks, but she wasn't sure those would last her until her new bank card and credit cards were sent. This might not be a bad solution until she could find an apartment and a steady job.

She glanced at Sebastian, who watched her intently.

Still, she didn't know these men. They could be serial killers for all she knew. Weirder things had happened—most of them to her in the past two days.

No, Sebastian and Rhys didn't look like homicidal maniacs. Of course, she'd already proven she wasn't the best judge of character.

"And," Sebastian added, pointedly, "Rhys was there for you when you needed him."

He had her there. Rhys had saved her life. Did serial killers bother to save a person just to kill them later? She wasn't sure, but she decided it was unlikely. Plus, something inside her did trust Rhys.

She hesitated a moment longer, then said softly, "All right."

Smug satisfaction filled Sebastian at his well-executed lie. He hadn't even felt remorse at her pained look when he'd thrown out his ace in the hole, Rhys saving her. Okay, maybe he felt a twinge of guilt, but it was worth it. Rhys needed this woman.

And, man, did she ever want Rhys. He'd felt flashes of overwhelming desire throughout their conversation. All he had to do was mention Rhys's name, and she exuded longing. Damn, he wished he had a sweet thing like her lusting for him. Oh, wait, he did. Lots, actually.

But he didn't get too long to bask in his success.

Jane straightened in her chair and said in a firm voice, "I will stay—but only a week. That should give you time to find someone else to watch Rhys, should he need it. And that will give me time to find my own place."

A week? Sebastian frowned. Rhys needed more than a week to get this woman to fall for him. He breathed in with frustration, ready to argue, when he smelled again the lust that was permeating the apartment. Damn, a week just might be plenty of time. If they needed more, he'd worry about it later. Right now, she was staying. Good enough. And she would keep Rhys in the apartment. Sebastian needed that time to figure out who had attacked Rhys and why. Rhys, in his confused state, would be an easy mark if the attacker had been after him specifically. It was best to keep him here—safe.

"A week is great."

She nodded, obviously relieved he hadn't pushed for longer.

But now Sebastian had the peculiarities of being a vampire to deal with. Being a vampire was easy. Being a vampire who didn't know he's a vampire; that might be tricky. Rhys could end his existence with one short stroll in the sunshine. Or if his hunger wasn't appeased regularly, Jane could die from one overzealous chomp.

"Watching Rhys should be quite easy," he said, contradicting his thoughts, but he didn't want to scare her away. "There are really only three things you need to be careful about."

Jane listened, her green eyes wide.

"He has an allergy to the sun, so he cannot go out in the direct sunlight, which generally isn't a problem. Since we work nights, his sleep schedule usually keeps him out of the sun anyway." All of that was basically true.

"Can he go out on overcast days?"

"Yes. But only totally overcast. Sun is poison to him." She nodded.

"Also, Rhys has a lot of weird food allergies, so he generally sticks to a high protein drink."

"He doesn't eat?" She looked dubious.

"He does, but only rare meat. Very rare. He's doing this weird, Atkins type thing, too. It seems to keep the whole allergy thing under control." He threw up his hands as though the whole concept was strange to him, too. "I don't even ask."

"But will he remember that?"

"I don't know, but I think we better continue it. He's lived on this stuff so long—I wouldn't want to screw up his digestive system or something."

She nodded, but the slight wrinkling of her nose stated she still found the idea odd.

"And—and this was exactly what the physician told me—we must humor Rhys for the time being. That is important. Otherwise we could fracture his memories, again the doctor's words, and his real memories might be lost permanently."

Jane looked stricken.

God, he was good.

She still appeared apprehensive, but she said, "Okay."

"Great. So let's discuss money. How is fifteen hundred dollars?"

Sebastian didn't think it could be possible, but her eyes widened more. "That—that's too much."

Sebastian shrugged. "I love my brother. And I want to see him happy."

"I can't take that kind of money. That is . . . It's too much."

Sebastian smiled, impressed by her shocked reluctance. He'd thrown out a large sum, assuming the amount would definitely clinch the deal, but obviously he hadn't needed to. Jane was too ethical to accept it comfortably.

"If I didn't want to pay it, I wouldn't."

She hesitated again, but after a moment, she offered her hand to him. "Okay."

He smiled. Did he mention he was good?

Chapter 7

Jane couldn't believe this. She had agreed to live with two men she didn't know. One of them was paying her an inordinate amount of money to do so, and the other . . . the other thought he was engaged to her. Oh, and he thought he was living in nineteenth century England.

Who was the crazy one in this whole scenario? They'd probably have to draw straws at this point.

She looked around the bedroom that Sebastian told her would be hers during her stay. Well, the digs were definitely good.

She wandered to the bed, running her hand over the luxurious blue velvet duvet that covered the mattress. Then her fingers brushed the wispy silk that created a canopy over the top and around the perimeter. Definitely a lot different than the creaky brass bed she'd slept in most of her life.

She moved over to the windows and parted the thick damask curtains. It was evening, but she couldn't even make out the city skyline. Thick frosted glass muted all light.

For a moment, she was disappointed. She wanted to see the view and, hopefully, get some bearings of where she was. Then she realized the windows must be for Rhys. To protect him from the sun.

Rhys sure had a lot of strange ailments. He didn't look like a man with any afflictions. Physically, he appeared perfect.

She pushed the image of that perfect body out of her mind. She had to get her attraction to him under control—somehow.

She thought again about his allergies. How strange to never go out in the sunshine. But she supposed she didn't spend much time in the sun, either. She hated sun bathing—it just made her freckle and burn. And she always got her second wind in the evening—often reading into the wee hours of the night.

Food, however, she couldn't give up. Who didn't love a yummy hot fudge sundae or a gooey pepperoni pizza?

Sighing, she let the curtain drop and headed to explore the bathroom. She had her own bathroom, another convenience she'd never known in her house. But this bathroom went far beyond simple convenience. It was downright opulent.

She touched the smooth white marble of the sink. Then she wandered over to the tub. The huge, inset tub was easily big enough for two. Then there was a separate shower. This was luxury.

But as luxurious as it was, she knew she couldn't stay any longer than it took her to sort out her finances.

She walked back out to her bedroom and moved her new suitcase over the bureau. Someone named Mick, a security guy for the club, had driven over to her hotel and gathered her stuff. She unzipped the case and started to pull out a stack of clothes, to place in the dresser. Then she rethought the idea and dropped the clothes back into her luggage.

There was no point in unpacking or getting too comfortable. Even though she'd like to cling to the reasoning that the situation was just too strange, the real reason she couldn't stay was that she was so ridiculously attracted to Rhys. And she couldn't be attracted to a man who didn't even know who she really was. Heck, he didn't know who he was. That was a relationship that was doomed from the get-go.

She sighed and pulled out a clean pair of jeans, a green turtleneck sweater and underwear.

Maybe a long, hot bath would help her put things in perspective and maybe even help her remember what happened last night.

The only explanation she'd been able to come up with for her lost memories was the tequila. Or maybe a combination of the tequila and the stress of all the horrible events of yesterday.

But what had happened to cause Rhys's amnesia? Could both their memory losses be connected? Short of alien abduction, which probably wasn't out of the question given how weird things had been, she couldn't figure out what could have happened to them. Maybe she would talk to Rhys's doctor, too. He might have some ideas. About mass amnesia? Yeah, right.

She dropped her clothes onto the closed lid of the toilet, then perched on the edge of the tub to close the stopper and turn on the faucet.

She watched the steaming water for a few moments, then went to the sink to look for soap. As she searched, she caught her reflection in the mirror over the sink.

She looked a wreck. Her hair stood out all over her head, and she had traces of mascara under her eyes. The smudged makeup made the purplish circles under her eyes look even darker.

Why would a gorgeous hunk like Rhys be fascinated with her? Sebastian had to be mistaken. But she had been in bed with Rhys. And he'd . . .

Her cheeks flamed, making her complexion a colorful pink, mottled against the purple under her eyes.

She closed her eyes, releasing a hitched breath. She couldn't remember last night, but she could certainly remember the feeling of Rhys's hands on her when she woke up.

Heat drained from her flushed cheeks to pool in her belly, then lower. She'd never felt anything as wonderful as Rhys's fingers against her.

As if by their own will, her fingers moved to the buttons of her blouse. Not opening her eyes, she pretended it was Rhys's fingers loosening the buttons, parting the white cotton. The wisps of steam from the hot water filling the tub moistened her skin, and she pretended it was Rhys's kisses warming her flesh.

What was she doing? She'd never been the type to fantasize about men. And especially fantasies like this. But she'd also never had a man touch her like Rhys had. It had been so . . . thrilling.

She let her blouse fall to the floor, and she moved her fingers to the front clasp of her bra. The filmy material separated, and her nipples peaked against the humid air.

Embarrassed, but unable to stop herself, she brushed her fingers over them, trying to remember exactly how Rhys's lips had felt suckling her.

Her eyes snapped open at the sound of a quiet cough, and she spun toward the open doorway.

Rhys stood there, watching her.

She crossed her arms over her chest, trying to hide herself and to somehow hide what she'd been doing. But she could tell from the smoldering glow of his eyes, he'd seen.

The burn of embarrassment mingled with the fire those intense eyes created inside her. She so wanted this man.

His gaze left her covered chest, and he held her eyes with his.

She shifted slightly under the hunger she saw there.

"Sorry," he said, his voice huskier than usual. "I thought I heard you calling me."

She stared at him. Well, her body had been calling him, but she didn't think her voice had. "I . . . No."

He nodded sharply. "Then I will leave you to your bath."

They stared at each other for a moment longer; then Rhys bowed slightly and left, pulling the door shut behind him.

Jane sagged against the sink, still clutching her breasts. This was impossible. It had taken every bit of her rational mind to not invite him to join her in the tub. What was wrong with her? She'd always been so practical, so reserved. Now she was acting like a wanton.

Rhys shut both Jane's bathroom and bedroom door, and he still seemed to sense her desire pulling at him, begging him to come back to her. He stopped in the hallway, his own desire telling him to go back. She was his betrothed after all. They weren't married yet, but they would be soon, as soon as he could arrange it, and then that delectable body of hers would be his.

He nearly groaned, thinking about what she'd been doing when he arrived at her bathroom door. Her hands caressing her creamy skin. Shaping themselves to the rounded curves of her breasts. Her fingers teasing her swollen pink nipples.

He still remembered the taste of them. The heat of her body. His cock pulsed painfully in his trousers.

She was already his, but soon, he'd have her beside him every night.

Forcing himself to ignore his overly enthusiastic body, he searched for Sebastian. His brother had left him after their celebratory drink to talk with Jane again. Rhys was curious to see what Jane had told his brother.

Sebastian was in his room. He finished buttoning his shirt, then shrugged on a jacket.

"Where are you off to?"

"To the club." Sebastian combed his fingers through his blond hair. The locks fell into their usual unruly tangle.

Rhys nodded. "I would join you, but I'm certain Jane already believes me a complete reprobate. I believe I should stay with her this evening and try to convince her otherwise."

Sebastian smiled, a puzzlingly amused twist of his lips. "Yes, I think you should."

Rhys frowned slightly, then went over to pick up a tie lying on Sebastian's bureau. How on earth would anyone get a proper cravat out of that skinny thing? He tossed it back onto the bureau.

"Where is Wilson?" Rhys had not seen their valet all

evening. Not that any of the brothers utilized the man much. They all agreed that if a man couldn't dress him-self—well, he was truly inept.

Sebastian frowned; then his eyes widened. "Oh, Wil-son. We gave him a holiday—for Christmas."

Christmas? That was right. Today was Christmas. Good Lord, Jane must think she was the one about to wed a savage. He hadn't even wished her a happy Christmas. And what of a proper Christmas meal—surely the staff hadn't forgone the meal because Elizabeth and Christ-ian were away? And they had left on Christmas, too?

Rhys frowned. How very curious.

"I won't be at the club long," Sebastian said. "But I thought it would be nice for you and Jane to have a lit-tle time alone."

Rhys glanced at his brother, no longer bothered by his siblings being away. In fact, he quite liked the idea of having Jane to himself, too. He just wished he had thought to arrange a proper Christmas celebration, even if it was only for the two of them. He had so much to make amends for—he hoped she was an understanding woman.

"Have fun," Sebastian said. Again that knowing little grin was on his lips.

Rhys supposed his brother found him actually being taken with his betrothed quite humorous—especially after all the objections he'd had. Rhys had to admit it was mildly amusing. If he'd known what he was missing, he would have arranged for her to join him sooner.

The bath didn't have the desired effect Jane had hoped it would. She was too unnerved by all the events of the past two days to relax. Not that she wasn't tempted to hide in her room the rest of the night. But she was supposed to be watching Rhys.

She finished drying her hair, then brushed on a little mascara, hoping it would make her look a little less tired. Examining her reflection, she decided it didn't help much, but at least she was suitably clad, her turtleneck and jeans very modest.

She took a fortifying breath, then exited her room, going to find the "beautiful brothers."

She walked down the hall toward the living area. She pushed open one of the dining room doors, but no one was in there. She paused, her hand still on the door, and listened.

The whole apartment was silent as if not another living soul was there. Worry filled her. What if Rhys wasn't here? What if he'd left the apartment?

She softly closed the door and hurried farther down the hall. The hall opened out into a large living room. It was as lavish as the rest of the apartment with more dark antique furniture covered in rich upholstery. But other than a cursory scan of the room, she didn't stop to study the decor too closely.

She rushed straight to another door at the far end of the living room. The door was ajar. She pushed the wood panel open and stepped inside.

Rhys stood in front of a huge stone fireplace, his profile to her, a drink held loosely in his hand.

She didn't say anything for a moment, too captivated by how gorgeous he was. The firelight glinted off his hair. The simplicity of the black sweater and black pants he wore seemed to enhance the width of his shoulders and the narrowness of his hips.

After a few moments, he glanced over at her. "Do come in. I promise I won't bite."

Jane felt her skin burn again from the mixture of mortification and the yearning his words sent through her. She could vividly recall him nipping her, and her breasts ached at the memory.

She sucked in a calming breath and walked into the room, her legs only a little unsteady. Perching on the edge of one of the soft, cushy chairs, she made herself focus on the room.

This room, like all the others in the apartment, was huge. One wall was taken up almost completely by three arched windows. The glass in here was clear. Outside, she could see the twinkle of the city lights.

The rest of the free wall space was filled from floor to ceiling with hundreds and hundreds of books. Despite the size of the room, the space somehow felt cozy. Maybe it was the fire. Or maybe it was the warmth of the shiny wood floors stained a deep brown. Or it could have been the large, overstuffed furniture and the piano in the corner near the windows. But Jane fell in love with the room.

She stood and walked over to the windows. The view was incredible. The windows looked out over the city. Lights twinkled, and snow swirled softly in the winter air.

"This is my favorite room."

Jane started. Rhys was right beside her; she could feel heat radiating from him.

He continued to look out the window. "The view is amazing, is it not?"

"Yes," Jane agreed, turning to admire the view again, too. "It's beautiful, and so different from where I lived."

He turned his head toward her. "I forgot this is all new to you. I must show you all the sights."

Jane smiled. Exploring New York with Rhys—that sounded wonderful. "That would be nice."

"London can be daunting, but you will soon feel comfortable here."

She blinked, and the reality of her situation came back to her. He didn't even know he was in New York. And he couldn't show her around, not until his memories returned, and by then, she would have to move on and out of this strange world in which she now found herself.

"What is America like?" he asked, moving away from the windows and back to the fireplace.

She didn't know how to respond. Did she tell him about Maine? Did she modify her responses to fit the time period he believed he was in?

"It's—different. Very rural. Lots of trees and lakes and wildlife." All true and nothing that would confuse him.

"It sounds like my estate in Derbyshire. We will spend our summers there. The manor is set amongst rolling hills, and there is a pond, where we often swim."

Jane smiled. She wished the place he described existed. It sounded lovely.

"I also have another estate much closer to London. That is where Christian and Elizabeth are currently. They are attending a house party at the Earl of Barrington's. He hosts a gathering every year at this time. My little sister, Elizabeth, hates to miss the event as she loves to wear her prettiest dresses and dance. Not to mention the fact that she is also quite taken with the duke's son, Lord Granford. She is a hopeless romantic." He smiled with fond indulgence.

Jane smiled back, finding his affectionate expression very endearing, so different from the unreadable man who had walked her back to her hotel.

"Now, my brother Christian is quite the opposite. I fear he is the troublemaker of the family. He's quite the scoundrel and inordinately proud of it." Again, Rhys didn't seem upset by his apparently wild sibling.

Jane caught herself. It was so easy to forget that these people were all figments of Rhys's imagination. He spoke about them so easily. Then again, maybe they weren't imaginary. Maybe Rhys did have a sister and another brother.

"Christian is the reason I owe you an apology. He is notorious for getting both Sebastian and me into all manner of debacles, which was why I was in the state I was in last night. But I assure you that will not happen again."

She nodded, unsure what to say since she really had no idea what he was talking about.

But Rhys seemed to mistake her confusion for doubt. "I hope . . ." He cleared his throat. "I hope that the evening was—enjoyable to you, despite my condition and my far too bold behavior."

She blinked again. Following his words was like trying to sort out a riddle—in another language.

"It was—very enjoyable."

Relief washed over his face, but then the earnestness returned. "I will, of course, call for our banns right away."

She nodded. What on earth was he talking about? She thought back to the several Regency romances she'd read. Did they talk about banns?

She couldn't remember, so she finally said, "Okay."

Rhys smiled, apparently relieved again by her agreement. But the smile disappeared as his eyes roamed over her. His gaze lingered on the fit of her sweater and then dropped to her jeans.

Suddenly her unexceptional outfit seemed very daring.

"American men must be very liberal. Your style of dress is far more revealing than what English women are encouraged to wear."

She stared at him. He didn't intend for her to wear a bustle or something? No, they wore empire waists and petticoats. She knew she was supposed to humor him, but there was only so much she would do.

"This outfit is considered very practical."

He walked up to stand before her. "I am sorry. I imagine many of our ways will be different. And it is not my intention to make you feel uncomfortable." He leaned back slightly to look at her clothes again. "Plus, I must admit I rather like this look." He reached out and traced a finger along the seam of her jeans, running it slowly down over her hip.

Jane gazed at him, amazed she could feel the light touch so unmistakably through the thick material.

One finger joined another until his broad palm was pressed to her hip.

Then, just as she thought he would stroke his full hand over her, he removed it and stepped back from her.

"And I certainly cannot talk about style," he said, his voice self-disparaging and far steadier than Jane felt. "Wilson, my valet, has chosen some interesting clothing selections for me as well." He pulled his sweater away from himself and frowned down at it. "This is different. And he didn't pack me a single cravat or proper dinner coat."

"The times they are a-changin'," she said distractedly as she still struggled with the longing in her belly, in her limbs.

Rhys laughed, the sound deep and rich. "Indeed they are."

Jane stared at him for a moment, amazed that everything about this man could be so unbelievably attractive. She forced herself to look away. She wandered over to the piano, running a hand over the glossy black lid.

"Do you play?" Rhys asked.

She shook her head. "No. My mother did."

"Did?"

"My mother died when I was ten."

Rhys looked genuinely sorry. "That must have been difficult. Do you have siblings?"

"No, I'm an only child."

"Yet, your father sent you so far away to marry and live. That must have been painful for him."

A dull pain squeezed her chest as it always did when she thought about the loss of her father. "He passed away, too. Almost a year ago."

Rhys stared at her for a moment, then crossed the room, coming to stand in front of her again. "We have that in common, then. My parents died a little over three years ago."

She nodded, wondering if he then understood the loss and the loneliness that accompanied death. When her father passed away, she lost the only world she'd ever known.

Then she realized maybe Rhys's parents weren't even dead. He was telling her about a life that didn't exist. Or maybe it did. Maybe he did understand.

"Jane," Rhys said softly, pulling her from her sorrow. His hand came up to cup her face, his fingers strong and warm. "I want you to know that I will take good care of you. You will want for nothing, and—I believe we can find happiness together."

As crazy as it was, she'd never wanted to believe someone's words more—to finally have someone care about her. To have someone to help her. To not be alone.

Then reality hit her again. This man believed they were engaged. He believed they would marry soon. He believed they would have a life together. But none of that was true—especially the happily ever after.

Still, she reached up and held his hand, pressing the palm to the side of her face, savoring the slightly rough texture of his fingers and palms. It was nice to feel kindness and compassion, and not feel alone—even if it was for just a few moments and it was all pretend.

His thumb moved to caress the sensitive flesh of her lower lip. He stared down at her, his eyes golden in the firelight.

"Has anyone ever told you how beautiful your eyes are, guileless and as green as new grass?" His voice was low and husky, slipping over her skin like his fingers.

She shook her head, just a slight movement against his palm.

"No? How about your lips? Has anyone ever told you how soft and delectable they look?"

The lips he described parted, and a small breathless noise escaped them. Again she managed a tiny shake of her head.

"Hmm," he said. "That has been a major oversight by the male population in general. But I must say, I am very glad I'm the first to tell you."

She was, too. She couldn't imagine wanting anyone else to compliment her like this.

"Now, my little betrothed, I should warn you that you might want to close those lovely eyes—because I intend to sample those pretty lips." His head lowered, and his mouth caught hers.

Jane did close her eyes and twined her arms around his neck, his hair tickling over the backs of her fingers.

She knew at the moment she was living in as big a fantasy world as Rhys, but she didn't care. It simply felt too right.

Rhys tasted Jane, savoring her softness, her delicious taste. Had any other woman ever felt this perfect in his arms? He certainly couldn't remember.

He traced her soft lips gently with his tongue, begging her to open for him so he could taste her fully, feel her heat.

She did, her own tongue darting out to touch his delicately, tentatively.

Her timidity was more arousing than any practiced move by an experienced lover.

He kissed her for a moment longer, then ended the embrace, feeling as though he was losing control too quickly. Damn, he wanted her.

He looked down at her; her green eyes were hazed with passion, and her sweet lips were still parted.

Possessiveness fused with his need, making his longing even more intense. He had meant every word he said to her. He planned to make sure she was happy, cared for, safe. And for some reason he couldn't understand, he knew he needed to keep her safe.

He supposed it was because she was alone in the world. Still, something niggled at the back of his brain. He couldn't figure out what—but it didn't matter; he'd be there for Jane. Forever.

He reached up behind his neck and captured one

of her hands that were still around his neck. Linking her small fingers through his, he led her to the carpet in front of the fire.

"Sit," he said with mock sternness. "I have something for you."

She obeyed, curling her legs under herself, watching him with curious eyes.

He went over to the table and retrieved a rectangular, green velvet box.

He seated himself down beside her, stretching his long legs out in front of him, then held out the box.

She frowned at it, her eyes darkened with confusion. "Rhys, what is this?"

He smiled wryly. "Well, you have to open it to discover that." He offered it to her again.

She still hesitated, but then took the box. She glanced at him again, before she opened the lid. Her eyes widened. She shook her head, trying to shove the case back at him.

"No, Rhys," she said adamantly. "No. I can't accept this."

Rhys chuckled at her shaken expression. "Of course you can. You are precisely who was intended to accept it."

His mother had left him several pieces of jewelry that were to be given to his wife one day. He had never really thought about them over the years, but now, he wanted this woman to have the heirlooms.

He plucked the necklace out of the box and held it up. Firelight danced in a single golden topaz and made the surrounding diamonds twinkle. He slid closer so he could loop the chain around her neck.

She remained perfectly still as he hooked the clasp. Then she shifted to face him. The necklace hung low enough to nestle in the faint valley between her breasts.

The top she wore, which had seemed so improper only moments before, suddenly covered far too much. He wanted to see the glittering pendant against her pale skin. He wanted to make love to her while she wore nothing but the necklace—a sign that she was his.

"Rhys, please, I can't take this."

He studied her for a moment. "I want you to have it. Not only as a gift to my betrothed, but also to celebrate our first Christmas."

Her green eyes began to glitter like large polished emeralds as they welled with tears.

He frowned, concerned. "Why do you cry?"

"Because I wish this was real," she said, then bit her lower lip as if she thought she'd said something wrong.

He captured her chin gently with his forefinger and thumb. "Jane, this is very real. More real than anything has ever been to me." He couldn't say why he felt that way, but he knew it was true. "Please wear it. For me."

She stared down at the pendant for a moment. Then she nodded, a minute movement of her head, which he was starting to recognize was how she reacted when she was unsure.

Rhys smiled. Then he pulled her to him, situating her between his long legs. She leaned uneasily against him, her ramrod straight back to his chest. But she didn't pull away.

They sat that way, quiet, watching the fire. Contentment filled him. And he knew this was a rare moment, a rare sensation in his life, that happiness had eluded him for a long time.

But why? He should be very happy with a wonderful family and all the trappings of the well-to-do. Why did he suddenly think the past had not always been this satisfying?

He breathed in deeply, trying to understand his nebulous thoughts, when her clean, flowery scent reached him.

He couldn't resist nuzzling the softness of her hair. His arms tightened around her waist, and he noticed she didn't seem as stiff against him.

Suddenly his indistinct recollections didn't matter. He was happy right this minute and vowed that Jane would also know the same happiness.

He'd make sure of it—just as he was sure he was the fifth Viscount of Rothmere.

Chapter 8

Jane lay in bed, holding the necklace up in front of her, watching it sway and glimmer in the lamplight. The center stone was larger than a silver dollar, oval cut and multifaceted so it seemed to capture light in its golden depths. Square-cut diamonds encircled the large stone and twinkled like a dozen stars.

She wouldn't even hazard a guess at how many carats it was or how much it must have cost. And she didn't doubt the stones were real. She shook her head, disgusted with herself. She shouldn't have taken it, even in pretense. That was a necklace intended for someone else—not a woman Rhys didn't even know.

Why had she accepted it? She could have argued. She could have convinced him it was too soon in their engagement. Anything. But she had taken it, and worn it. And for a brief moment, she pretended the exquisite gift was really for her. Not because the item was obviously expensive, or beautiful, but because the necklace made her feel as though she belonged—to him.

She rolled over and gently placed the pendant on

the nightstand, the chain pooling like liquid gold around the jewel.

Resting her hands under her cheek, she continued to stare at the present.

Sadly, this had been one of the nicest Christmases she'd ever had. What did that say about her life?

She let her eyes drift shut as memories of her life in Maine came back to her. Christmases in a run-down, eerie old house, her father too lost in his fantasy world to give his daughter the attention she ached for. The loneliness.

As always, guilt filled her. Her father had done the best he could. And maybe she had always expected too much.

She opened her eyes again and gazed at the necklace. She'd just hold on to this night for what it had been—a lovely time. The gift and the snow and the fire. That had all been so nice. And Rhys's kiss. So very nice.

She rubbed the knuckle of her forefinger over her lips. The soft skin tingled even now from the memory of Rhys's kiss. His touch had been so wonderful, so perfect. And while he was holding her, the thought hadn't even entered her mind that she shouldn't be returning the kiss. When he touched her, it was as if everything was okay and suddenly made sense.

The night had been wonderful, and she would remember it that way—even after the real world came tumbling back to them both.

She closed her eyes again, exhausted. Who knew, maybe this was all just a dream anyway, and tomorrow she'd be home in Maine. Alone.

Jane started, her eyes snapping open as she tried to get her bearings. She was in Rhys's apartment, in the lovely blue and white room. But the room no longer felt comfy or safe. Something hung in the air, eerie and sinister.

She held herself very still, barely breathing, the covers up to her chin, listening. The room was absolutely silent; not even the sounds of the city penetrated the stillness. But she didn't need to hear whatever was in the room. She could *feel* it. Dankness hung in the air and crept over her skin like cold, clammy hands even under the thick covers. She fought back a shiver, remaining perfectly still.

The sensation didn't subside. In fact, it grew stronger. The clamminess encircled her legs, moving up them. It swirled around her arms, pressing down on her, restraining her.

Moving only her eyes, she glanced at the clock. It was after six-thirty A.M. The room was still softly lit by the lamp on her nightstand, and soon the sun would rise. She knew she was being ridiculous, but none of that seemed to matter. She still felt someone there. Someone or something that she could only describe as evil. And she knew she had to run. The pressure was increasing, suffocating her.

Mustering her courage, she held her breath and shoved out of the bed. She leapt over the platform, directly to the floor. The action might be the behavior of a frightened child, afraid of a monster under her bed, but she didn't care. She just knew she had to get out of that room.

She raced past Sebastian's door, even though his room was closer. Her only thought was to get to Rhys.

She didn't knock, but thrust the door open and ran inside. She slammed the door behind her only to realize that left her shrouded in complete blackness. She cracked the door just slightly to allow a hint of light from the hallway and rushed to the bathroom. She flicked on the light switch, then ran back to the door and closed it again. This time she flipped the lock, too.

She peered at the bed where Rhys lay on his back, the blankets covering him from the waist down, leaving his chest bare. His eyes were still closed.

How had he slept through her running around, slamming doors?

She crossed to the bed and touched his shoulder. The coolness of his skin surprised her.

"Rhys," she whispered.

When he didn't move, she whispered his name louder.

No response. Panicked, she jostled him, practically shouting his name. What if the evil she'd felt in her room had gotten to Rhys first? He wasn't moving, and in the dim light, she couldn't tell if his chest was rising and falling as he breathed.

Just as she was about to leave to go check Sebastian, Rhys's eyes fluttered open. "Jane?"

"Oh, thank heavens," she cried, and flung her arms around him as much as his reclining position would allow.

Lethargically, almost as if he was drugged, his arms came up to hug her back. "Jane—what is it?"

She pulled away from him. "Someone is in my room."

Rhys frowned up at her, confusion clear on his face. "What?"

Jane could tell by the heaviness of his eyelids, it was his exhaustion rather than her words that confused him. So she said them again slowly, "Someone is in my room."

"Did you see someone?"

"No—but I could tell he was there."

He nodded, although she was fairly sure he didn't believe her. He patted the other side of his bed. "Get in."

She hesitated, then scooted around the bed and scrambled under the covers. She turned to face Rhys, but she could tell he had already fallen back to sleep. He was once more totally still.

She rolled back over and stared at the closed and locked door. The cold, creeping feeling on her skin was gone. Everything felt normal, but there was no way she was stepping back into that hallway. Or back in her room.

She shivered and pulled the covers tighter over her. Maybe it had been a nightmare. Or residual anxiety over what had happened to her with the guy from the bar. Or even the mugging. But it didn't really matter, because she was staying right here—even if Rhys did think she was a big chicken in the morning.

Christian materialized into the derelict building that he had converted into his makeshift home just as the first rays of sun peeked over the city's skyline.

He crawled onto the mattress he'd situated in the center of the building, where those lethal rays couldn't reach him.

Exhaustion overcame him as it did for all his kind, especially on a day that was clear and the sun was bright.

But his last thought before he sank into blackened oblivion was that Rhys had a woman. He'd gone to see if he could sense how Rhys had fared his attack, and he found the little mortal from the alley. And he could sense Rhys's possession all over her.

Very interesting.

He would have to keep an eye on that.

Rhys leaned on an elbow and watched Jane sleep. Both of them had managed to sleep the whole day away.

She lay snuggled against his side, her head nestled in the crook of his arm. Even, quiet breaths whispered warmly over his chest and shoulder.

He didn't understand what he found so fascinating about just watching her breathe. But there was something so mesmerizing about it. Something thrilling about the tiny flutter of her pulse just above the slight jut of her collarbone.

He lifted his hand to touch the spot, but instead brushed a strand of her cropped hair away from her cheek. His fingers lingered, and he marveled at the softness of her skin, the flawlessness of her complexion like porcelain decorated with pale pink. A single finger trailed down to her lips, the skin there pinker and even softer.

He moved his hands away, hating to disturb her sleep. She looked so relaxed, so unguarded—not at all like the often wary, uncertain woman from the night before.

Of course, he could understand her apprehension. She had been uprooted from everything she'd known and thrust into a whole new world, surrounded by strangers who were completely different from her.

Too different, his mind warned, but he pushed the thought away. No—he had gone about things wrong. He just needed to make sure she understood, truly understood that he intended to care for her. He sensed boldness buried under that uncertainty. She would be fine here.

He moved his hand to rest on her waist and held her.

She burrowed against him with a content sigh. Then her eyes flew open, and she stared up at him, all that trustfulness gone.

"Good morning."

"Hi," she said, shifting away from him.

He knew he should let her go, it was the gentlemanly thing to do, the appropriate thing, but his hand held her fast.

Her eyes widened more, but she stilled against him. She swallowed, then said, "I shouldn't have come here. I—I thought there was someone in my room. But I think it must have been a nightmare."

He nodded. He remembered. "I will check your room for you. I should have checked last night, but I must have been more tired than I realized."

"Then I should let you rest." She tried to slide across the mattress again.

He had been tired, more exhausted than he could ever recall feeling. Sleep had fallen over him like inescapable blackness. But now he felt incredible. Rejuvenated, energetic.

"I'm very well rested," he assured her, allowing her to put a little space between them, but not releasing her waist completely. He rubbed his hand gently over her side, the touch not insistent or aggressive but rather lulling, coaxing.

She quieted again, those green eyes holding his.

"I know I should let you go," he told her honestly. "But I love holding you. Touching you."

Nervousness filled her eyes, but Rhys knew it was desire that darkened them to the shade of evergreens at dusk.

She didn't say anything for a moment. Then she admitted, "I like you touching me, too."

Her tentative words were all the encouragement he needed. He pulled her against him and pressed his mouth to hers.

Jane kissed him back, her arms coming up to clasp around his neck. Her rational mind still insisted this was not the right thing to do, that she could get hurt. That it wasn't fair to Rhys either. But her body was merrily singing, *tra la la*, and completely ignoring her mind.

She gave in to her singing body, which now hummed as well with a combination of nervous excitement and passion. She sank her fingers into Rhys's silky hair, pressing tighter to his hard length.

His mouth molded to hers, caressing her, tasting her. His teeth nipped gently, and his tongue teased.

She moaned, loving each different touch, mimicking them, wanting him to feel exactly as she did. On fire.

He responded with a groan of his own and deepened the kiss.

His hand continued to stroke her through the thin cotton of her pajamas, sliding slowly upward and then down, then back up again. His palm felt huge and hot, his fingers magical. She wanted them on her bare skin, all over her. She didn't know she could feel this way or want so badly. And even though she was nervous and uncertain of what exactly to do, she didn't want this to ever stop.

But it did. His lips left hers and he stared down at her. The room was illuminated only by the faint light from the bathroom, but she could see his eyes, burning as if flames blazed in their amber depths.

"Jane, tell me to stop. Tell me this is unfair to you. Tell me we should wait."

She stared up at his beautiful face, at his wide, sculpted lips and the arrogant flare of his nose. And those eyes that seemed to penetrate deep inside her.

She reached up and brushed a lock of his hair back from the chiseled line of cheekbone. This was the time to do the right thing. To stop.

"I can't," she whispered. She wanted him too much, and she'd waited so long to feel this way.

He groaned as if her words caused him pain, but his lips returned to hers with such fierce hunger she couldn't feel any shame in her weakness. Everything felt too right.

One of her hands caressed the smooth skin of his shoulders, delighting in the ripple of his muscles under her fingertips as he levered himself over her.

The hand at her waist caught the hem of her camisole pajama top, pushing it slowly up her stomach, his broad palm velvety against her skin. He nudged the material upward until her breasts were bared. He drew back, his gaze roaming over her.

"Oh, God, Jane, you are so beautiful."

Bliss skipped through her veins, over her skin. She'd never felt this way. She'd always thought she'd be embarrassed for someone to stare at her naked, too self-conscious, but she felt no embarrassment, only deep, agonizing need.

Her breasts ached and throbbed. Her nipples tightened, ordering him to touch them. And he obeyed, swirling the hardened peaks gently with his fingers and thumbs. And still he watched her. He watched his fingers teasing her, and her reaction as he did so.

She groaned and arched into his touch, begging him for more.

Again he obeyed, leaning forward to capture one of her nipples in his mouth, suckling her, carefully rasping the tender flesh with his teeth.

She gasped and squirmed against his length, registering for the first time that he was naked as she felt his hard arousal sear her thigh. Her surprise was quickly overwhelmed by the heat of his mouth on her, suckling her.

His mouth moved to lavish the same excruciatingly wonderful attention to the other nipple.

"Please, Rhys," she begged.

"Please what, Jane?" he asked, his voice breathless, his eyes glowing even brighter than before.

"I—I don't know how to tell you what I want."

His eyes held hers. "Just tell me. You can tell me anything."

Her heart hammered in her chest, in her ears. *Anything?* His words were the most thrilling fantasy she could imagine.

She stared up at him. He was so beautiful, the cut of his jawline, the shape of his lips, his silky hair framing his face. And his body. He was truly a fantasy personified.

And she didn't have a clue what to do with him.

"How about this," he said as he leaned forward to nuzzle her ear, his breath caressing her skin, his words soft and rich like brushed suede. "I'll do something, and you tell me if you like it."

She nodded, letting her eyes drift shut, savoring the feeling of his lips so close to her earlobe.

He nibbled the soft flesh there.

She whimpered, feeling the tiny bite throughout her body.

"Do you like that?"

She nodded again.

He kissed her neck, his lips teasing the sensitive skin below her ear.

She shivered, again feeling thrill dance through her limbs.

His lips lingered for a moment, before he asked, "Did you like that?"

"Yes." Her voice was breathy.

"Should I stay here?" He licked her neck. "Or move back to these?" He lifted himself up on one arm, so he could move a hand to her breasts, lightly brushing his palm over her so it barely skimmed the erect, aching points of her nipples.

She gasped, the sound almost anguished. "My—my breasts. Please."

He grinned at her, the curve of his lips so arrogant, yet his eyes were filled with so much desire that he was breathtaking. Then his finger plucked at one of her swollen nipples, and her breath rushed back in a low hiss.

"Do you like this?" He squeezed the hardened bud again, rolling it gently between his thumb and forefinger. "Or this?" He replaced his fingers with his mouth.

"Rhys." His name was a broken cry on her lips.

He continued to draw on her aching nipples, pulling them deep into his mouth, using his tongue to tease her.

She held her breath, the ache inside her so strong and intense it was almost unbearable. Is this how making love always felt? As though she was careening toward something she didn't quite understand, and Rhys was the only one who could save her.

"I love touching you," he murmured against the swell of her breast. He rasped his tongue over her other nipple. "I love tasting you."

She writhed under him, her body begging for the things she couldn't voice.

"Where should I touch you next?" His question would have sounded offhanded if his breathing wasn't as labored as hers.

She wiggled against him again. One point on her body, centered between her thighs, desperately pleaded for his attention. But she still couldn't tell him what she wanted.

"Maybe you would like to be touched down here." He trailed a finger between her legs, a faint brush against where she was desperate for him to caress, to touch.

Her hip instinctively lifted, pressing herself against his hand.

He groaned deep in his throat, then muttered roughly, "Janie, you are enough to kill a man."

She wasn't sure that was a compliment, but she didn't have much time to contemplate his words, because his fingers hooked the waistband of her pajama bottoms and tugged them down. Then his finger parted her to touch that one focal point. That one spot that would both drive her mad and give her back her sanity.

He stroked her, until his name was just a mindless mantra that she repeated over and over. And several times she thought the wonderful magic of his fingers against her and her repeated prayer were going to give her release. But just as she was on the edge, he'd pull back.

"I—I can't take anymore," she panted at him. She blinked up at him, her eyes clouded with passion.

He grinned at her, his own eyes dark with desire.

"Then tell me what you want? You have to invite me in."

"I can't."

"You have to."

She stared into his eyes, and the hunger she saw there gave her courage. It stole away her inhibitions.

"Rhys, I want you inside me. Please."

Then he moved so the full, hard length of his body was on top of her. Skin against skin. Muscles flexing. Heat burning.

She gasped again.

He braced himself, lifting some of his weight off of her. "Are you all right?"

All right? She sighed, moving her hands to stroke the muscles of his back, drawing him more fully against her. "I don't think I've ever been better," she said sincerely.

He stared at her for a moment, then gave her a smile, rich with desire and awe. "Nor I."

His head came down, and he kissed her again. His body rocked gently against her, a wonderful friction along her breasts and belly. But she wanted more. She wanted all of him.

She parted her legs, cradling his hips, feeling his heavy erection against her.

He continued to kiss her, his tongue swirling with hers as his hand moved down between her spread thighs. His fingers parted her, and he swirled a finger around her clitoris.

She moaned into his mouth and writhed.

"Please," she begged again, against his lips, and she felt him smile.

His hand left her to position himself to enter her. Moving carefully, he held her gaze as he penetrated her, inch after inch of heavy, thick pressure.

"Are you all right?" he asked when he was deep inside her.

She nodded. She felt stretched and sensitive, but she also felt wonderful, full of this gorgeous, powerful man.

Rhys remained perfectly still. It was damned near killing him, but he wanted this to be good for Jane. He wanted to show her that she was marrying a generous lover—not the beast from the other night. That she would never regret becoming his.

But damn, she felt good. Tight and hot and so wet.

He ground his teeth and kept his hips motionless. Balancing his weight on one hand, he slid his other hand over Jane's body. He teased her puckered, rosy nipples, but when she began to squirm, he slipped his hand down between their joined bodies.

She was parted wide, filled with him. Her clitoris bared to him. He touched the tiny, engorged nub, brushing over and around her until Jane's hips began to move, slight jerks up and down his erection. A miniature imitation of the hard, deep thrusts he planned for later. But right now, this was about exquisite torture for both of them.

He increased the pressure of his fingertip on her.

She moaned, the sound almost pained. Her hips lifted higher, forcing him deeper. Her muscles flexed, pulsing around his erection.

He pressed his finger harder against her, quickening his pace, a rapid, relentless flutter until she cried out and contracted violently around him, nearly pulling him over the edge with her.

He watched her as she closed her eyes, her pants gradually turning to slower, deeper breaths. Finally she blinked up at him, her eyes clouded with dazed satisfaction, her cheeks pink.

"Oh, my," she managed in a breathy voice.

He smiled. That seemed to be her favorite response to an orgasm.

"Good?"

She nodded, the pink in her cheeks deepening to red.

"How about this?" He pulled the full length of himself out of her body, until only the head was still inside her warmth. Then he slowly but steadily entered her again.

Her eyes widened. "Oh, my," she breathed, her hands pressing against his back.

He grinned, and then moved again. And again. Thrusting harder and deeper until they were both straining and panting, and this time he didn't stop until they both cried out in ecstasy.

Chapter 9

Jane whimpered softly when Rhys withdrew from her. As strange and foreign as it had initially been to have him filling her so completely, it felt even odder to have him gone.

He rolled and pulled her with him so they were face-to-face, legs tangled, hands still touching each other's warm bodies.

"Are you all right?" he asked.

"I'm—wonderful," she told him. "Beyond wonderful." And that was absolutely true. She couldn't imagine anything more perfect with a more perfect man.

"It was perfect," he agreed as though he could hear her very thoughts. He stroked his large hand up and down her hip, the touch tender.

She sighed. So this was what girls had giggled about in her high school locker room and young women had discussed over their coffees in the college snack bar. Jane had always felt different from those women, too busy with her studies and her strange home life to experience romance and boys. Now, at twenty-five, she understood. Before she thought better of it, she added, "I finally feel normal."

Rhys's eyebrow shot up and he gave her a wry grin. "Normal? Not exactly the result I was hoping for."

Why had she said that? "I—I . . ." She winced, as she struggled for the right explanation. "I meant that I now understand what I have heard other women talking about."

His smile broadened. "Women talk about bedding men?"

She widened her eyes, surprised by the question. "Oh, yeah. All the time."

Rhy's expression appeared caught between amusement and surprise. "Really? So all those proper ladies are not nearly as proper as they seem, then?"

She frowned. She'd managed to forget again that Rhys wasn't living in the same time period as everyone else. "Well—I suppose *proper* women don't talk about that sort of thing too much."

"Are you trying to tell me that you didn't associate with proper ladies?" He grinned and pulled her closer to him. "Or that *you* aren't a proper lady?"

No, she wasn't a proper lady, that was for sure. If she'd had a respectable bone in her body, she wouldn't have allowed this to happen. She would have left his bed as soon as she'd woken. But as usual all her appropriate behavior and rational thoughts fled at the sight of him.

"I . . . I'm certainly not the woman you think I am." She sighed, wondering what he'd think of her when he got his memory back. She didn't imagine he'd have a very flattering picture of her.

Rhys shifted away from her, his eyes locking with hers. He regarded her silently for a few moments. "Why do you say that?"

What could she say? *I'm not your betrothed. I'm some woman you met in a seedy bar.*

"What do you mean?" he asked again, his voice lower, more demanding.

"I—I just mean . . ." She didn't know what to say.

He moved suddenly, his weight pinning her into the mattress—his face above hers. "I don't care who you were, Jane. Because now, now you are mine."

His mouth came down on her parted lips, capturing her startled gasp. The kiss was possessive, insistent, leaving no room for her to deny him. Not that she wanted to. She wanted to be his—desperately.

He ended the kiss as abruptly as he'd started it. Peering down at her, his eyes roamed her face, and for the briefest moment, Jane wondered if he was remembering something. Remembering who he was—who she was.

"You are exactly who I thought you were," he said softly, his voice rasping over her like velvet. "A beautiful, sweet, honest, and so, so desirable woman."

The words should have melted her into a delighted puddle in the center of the mattress, but they couldn't—not when they weren't true. Especially not the honest part.

He sighed, his brow creasing. "Again, I am not achieving the desired effect." He tempered the grim look by brushing back a lock of her hair from her cheek.

"I feel . . ." She struggled for the truth. A truth that Rhys could hear, that wouldn't upset the world he'd created. "I feel like I'm taking advantage of you."

He stared at her. Then he laughed, rolling back to his side, hugging her against him. The rumbling in his chest created a warm vibration throughout her body.

He shifted back so he could see her face, but their chests continued to be pressed together. "I rather like that. Now *you* will have to make an honest man of me."

She smiled back, but guilt made the gesture strained. Honest. There was that word again. She was the one "bedding" him under false pretense. She felt like a total . . . what was a good historical term? Trollop? Yeah, that one fit.

Somehow she didn't think this was what Sebastian had in mind when he hired her to take care of Rhys.

Sebastian sat in the living room, reading *Salem's Lot*, when Rhys strolled into the room. Whistling.

"Good morning."

Sebastian gaped at his brother. Rhys did not whistle. And he was never agreeable when he first arose.

And what was he wearing?

"What do you have on?"

Rhys glanced down at his clothes, a dark brown, button-front shirt and faded jeans. He smiled again. "Jane brought these from America for me. At least I think she did, and I thought it would be rude not to wear them." He examined them again. "They are actually rather comfortable."

Sebastian had no idea what to say. Rhys in jeans. He was too morose for normal clothes like that. He always wore black. In fact, Sebastian was surprised that Rhys hadn't resorted to dressing like Dracula—lurking around like a menacing head waiter.

Rhys flopped down in a chair and put his feet up on the coffee table, crossing them at the ankles. He smiled broadly.

Sebastian blinked, then finally found his voice. "You are certainly . . . happy." Lord, it would take some time to get used to using that word to describe Rhys. And he kept smiling—it was actually a bit unnerving.

"Well, it seems that my betrothed feels as if she has taken advantage of me." He sighed with satisfaction. "I'm well and truly compromised."

Sebastian smiled himself. Ah, so Rhys had gotten himself laid. That certainly explained a lot. And it hadn't taken the two of them long. He'd thought one of them would fight the attraction—for a while anyway.

"That's great. You've needed to be compromised for a long, *long* time," Sebastian pointed out.

Rhys grinned. "I suppose she will have to marry me now."

Sebastian rolled his eyes. Leave it to Rhys to still be morally uptight—even in his delusions.

Rhys grew serious. "I do need to call the banns. I should go now. I think I will go have Spencer ready a carriage." He stood up.

Sebastian jumped up, too. "You—you did that already."

Rhys frowned. "I did? I already requested the banns? Or told Spencer to have the carriage readied?"

"The banns. Right after Jane got here—on the way from the boat—I mean, ship."

"I did? While drunk?"

Sebastian gave him a shrug and a nod. "You liked what you saw, so you figured why wait."

Rhys rubbed a hand over his face, then peered at Sebastian. "As if she was some horse I decided to buy on impulse? Good Lord, it's little wonder she didn't flee right then and there."

"She seems to like you."

"I cannot imagine why. Or how I will make all this up to her."

"I'd stick with the sex. She seems to like that, right?"

Rhys gaped at him. "And to think, mother wanted you to go into the church."

Sebastian shuddered. Yes, he'd dodged a bullet of his own by choosing vampirism. Mother would be proud.

Rhys shook his head, obviously still aggrieved by his imaginary bad behavior. "I should go see what Cook has prepared for breakfast. Jane must be famished."

Sebastian stepped forward to block him. "Holiday," he said quickly.

A puzzled frown creased Rhys's brow.

"Cook—all the staff actually—are on holiday."

"All at once?"

Sebastian nodded. "It seemed like a good decision at the time."

"Let me guess. While we were drunk?"

"Yeah."

"Remind me again why I ever trust Christian," Rhys muttered more to himself than Sebastian, then left the room, heading toward the kitchen.

Well, Sebastian thought as he fell back into his chair with a sigh of relief, so far so good.

Except for the lack of food in the apartment. He kept forgetting that mortals needed to be fed. He would have to call down to Mick and ask him to go to the grocery store. But other than that, things were going better than he could have anticipated. Certainly faster.

If he could keep Rhys believing he was mortal for a while longer, maybe Rhys would realize that he could have Jane—even as a vampire. Plus, Jane would also need time with Rhys to accept the truth. Some mortals were squeamish about the whole undead thing. For some reason, he didn't think Jane would be one of them. He could feel something when he talked to her. She knew about death.

But the main thing Rhys and Jane had going for them was their connection. It was stronger than he'd ever sensed, even between most mated vampires.

Maybe his Dudley Do-Right brother *would* do the right thing and cross this woman over and marry her.

Jane peered at herself in the mirror. The simple A-line skirt and tailored shirt were very respectable. Very proper. No one would guess she was a complete wanton with absolutely no ability to control her desire. She couldn't believe it herself.

She'd just had sex with Rhys!

While she was in his arms, being with him had seemed so right, so natural. But now . . . Now she couldn't believe what she'd done. How had her life gotten so out of her control? When she'd decided to leave Maine, she made up her mind she would do the normal things other women did. She'd date. She'd discover the intrigues of intimacy. She'd have friends and fun times. So far, she'd skipped right over all of that straight into the intimacy.

Her heart pulsed wildly in her chest, and heat tingled through her limbs and belly, before centering on the sensitive flesh between her thighs. Oh, she'd definitely experienced intimacy—and it had been so, so wonderful.

But she wouldn't allow it to happen again. No matter

how attracted to him she was, they would not have sex again.

At least not until he was well. It just wasn't right.

But it sure as heck felt right.

She glared at herself in the mirror. She couldn't think like that. She wouldn't.

But maybe—maybe one day, when Rhys was well, they could start again. She could know the real Rhys. And maybe he wouldn't think poorly of her one transgression, and they could—date.

And maybe Rhys was a real viscount.

The more likely outcome would be that Rhys would get his memory back and promptly remember he liked women as stunning as himself. Not short, mousy women with the morals of a tramp.

She adjusted her skirt, smoothed her hands over her shirt and left her room to find him—to explain that they should wait. He'd, of course, think she was referring to until after their wedding, which was fine, since there wouldn't be a wedding.

But instead of Rhys, she found Sebastian. He looked up from the book he was reading as she entered, greeting her with a warm smile.

"Hey there. You look nice."

She smiled, but barely registered the compliment. Her mind was on what she needed to do. "Have you seen Rhys?"

"Why, yes, I have." He smiled, a knowing look in his hazel eyes.

Oh, no. Her stomach sank. Sebastian knew.

"So I hear from a very happy Rhys that you have compromised him."

She blushed and fought back a groan. "I'm really

sorry. I know I shouldn't have allowed it to happen—
and I have no excuse. I can leave right away." She had
no idea where she'd go, but she'd just have to figure
something out.

"Are you kidding? Leave? Jane, this situation is perfect. I mean, you'll know exactly where he is if he's in
bed with you, right?"

Jane gaped at him. With each passing day, it seemed
that both brothers were nuts.

"But it's unfair to him. He thinks he's engaged to
me. Plus, you are paying me. There's something just—
wrong about all of this."

"So," Sebastian said slowly, "you are having moral is-
sues with this?"

"Yes."

He shook his head, amazement clear in his hazel
eyes. "Damn, you two are perfect for each other."

She frowned, unsure what he was talking about.

"Listen," he said, "do you like Rhys?"

She nodded.

"And do you want to be with him?"

She considered lying, but she couldn't. She did want
to be with him—desperately. She nodded.

"Then I don't see a problem. I certainly don't think
Rhys's amnesia would somehow make him attracted to
you when he normally wouldn't be. Hell, nothing
would have made him attracted to his real American
betro . . ."

Jane gaped at him, eyes wide, her mouth falling
open. Was he saying that Rhys had a real fiancée? Dizziness whirled through her.

Sebastian immediately came to stand in front of her.
He caught her arm, as if he knew she was woozy.

"I said that the wrong way," he told her, his voice

steady and apologetic. "Rhys seems to think he is an ancestor of ours, and I have seen pictures of the American woman the real viscount married. She was—unattractive."

Jane felt relief clear away some of the dizziness. At least she didn't have to add adulterer to tramp.

"Jane, Rhys is happier than I have seen him in years. And that isn't because of the amnesia; that is because of you."

Her heart leapt in her chest at the idea that she was making Rhys happy—but something seemed odd about Sebastian's assurance. Why would he be happier with the amnesia? Were there things in his real life he needed to forget? Or maybe she was just reading too much into Sebastian's words.

She studied him, trying to decide which it was, but his hazel eyes revealed nothing.

She sighed. "Rhys and I don't even know each other. And we can't get to know each other, because he thinks he's a viscount, and I'm pretending to be his fiancée."

"But it won't always be that way. And you are good for him."

She wanted that to be true.

"Jane, I know my brother. He is very particular, and if he is with you, it's because he wants *you*. Not because you just happen to be part of his current delusions. Just have fun."

How easy it would be simply to accept Sebastian's advice. But she still thought it was wrong to continue a physical relationship. She had to wait until they could honestly know each other.

"You will stay, won't you?" he asked.

She nodded. She would stay. She would continue to hang on to the excuse that this arrangement made the most sense with her financial situation, but she knew she was lying to herself. She wanted to be close to Rhys. But she also needed to know more about the man. To understand him.

"Yes. I'll stay, but I can't take your money," she said resolutely. "It makes what happened between Rhys and me feel—cheap. I'll stay because I owe Rhys to help him if I can. Also . . . Can you tell me something about him—his real life—so I at least feel as though I know something about him?" *So I didn't just sleep with a total stranger.*

"What—what has he told you?"

Jane frowned. Why should it matter what Rhys had told her? He was the one with amnesia, wasn't he?

But she finally said, "He told me your parents passed away?"

"Yes, when I was twenty-two and Rhys was twenty-six."

Jane nodded, so Rhys did understand loss. They did share that.

"Do you really have two other siblings?"

"Yes."

Jane nodded, gladness warring with envy. He had other family to care about him, to love. She didn't be-grudge him that. She wanted him to have others in his life. His siblings just made it all the more clear that she was alone. And once Rhys was better, she might be to-tally alone again.

She straightened. Perhaps it was best, despite the in-timacy she'd just shared with him, to prepare for that possibility. Maybe that would make things easier in the long run.

"I will stay," she told Sebastian again, "for the time we originally agreed on. But I do need to be searching for my own place and a job."

Sebastian opened his mouth as if he planned to argue. Then he closed it. He looked at her speculatively, then asked, "What do you normally do for work?"

"Normally, I ran a funeral parlor. But I actually have my BA in accounting. That was what I intended to do here in New York."

"A funeral parlor?"

"My father was a mortician." She waited, expecting one of two typical responses, repulsion or morbid curiosity.

She got neither. Instead Sebastian chuckled, shaking his head. "I swear you two are a match made in heaven."

But before she could ask him what he meant, he asked, "Would you be able to handle the finances of a nightclub? Accounts payable? Ordering supplies? Payrolls? Taxes—that sort of thing?"

She frowned. "I don't see why not."

"Great! You're hired. Rhys and I stink at the financial end of the nightclub. I do it, but I truly hate it. I'd be thrilled to lose the job."

She shook her head, that dizzy feeling coming over her again. "You want me to work at the club?"

"Sure. It's the perfect solution. You won't be taking money for doing the dirty with my brother, yet you'll still be here and financially stable."

"But I won't be watching him, which is the reason for me to stay here in the first place."

"Oh, well, I wouldn't want you to start until after the New Year, and who knows, by then Rhys could be fine again."

She frowned. Something just didn't add up here. Why was Sebastian so set on her staying here? And she still got the feeling that Rhys's ailment wasn't distressing Sebastian in the least. The doctor hadn't even come today as he had said he would.

"I thought the doctor was supposed to come today to examine Rhys."

He was nodding before she even finished her sentence. "I did, too. So I called, and it seems I misunderstood. He said tomorrow, because of the holidays, you know."

She nodded. Okay, but that still didn't explain why it was so important that she stay here.

"If I do take the job at the club, I will still be leaving to live in my own place—after you figure out another arrangement for Rhys."

Sebastian shrugged. "That's fine." He picked up his book as though he planned to start reading again. Then he paused, the book in his lap. "I just thought, since we have this big apartment and you don't have a place, it would be easier for you to just stay here. Finding good rentals in this area can be tough, but I suppose you could leave . . ."

Suddenly she felt a tad silly, and more than a little overly suspicious. He was just being kind, and she was looking for ulterior motives.

"You'd love working at Carfax Abbey, I think. It's a fun place."

When she frowned with confusion, he clarified, "The nightclub."

She nodded. She *did* need a job, and Sebastian was offering a real one this time. In a nightclub, which was infinitely different than a funeral parlor. It could be exciting and fun. She loved the idea of being surrounded by people out for a good time. Dancing, socializing, living.

She wasn't going to even speculate on the faint rise

in her pulse when she thought about the fact she'd be working with Rhys. Given how uncertain everything was with her relationship with the man, it wasn't wise to take a job with him. She had to keep reminding herself that things could change. Would likely change.

But on a practical note, Sebastian was offering her an exciting job, a good job. She'd be a fool to pass up the deal. And if the situation changed once Rhys regained his memory, well, she'd figure that out when the time came. Right now, she wanted to stay, although she did intend not to let things get out of hand like they did last night. She still believed she and Rhys should wait to continue the physical side of their relationship until they both understood what was going on.

"Okay," she said slowly, "I'll take the job."

Chapter 10

Rhys scrutinized the kitchen. He couldn't put his finger on it, but something didn't look like he remembered. Didn't the kitchen have a fireplace? And he could have sworn Cook kneaded bread on a large wooden table. Granted, he hadn't been in the kitchen since he was a child. Or perhaps he was remembering the Derbyshire estate. That had to be it.

The door swung open, and Jane walked into the room. She wore an unfussy skirt in dark blue and a white top with a single row of buttons running down the front. The neckline was opened slightly, revealing the hollow at the base of her throat and a little vee of the creamy skin underneath.

"Hello," she said with a shy smile.

The changes in the kitchen suddenly didn't matter.

He walked over to her and pulled her against him. She squeaked at his abruptness, but the sound was lost against his lips as he kissed her. She returned his embrace after only a moment's hesitation.

"I like this," he said when they finally parted. He toyed with a button on her blouse.

She blushed. "You are very easy to please."

"Actually, I am rather difficult to please. Very exacting. Very particular. You just happen to be perfect."

She made a noise somewhere between a laugh and a snort.

"You don't believe me?"

She shook her head. "It's funny, though, your brother just said the same thing about you being particular."

"Did he? For once Sebastian is right." He caught her hips and walked her backward across the kitchen until her bottom hit the edge of the kitchen cupboards.

Her surprised laughter filled the room, a sweet, joyous sound.

Rhys smiled down at her. His pelvis and his hands pinioned her there against him and the counter.

Her smiled faded, and she looked up at him with wide, serious green eyes.

"You keep doing that. Giving me reactions very different than the ones I've been aiming for."

She smiled, although it was only a bittersweet half smile. "I'm sorry, this is all just so new to me—and I'm just sort of flying by the seat of my pants here."

His smiled broadened at her description. "Why do you feel that way?" he asked.

"I . . ." Her cheeks grew pink. "I really liked what we did earlier . . ."

"Mmm, I did, too." Really, really liked it. He leaned forward to steal a quick kiss.

Pink deepened to red. "But I think we shouldn't do it again."

His smile disappeared.

"I know I told you that I didn't want to wait—but I think we should. Wait. Until we are—until our situation is different."

Jane didn't know how she'd expected Rhys to respond, but it definitely wasn't the reaction she got.

He spun away from her and shouted, "Sebastian!" in a loud, commanding voice.

He waited for a moment and then shouted his brother's name again.

After several seconds, Sebastian strolled into the room, looking as though he hadn't even heard his brother's wall-shaking bellow.

"Good God, Rhys, haven't you ever heard of simply walking into the room where the person you want to speak to is—and talking to said person in a normal voice?"

Rhys didn't answer him, instead saying, "Please tell me that we have at least one servant who isn't away on holiday."

"What? Why?"

"Because Jane and I need to go to the vicar—this instant."

Sebastian threw a bewildered look at Jane.

She shook her head. She had no idea what to say or do. But apparently Rhys had agreed to wait until the circumstances were different. He just intended to change the situation as soon as possible by getting them married. Too bad that wasn't the circumstance she hoped would change.

"A servant?" Rhys asked again impatiently. "I don't intend to show up at the church with Jane and me on the back of the same horse."

"Well, there aren't any servants. So you will just have to wait," Sebastian told him flatly.

Just then the kitchen door opened, and a hulk of a man with a bald head and neatly trimmed goatee entered the room. He glanced at everyone, but his face remained impassive.

"Mick," Sebastian greeted, then gestured to the two white plastic sacks Mick had set on the floor. "Thanks."

Mick nodded and started to turn to leave.

"Mick?" Rhys said.

The hulk stopped and looked back at Rhys.

"Mick," Rhys repeated. "You work for us."

Mick did raise his eyebrows in response.

"Thank God, man." Rhys walked over and clapped the giant on the arm. "Ready me a carriage. Immediately."

At that, Mick's brows shot up even farther, an almost laughable expression of perplexity coming over his stoic features.

Sebastian stepped forward. "No. Don't ready—a carriage, Mick."

"Okay," the huge man agreed, the word rumbling low in his throat like the distant echo of thunder.

Rhys turned to glare at his brother. "Why ever not?"

Sebastian hesitated for a moment, then stated, "It's after nine o'clock. Too late to go to the vicar. He will be asleep."

Rhys pondered that, then nodded. "Perhaps you are right." He turned back to Mick. "But please do have a carriage readied first thing tomorrow morning."

Mick looked at Sebastian, who nodded. The hulk nodded, too. "Okay," he said again, confusion clear in the low rumble.

"Thanks, Mick," Sebastian said.

"Okay," Mick said once more, then left.

Rhys crossed back to Jane and caught her hands,

rubbing his thumbs back and forth over her knuckles. "We will go to the church first thing tomorrow morning and get married."

Sebastian came up behind him. "You can't do that."

Rhys glanced at his brother over his shoulder. "Yes. We can."

"No. You can't."

Rhys released one of her hands and turned to face Sebastian. "And why can't we?"

"Well . . ." Sebastian rolled his eyes upward for a moment as if he was inspecting the kitchen's high ceiling. "You just called the banns," he blurted out, then smiled smugly. "It's still going to be over two weeks before you can be married."

Rhys glanced at the floor, considering that announcement.

Sebastian cast Jane a quick look, wiggling his eyebrows proudly.

Jane forced a slight, bemused smile back. The argument would have been quite funny if it hadn't been so odd.

"I will go to the archbishop and tell him that a special license is required." Rhys gave his brother a significant look, although Jane didn't understand the significance.

Sebastian gaped at Rhys. "You would do that? You would besmirch Jane's reputation like that?"

Rhys gave Jane a sheepish look.

Jane stared back at him, stuck on the fact Sebastian had actually used the word "besmirch."

"I would, of course, require the vicar's discretion on the details of the ceremony. But I do, in fact, think Jane stands a larger threat of being ruined if we wait. After all, she has no chaperone—not even a servant. And she could very well be with child already."

Jane gaped at the brothers. Rhys was suggesting that they had to marry because she might be pregnant! Her heart did several somersaults in her chest. She *could* be pregnant.

She sank back against the counter, her sudden movement drawing Rhy's attention to her.

"Are you all right?" he asked, his eyes scanning her face.

"You don't really think I'm pregnant, do you?" Her voice sounded reedy, not at all like her own. How could she have been so careless, so—so dumb. She could be pregnant. Of course she could.

Rhys gently squeezed her fingers. "It is certainly a possibility."

She blinked up at him, shock still making it difficult to comprehend much of anything. Then she noticed Sebastian over Rhys's shoulder. He adamantly shook his head and waved his hands repeatedly, while mouthing the word "no."

She frowned. What was he trying to tell her? She tilted her head and gave him a confused, questioning look.

"Sebastian? What the hell are you doing?" Rhys asked sharply, following her gaze over his shoulder toward his brother.

Sebastian immediately dropped his hands, his mouth snapping closed. Then he said in an offhanded voice that belied the fact that he'd just been motioning like a mime gone mental, "Fine. We will get a special license, but let me do it. I'll go to the archbishop, and then I can bring the vicar back here to perform the wedding. That will decrease the risk of scandal."

Rhys considered that plan, then nodded. "That is probably a good idea."

Sebastian breathed out a sigh of relief. "Good. Now, if there are no further crises, I think I should head to the club."

"Another good idea," Rhys agreed.

Sebastian shot Jane a reassuring smile, then left the room.

She remained against the counter, her hand in Rhys's, feeling more than a little dazed by the events of the past few minutes.

"Janie, you are all right, aren't you?"

She swallowed and forced herself to meet Rhys's riveting, amber gaze. Could she really be pregnant with this man's child? The chances were slim—but not impossible.

"Yes, I just hadn't even considered pregnancy as a factor when we . . ."

He smiled. "We weren't thinking about much aside of each other."

"No."

"Listen, you must be starving. Why don't you see what we have for a simple meal, and I will go in the library and start a fire. We can dine there."

She nodded, still feeling too stupefied to consider eating.

Rhys leaned down and captured her lips, giving her a tender kiss, only the gentle caress of skin against skin.

"It will be fine," he assured her again.

She forced a smile and watched him leave the room, his walk graceful and confident.

She took a deep breath—just when she thought things couldn't get any weirder. She doubted that she was pregnant. It wasn't the right time of the month—she didn't think. She'd never thought about the ins and outs of getting pregnant. She'd never needed to. But she should have been more cautious for many reasons.

It was as if she saw Rhys, and she lost her mind.

"Good, you're alone."

Jane popped out of her reverie to see Sebastian, peeking in the doorway.

"Yes."

He stepped inside the kitchen. "What the hell brought on the sudden and immediate need to get married?"

Jane didn't really want to talk about it. As far as she was concerned, Sebastian already knew too much about her sex life. But as he didn't seem to be leaving without an answer, she finally admitted, "I tried to tell him that we should stop being—intimate until our situation changed. Meaning his memory loss."

"But he, of course, thought you meant your marital situation."

She nodded.

Sebastian chuckled. "Well, you gotta be sort of flattered about that. He was going to marry you tonight to get you back in his bed."

"Yeah, that was real flattering," Jane agreed dryly. "In a crazy Regency sort of way."

Sebastian's grin slipped. "I'm sorry, I don't mean to make light of this situation."

Jane sighed. "Okay. But I do think he needs to see a doctor soon."

He nodded. "I agree."

He picked up the two plastic shopping bags that Mick had left by the door and brought them to the counter. "Here is some food."

"Thanks," she said, staring at the bags, but her mind was back on the stupidity of having unprotected sex.

As if Sebastian was reading her mind, he gently touched her shoulder and said, "Don't worry. You aren't pregnant. Rhys can't have children."

"He can't?"

"No. He had a bad—animal attack when he was younger. A—bat."

Jane frowned. A bat? "How—"

"The bat was carrying a disease that rendered Rhys sterile."

Severe sun and food allergies, amnesia and sterility. Rhys was exceptionally unlucky. "That is—unbelievable."

"Yeah. You don't even know the half of it."

Relief with a hint of disappointment mingled in her stomach. She was honestly glad she wasn't pregnant. This was not the time or the circumstance for that. But she did feel bad that Rhys couldn't father children.

"Okay," Sebastian said. "I'm headed to the club. I hope things go smoothly the rest of the night."

So did she.

Chapter 11

Jane finished arranging her turkey sandwich on a plate and added a handful of potato chips. She reached back into the open bag for two more slices of bread, then stopped.

Rhys didn't eat bread. Just protein drinks and raw meat.

She shuddered and popped one of the salty chips in her mouth for good measure.

"Protein drink," she said thoughtfully, then decided to check the refrigerator first.

Sure enough, there were several plastic pouches labeled "For Rhys." She took out one of the bags and flipped it over in her hands, looking for directions. None.

She debated what to do since Sebastian was down at the club, and Rhys probably wouldn't remember how to prepare it.

The viscous liquid squished around in the plastic pouch looking like chocolate syrup and cherry syrup all mixed together. He probably wouldn't even drink the stuff anyway. It certainly didn't look like a health drink; that was for sure.

With a grimace, she headed back to the cupboards and took down a tall drink glass.

She frowned at the pouch. The clear bag had two plastic stoppers at the top, and it didn't seem to make much difference which one she opened.

After a struggle, she got one of the caps off and poured the syrupy liquid into the glass. She quickly snapped the cap back on and took the remaining concoction back to the fridge.

Picking up her plate in one hand and the drink in the other, she lifted the glass to her nose to sniff the dark liquid. The scent of copper mixed with a sweet, almost rusty smell assaulted her nose.

"Ick," she cringed, but headed to the library with the drink still in hand.

Rhys sat in one of the overstuffed chairs. He rose when she entered the room and took the plate from her, frowning as he set it on the table.

"Is this punishment for having to prepare your own meal?"

It took Jane a moment to realize he was referring to the fact she brought in only one plate.

Her far more appetizing dinner *was* going to make it rather difficult to convince him the slimy beverage was his meal.

"Sebastian said that you . . ." She supposed it couldn't hurt to just tell him the truth. "He says you have food allergies, and this is what you usually eat." She held it out to him.

Rhys peered at the glass, a look halfway between amusement and disbelief on his face. "He did, did he?"

She nodded.

"Are you sure you aren't trying to poison me because I've been such a wretched cad since you arrived?"

"You haven't been wretched or a cad."

He smiled, apparently pleased. He accepted the glass, looking at it closely before taking a tentative sip. He swallowed with a thoughtful look, then nodded approvingly. "It's actually not bad." He took another sip. "It would be better warm."

"I'll take your word for it." She settled onto her sofa to eat her sandwich.

Rhys sat beside her, and although he was a few inches away, his large frame seemed to overwhelm her. His presence enveloped her. Suddenly the turkey sandwich didn't seem nearly as mouth-watering as he did.

"Is everything to your liking?"

When she simply stared at him, he gestured to the sandwich half, forgotten in her hand.

"Oh," she said with a self-conscious laugh. "Yes, it's great."

"I am more than a little humiliated that I haven't been better able to see to your needs."

Her gaze dropped to his lips as he said, "needs." Was he doing that on purpose?

"My—needs have been met nicely," she said, avoiding his eyes. But she did catch the faint hint of a smile on his wide, well-formed lips before she determinedly focused on her sandwich.

But all too quickly her meal was gone, and then she was forced to diligently pick the crumbs off her skirt. Then she had to gather everything to be taken back to the kitchen.

Rhys placed a hand over hers as she reached for his empty glass.

"Why are you so nervous?"

She stared up at him, his whiskey-colored eyes luminescent in the firelight. She could get lost in those eyes.

She straightened and carefully extracted her hand from underneath his. "I'm not nervous. I'm just . . ." She didn't know what to say. She was just trying not to be so darned attracted to him. She was just trying to act as though she had no idea what it felt like to kiss him, or be held by him, or make love with him.

"Jane, we will wait. You want to wait, and we will. But I cannot act like I'm not attracted to you."

Her heart fluttered in her chest. "Okay."

"So come here." He tugged her hand gently, indicating he wanted her to move closer to him. "I just want to hold you."

She hesitated, but then slid closer. Rhys nestled her against his side, looping an arm around her shoulder.

She remained stiff for a few moments, feeling as though even this contact was unfair to them.

But Rhys didn't do anything other than hold her, his large hand motionless on her arm, his thigh pressed tight against hers. Slowly, between the feeling of his strength and his warmth and the soothing crackling of the fire, she relaxed. It felt so nice to be held, and again, she found herself wanting to believe in something that wasn't real. Maybe she could chalk it up to the lonely life she'd lived up to this point.

"So tell me about your life."

Jane stiffened slightly. How did these brothers do that? They both had the uncanny ability to read what she was thinking—or at least it sure seemed that way.

"What about it?" She wasn't sure how much she could share—or even if she wanted to. If he did give her the heave-ho when he got his memory back, she didn't want him pitying her, too.

"What was your home like?"

"It was a big, old Vic—an old house."

"Did your father do a lot of entertaining?"

Before she thought better of it, she laughed. "No, not hardly. My house would not be the type of place that people would come to for a party. And my father was a bit—eccentric."

"Really? How so?"

She shifted slightly so she could see Rhys. He watched her with those peculiar eyes, interest and curiosity adding to their glitter.

"Well . . ." She didn't know what he already believed about his American fiancée. Did he think she was a lady? Or a commoner? Probably not a commoner if he was a viscount.

She sighed. This was too hard. This was the reason she couldn't have close contact with him, because she found that she did want to share with him. She wanted him to understand her.

Maybe it was because they had been intimate physically, so it only seemed natural to be intimate emotionally, too. Or maybe it was because no one had ever really asked her about her father and her life. Not without the usual morbid curiosity.

"When my mother passed away, my father went kind of—mad." She glanced at him to make sure that didn't conflict with his preconceived beliefs of her.

He waited for her to continue, no judgment in his beautiful features.

She stared at the flickering flames of the fire and did continue. "He talked to my mother and generally acted as though she never died. And he wasn't really very—attentive to me after that." Then she quickly added, "He was kind and he did love me, but it was as if part of him was gone. He was absentminded and often in a world of his own, which was hard."

The usual guilt filled her, guilt over the resentment she'd felt toward her father. Guilt over the fact that she still wished he had put her, his living child, first over a memory.

She blinked, realizing that Rhys hadn't responded. Reluctantly she peeked up at him, but instead of the pity she was sure she would see, he frowned.

"It must have been very difficult," he stated, a hard edge to his voice. "You were a little girl—only ten. You needed your father."

Yes, she had.

"What did you do? How did you live?" he asked. His fingers stroked her arm, rubbing gently up and down over the cotton of her blouse as if he thought she was cold.

She shivered, even though she wasn't. "I grew up very quickly. As any kid would, I guess."

"Elizabeth has had to grow up quickly, too, but she lost both her parents at once. You had a father."

She didn't say anything, although she did feel a measure of comfort from his soothing touch and his quiet indignation. He understood and defended feelings that she'd begun to think were unreasonable and selfish of her. After all, her father had been mad with grief, and his fantasy world had allowed him a measure of peace.

How ironic that the only person who'd ever understood her anguish was living in a fantasy world himself.

"What was your life like? Tell me."

She didn't want to tell him everything. About the loneliness and awkwardness of being the crazy mortician's introverted daughter. So she simply said, "I was generally busy running the house, and helping my father with his business."

"Which was?" he asked.

She hesitated. "He was a mortician."

His hand stilled on her arm. She stared at the fire, avoiding his eyes. Indignation would be replaced by revulsion now.

"He was a mortician?" His voice did sound aghast.

She nodded.

"Did your father do his work right there? In your home?"

She nodded again. "It was a little strange, but since that was all I knew—"

"The man wasn't fit to be a father," he said flatly. "Making you help with a business like that—making you live with it."

She blinked, surprised at his anger. "Well, I only ran the business end. Meeting with the families, helping them make the arrangements, helping run the funerals."

"You were surrounded by death. It must have been horrible—frightening."

She considered that. Yes, she had always been surrounded by death, and it had been difficult, and at times depressing, but she couldn't recall a time when death hadn't affected her life. Death had stolen her mother, and her father long before he actually died. Death had made her different. Made her an oddity. But it had also been the only constant in her world.

"Death is easy for me," she finally said. "It's living that's scary."

Rhys frowned. Death easy? He didn't understand that. Losing his parents had been one of the most difficult experiences of his life. And losing Eliz . . .

No, he hadn't lost Elizabeth. What was he thinking? Why would he even make that mistake? Jane's confession had his mind whirring—jumbled.

"Death is easy?" He just couldn't wrap his mind around that idea.

"No, that isn't the right word. Death, the funeral parlor, that was what I knew. It's only now—when I'm trying to make a new life for myself—that I realize how very little I know about living."

He stared at her. She regarded him with huge, solemn eyes. How could she think she didn't know about life? She exuded vitality. Life danced in her green eyes and sparkled in her smile. Life scented her skin, fresh and dynamic. He tasted life on her lips when he kissed her.

Before he thought better of it, he captured those lips. His mouth clung to hers, tasting her. She responded immediately, her arms twining about his neck, her lips clinging to his.

Suddenly, he could more than taste her life, her vitality. He could sense her heart beating, the blood coursing through her veins. Her energy surrounded him.

His mouth became more insistent against hers, forcing her lips open, devouring her.

She whimpered at his forceful onslaught, but she responded, giving him what he wanted.

He caught her around the waist and pulled her onto his lap, so he had easier access to her mouth, to her warm, pulsing energy.

Jane's hands tangled in his hair, stroked his face. She seemed to be trying to calm him, even as she gave to him what he demanded. But gradually, he regained control of his desire, of his need.

He lifted his head and stared down at her where she lounged on him, her head in the crook of his arm.

"I'm sorry," he said, his voice lower and gruffer than he intended. "I'm afraid when it comes to you, I often seem to lose my self-control."

Her eyes glittered with the same passion he felt raging inside him, and it seemed at odds with the heavy sigh she breathed out. "I lose control, too."

He smiled. "I guess we will just have to get married soon."

She smiled in return, but Rhys couldn't miss the uneasiness that had replaced the desire in her eyes.

He repositioned her so she was no longer lying back, but against his chest, her head nestled under his chin. "Janie, you don't have to be worried. You will have the life you always wanted. You will be surrounded by my family and our love and our laughter."

But even as he made the assurance, something faint and undefined niggled his mind. A distant sensation that there was an important thing that he'd forgotten. But he simply couldn't figure it out—the memory was just beyond his reach.

He didn't want to remember it anyway. He didn't need to; he had Jane and that was all that mattered.

Although, he couldn't help but notice that Jane didn't respond to his promise. Did she doubt him? Should she?

Chapter 12

Jane splashed water on her face, then groped around on the sink counter for a towel. Finding the fluffy cloth, she patted her face dry, then left the bathroom before she caught even a glimpse of her reflection in the mirror over the sink.

She didn't want to see herself. The woman who so desperately and so pathetically wanted to believe Rhys. She wanted to believe every word he'd said. She wanted to be a part of his family. She wanted a life here. She wanted laughter.

She threw back the bedcovers with more force than necessary and crawled underneath, tempted to pull the blankets back up over her head in shame.

Instead she covered herself, crossed her arms over her chest and stared at the ceiling.

What was she doing? Instead of distancing herself, she was just getting more involved. But to be fair to herself, Rhys did have an intensity that was hard to ignore. She'd noticed that back in the bar, even before she ever spoke to him.

And he was pretty intent that he wanted her.

Even now, her heart sped up at the memory of the passion in the kiss he had given her earlier. It had been as though he wanted to completely possess her. And she had wanted to be possessed. Not one fiber of her being had told her to fight, to say no.

The physical attraction would have been a big enough problem, but tonight, he had also added to his emotional appeal, as well. He had understood her resentment toward her father right away. And he'd thought her feelings justified. That didn't alleviate the guilt she still felt and had felt since her father's death. But it had been so nice for someone to understand.

She closed her eyes. She was doomed. If she stayed in Rhys's presence—she was so doomed. He made it so easy to care about him, to want him.

But she would stick to her plan and try to distance herself until he had his memory back. Then . . .

Then she prayed that he would feel the same way about her, because she wanted him. She wanted him more than she'd wanted anything in her whole life. And given she'd lived a life filled with wants—that was saying something.

Jane woke instantly, and a slight gasp escaped her before she clamped her lips closed. A primeval instinct told her to remain motionless so the predator lurking in the dark wouldn't notice her.

But her first reaction didn't make a difference. The evilness, the same feeling she'd experienced the night before, glided over her like fog rolling in off the water, cold and damp and growing denser.

Her heart pounded in her chest, and she fought the

panic pooling in her belly and rising in her throat. This couldn't be real. It had to be a dream—a nightmare. But the sensation felt very real.

She peered into the darkness, trying to make out a shape or even a billowing mist, but she couldn't see anything. The room was absolutely black—the door shut, the curtains drawn.

Then the thickness began to settle on her, heavy and menacing.

She knew she couldn't wait any longer—she had to run. Had to get out of that room.

She had to get to Rhys.

She leapt from the bed and ran toward where she thought the door was. A terrified and frustrated sob strangled her as she fumbled for the doorknob.

The fog was intensifying around her again, clinging to her, suffocating her. Or was that her own blind fear?

She forced herself to calm her movements, to concentrate. With trembling fingers, she made steady sweeps along the wall. She cried out again, only this time because she located the knob, the metal rattling under her fingers.

She turned the handle and yanked the door open, half afraid whatever was surrounding her would slam it shut again. But thankfully, the "thing" didn't, and she raced down the hallway to Rhys's room.

This time she didn't bother with the bathroom light, or even trying to wake Rhys first. She slammed his door shut, twisted the lock on the doorknob and scrambled into the bed beside him.

Rhys didn't wake fully—he simply rolled over and pulled her against him.

She closed her eyes with relief, all the terror, all the

panic, slowly evaporating until she was left limp and exhausted in his arms.

Christian materialized in the shadows of the deserted bedroom. He grinned as he heard the sound of a door slamming and the jiggle of a doorknob as the lock was worked into place.

A locked door would hardly be a deterrent if he really wanted to get to her. Of course, the fact that his brother was also in that room was definitely a discouragement.

He knew his brother would protect her. Rhys had coupled with the mortal—Christian had smelled the fervor of sex as soon as he entered the room. Although the stupid fool probably would protect her without the incentive of sex. Not that mortal sex was appealing after his union with Lilah. Mere mortal sex was base and unpleasant comparatively.

But let Rhys continue his lowly affair. Christian even hoped he developed real emotions for her. He wanted Rhys to understand the pain he'd left when Rhys had taken Lilah. Of course, Rhys's pain would be even more horrendous, because after Christian took the little mortal, he was going to kill her.

When Jane woke again, she nearly groaned. She'd done it again. She was back in Rhys's bed. Even though he wasn't touching her, she could feel him beside her.

Reluctantly she lifted her head. Rhys leaned on an elbow, watching her. The covers had slipped down, revealing his muscled chest, flat stomach, and the jut and sinew of his hip. He was utterly magnificent.

And she had decided to stop touching all that magnificence? She was such a fool.

She quickly dragged her gaze back to his face. His slight, arrogant smile told her he knew exactly what she was thinking.

"I am not sure why we go to sleep in separate beds," he stated. "We always seem to end up in the same one by morning."

"Or by evening," Jane pointed out, opting to be nit-picky versus actually addressing his point.

He frowned at the radio alarm clock with its glowing red numbers. "So it is. Our schedules certainly are confused."

Everything was confused, she thought wryly. But now that he was sufficiently off the topic of why she was in his bed, she started to slip away from him, before she did something stupid. Something delightfully and so, so pleasurably stupid.

But his hand shot out to stop her, his fingers stroking the curve of her waist.

"Did something frighten you again?" he asked, his eyes serious and concerned.

She paused, loving the feel of his hand on her. Funny how just a touch from him could blot out all the fear she had felt the night before. As soon as she'd crawled into bed with him and he'd held her, a sense of safety had encompassed her. But now it wasn't safety that skipped over her nerve endings and made her skin tingle. Although this touch was equally as distracting.

"I think—I do think it must have been a nightmare." Now, lying here with Rhys, the sensations of the night before seemed distant and surreal.

"I really think you should consider just sleeping in

here from now on." Even though he sported a teasing grin, Jane didn't think he'd complain if she said okay. She wouldn't complain either.

But she determinedly shook her head. "Not until everything is—settled."

"Believe me, I'll be questioning Sebastian about that special marriage license later. First, however, I am going to steal a kiss."

He leaned forward and pressed a sweet, gentle kiss to her mouth. "And then I am going to take my betrothed out to see some of the sights."

It took a moment for the lovely warmth of his kiss to diminish and for his words to sink in. But once they did, she immediately sat upright. "No! We can't do that."

He frowned, although the amusement sparkled in his eyes. "Of course we can. I realize it is rather gauche to walk, since I have no coachmen available. But I could hire a hack. Perhaps we can see a play, if you like. There is an opera that I've been wanting to see, if you like opera."

"I think we should stay right here," she insisted.

His amused frown disappeared, replaced by a rather lascivious grin. "Right here? Did you have anything in particular planned?"

She would have laughed at the almost hopeful quality to his voice if she wasn't so concerned with how she was going to keep him in the apartment. And so determined to do the right thing.

"We could play a game."

He raised an intrigued eyebrow.

She nearly groaned. She was definitely giving him the wrong idea.

"Or—" She tried to think of something else, some-

thing with no connotations. "We could—we could find
Sebastian." She needed him to handle this.

"As I said, I intend to talk with him before we leave."

"I'll find him," she said, slipping out of his hold, and
dashing to the door.

"Jane?"

She paused at the door, looking back at him.

His eyes roamed over her. "I must request you dress
before approaching my brother. He is only mortal, after
all."

Jane glanced down at her pajamas, a T-shirt and
shorts set. It wasn't exactly skimpy—not by today's standards—but she was dealing with Regency standards,
wasn't she?

She nodded, then started to open the door again.

"Jane?"

She stopped again.

"Dress warmly. London can be very cold this time of
year."

She nodded and left the room. She needed to find Sebastian. Now.

Unfortunately, after much searching, she didn't have
any luck. The apartment was Sebastian-free.

She headed back to her room to dress and to decide
how to stop Rhys from leaving the apartment on her
own. All she needed was to have Rhys lose his memory
forever.

As she reached her room, her mind shifted to the
happenings of last night. She stood in the doorway, trying to sense anything strange. Could she feel something
oppressive in the air? Was there something lurking in
the shadows?

She took a hesitant step into the dark room, ready to run if she sensed anything—but she didn't. Chills didn't run down her spine. She didn't even feel nervous to cross the shadowed room and turn on the bedside lamp. The white and blue room felt like any other room. No evidence of anything eerie.

Although there was evidence of her rushed escape. The covers hung half off the bed from her mad dash out of the room and straight to Rhys.

As she made the bed, she half wondered if it was her subconscious coming up with excuses to be close to him. But as she fluffed a pillow and threw it beside its mate at the head of the bed, she rejected the idea. She must have had a nightmare—that was the only feasible explanation.

Maybe because of her lifestyle, living in a funeral home, or maybe because of her father's illness, she'd always discredited the supernatural. She'd decided at a young age there was nothing that went bump in the night. But the past two nights had seemed so real.

No, she told herself firmly. It was a nightmare—nothing more.

Sighing, she left the bed to search for something to wear. Warm, Rhys had said—but she didn't know if she should humor him. After all, the goal was to keep him in the apartment.

"Something to keep him here," she muttered as she sorted through her clothes. "Something to keep him here."

"I can think of several things that would keep me here," Rhys said from the doorway, causing her to drop the shirt she was holding up for inspection.

She spun toward him.

He crossed his arms and leaned a shoulder on the door frame. "But since we did agree to wait until after the wedding, I think we had better go explore London. Otherwise I will definitely break my promise."

His eyes wandered over that tiny outfit she wore, which hugged the lovely curves of her breasts and waist and revealed the enticing length of her legs.

He recalled those legs wrapped around him. His cock stirred.

He straightened and said more harshly than he intended, "Get dressed." Then he tempered his voice, since it was hardly her fault he could barely control his desire for her. "We have much to see."

He started to leave the room, when she said, "You know, I'm actually feeling a little sick."

He turned back to her, studying her coloring. She certainly looked fine. Much, much better than fine. Although unease did shadow her eyes.

He knew he should just give in to her wish to stay home, but he couldn't. He could not be here alone with her and keep his promise to wait until after they were wed to make love again. He wanted to spend time with her, but he also needed distraction.

"Well, perhaps you should just go back to bed, then."

She immediately looked relieved.

"In fact, I'll join you."

He knew that was low—and made him look like a man who didn't keep his word. So he was absolutely shocked when she said, "Okay."

She glanced at her bed and then at him. But he didn't see desire in her eyes, rather worry. Not the look he wanted from her when he took her back to his bed—or her bed.

Why would she change her mind about waiting? Just to get him to stay here? Something was not right.

"No," he stated, even though his body was calling him a thousand different kinds of fool. "Tonight we are going to have a proper outing."

She dipped her chin, the minute nod he knew meant she was agreeing, but she wasn't really sure she should.

He nodded, too, and then closed the door.

He headed to the living room to look for Sebastian. He'd originally stopped by Jane's room to see if she had located him. But then her sleepwear had distracted him—and then her proposition.

The living room was empty when he entered. He opened his mouth to yell for Sebastian, then snapped it shut. Shouting did get on his brother's nerves—and Rhys supposed it was a tad rude. He needed to watch himself if he was ever going to succeed in making Jane believe she wasn't marrying a total brute.

Tonight, he intended to make a good impression. Court her properly as she deserved. That was, of course, if he could get her to leave the house.

He walked to the library. The room was empty as well.

Where the hell was Sebastian? He paused and listened for a moment. He couldn't sense Sebastian in the house.

He frowned, wondering how he could be so sure he wasn't there just by listening. He didn't know how, but he was positive his brother was out.

Sebastian was at his club again, Rhys was sure. He

spent most nights there. Sebastian was obsessed with women.

For the first time, Rhys understood that obsession. He'd always enjoyed women, but he'd never been pre-occupied with them—until Jane. He'd do anything for her—to have her.

He went back to the living room to wait for her. Settling in one of the chairs, he reached for the book Sebastian had been reading. *Salem's Lot?* He flipped the book over and read the back cover.

Vampires.

He grimaced and dropped the novel back on the table.

Rhys glanced at the doorway, wondering if Jane would even appear. She really was adamant that they should stay here. Was she nervous about being in such a large town? He knew London was probably far bigger than any place she'd ever been, but he really believed she would enjoy the bustle once she got used to it.

To his relief, Jane did soon enter into the room—and he was rather surprised to see that she had on warm clothes and carried her coat.

He stood. "Are you ready, then?"

She nodded, another one of those tiny bobs of her head.

"You will see so many fantastic sights that you won't help but have a good time." He smiled reassuringly. "I promise."

Another slight nod, but when he turned to lead her into the kitchen, he heard her mutter, "They probably won't be as fantastic to me as they will be to you."

"Excuse me?" he asked, frowning. Why would she say that?

"I didn't say anything," she promptly replied, but he could see distinct discomfit in her eyes.

He decided to let the comment go for the time being. After all, she was going out with him, and he didn't want to ruin that success.

Chapter 13

Jane watched as Rhys grabbed a coat from the rack by the door. The same black coat he'd worn the night he'd saved her.

Guilt ripped through her—she didn't seem to be able to save him. But she'd done everything she could think of—including offer to go to bed with him. She probably would have been offended by his refusal if she wasn't so worried about him.

He shrugged on the coat and then opened a door off the kitchen, which led into a long, almost industrial looking hallway. Metal ducts and bare wallboard ran the length of it. At the end was a freight elevator, nothing more than a huge cage with a gate that manually pulled down once the individuals were inside.

How strange that the hall would be so different than the luxurious apartment. But what was even stranger was that she had no idea that this part of the building existed. It really was as if she'd been dropped into a fantasy world, unaware of anything outside of the apartment.

Not for the first time, it hit her how weird this situation was—and it was about to get weirder yet again. And potentially damaging to Rhys.

She just couldn't think of anything to get him to stay—outside of finding Sebastian. He was probably in the nightclub, but she didn't think bringing Rhys into a club with flashing lights and loud music would be good for his mental state. And she couldn't figure out how to get away from him. He was determined to take this outing.

They reached the elevator, and he easily lifted the grate, holding it for her to enter. Once she was inside, he got in and pulled down the metal grid. Without a moment's hesitation, he pressed the black button marked G for ground level.

Jane stared at the button, then looked up at Rhys's profile. His face was composed, serene.

He wasn't confused by the elevator. He understood exactly how it worked.

She frowned. Now that she thought about it, he wasn't confused by anything modern. Lights, plumbing, the digital clock this morning. Why hadn't she noticed that before?

"Do most buildings in London have elevators?" she suddenly asked him.

He considered the question, then shrugged. "I would think the bigger ones do."

"And do all the buildings have lights?"

He nodded. "Of course. We are hardly primitives here." He smiled at her as though he thought she must be daft.

Why hadn't Sebastian noticed this? Had he? Had he asked the doctor why Rhys's amnesia appeared to be selective?

"Here we are." Rhys threw up the metal gate as if it was little more than a rolling blind.

They stepped out into another hall that matched the one upstairs.

He led her to a heavy steel door with several dead-bolts. He unlocked them, then said loudly, "Mick, lock these behind us."

Jane glanced around until she realized there was a small room, back up the hallway.

The huge Mick stood in the doorway; the faint bluish light of electronics flickered behind him. He nodded in greeting as she stared at him.

She nodded back, then quickly glanced away.

Rhys stepped outside and waited for her, his hand extended to help her down the step. She accepted it and joined him outside. The heavy door slammed, and they were in a dim alley.

Back where they'd begun, she thought ironically.

Rhys must have caught her wry expression. "Not the best view to start your adventure with, but come this way."

Still holding her fingers, he tugged her toward the brighter lights of the street.

The faint rumble of bass sounded from inside the building, and Jane realized the noise must be coming from the nightclub.

They reached the street, and for the first time, Jane got to see the outside of the building where she'd been living.

It was a large, brick warehouse, although a gothic façade had been added to the front. Gargoyles and spires decorated the roof. The windows were stained glass, colorful patterns that glowed with each flash of the lights inside. Two more large gargoyles, crouched and poised to leap, guarded the front entrance. Over the double doors in scrawling blood red neon was the name Carfax Abbey.

She stopped, which forced Rhys to stop, too.

Again, she was struck by the surrealism of her situation, that she'd been living in a building that held three distinct worlds.

Two very odd looking characters, with ashen complexions, heavy eye makeup and black leather clothes, came up the sidewalk toward them. They gave Jane and Rhys curious looks before going up the few steps and into the club.

She hesitated a moment, then decided maybe she should risk taking Rhys inside the club to find Sebastian. She needed to tell him about Rhys's selective memory. "Maybe we should go in and look for Sebastian."

"Sebastian? Why would he be in there?" Rhys followed her gaze.

"This is his club."

Rhys snorted and cast a disgusted look at another crowd of goths as they approached the club. "No, no. These are hardly the sort of people our family would associate with."

Jane glanced at the group, giving them an apologetic smile. Once they passed, barely acknowledging either of them, she asked, "Where is Sebastian's club?"

"White's? It's not far. Although we cannot visit him there, it's a gentlemen's club."

Rhys didn't remember his own nightclub, the club he owned with Sebastian, but he did remember the name of a nineteenth century club. Why?

A yellow taxi honked loudly behind them, causing her to jump. Rhys didn't even react, except to look over his shoulder and frown at the driver.

Then he asked, "Should we take a public conveyance, or would you prefer to walk?"

She stared at him for a moment. "I think I'd like to walk." She needed the cold air to clear her head and help her make sense of all this.

They walked in silence, the sounds of the city making the quiet between them less noticeable. And it gave Jane a chance to watch him, to study his reaction to his surroundings. A police car with its sirens blaring. A youth with his ears, eyebrows and lips multiply pierced. Brightly lit signs. Skyscrapers. Traffic.

None of it gave him the slightest pause.

He definitely had selective memory loss, which made her think, again, that there was something in particular he was trying to forget. But was this type of amnesia more or less severe?

Part of her thought it might be less serious as he had fewer things to remember, because most of his memories were still there. But another argument could be made that the ailment was worse, because it wouldn't be as easy for something to jar his memory and force him to remember. He could just continue to adapt everything to his own belief system.

He needed a doctor. That much she knew for sure. And not the quack who had diagnosed him over the phone. He needed a specialist, and she was going to see that he got one.

"Look," Rhys said suddenly, grabbing her hand and tugging her toward a large plate-glass window. The storefront was filled with animatronic elves and reindeer. The holiday decorations were still up until the New Year.

The creatures worked diligently and repetitively to build the toys to fill Santa's sleigh.

"That is amazing," he said, his golden eyes filled with amazement and delight.

She couldn't help but smile. It was like watching a person see something for the first time. But he must have. Why would he forget something like that?

"Look at this one," he said, tugging her on to the next store before she could consider a reason.

Hand in hand, they walked down the crowded street, stopping to admire the beauty and whimsy of the holiday decorations. And soon, Jane decided to put Rhys's ailment out of her mind, just for tonight. He was obviously enjoying himself—and so was she.

"Elizabeth should be here," he said suddenly as they peered through a window at more automated creatures—this time old-fashioned dolls in Victorian clothes, waving candles and singing carols. "She used to be crazy about her dolls. She had dozens."

He glanced at Jane, an indulgent smile on his lips. "She was extremely spoiled being the only girl."

"I can imagine. It must be nice to have three older brothers."

"She is very easy to spoil," he said, casting one last look at the dolls before gently squeezing her fingers and starting down the sidewalk again. "She is very fragile, often sick. But she's always full of laughter, despite her health. She says that she can't be too serious—that it is my job to be the serious one."

Jane considered that description. The Rhys she'd met in the bar had seemed serious—more than serious, almost grim. But now, she couldn't correlate that person to the one holding her hand. This Rhys could be determined and serious, but he also smiled, a lot.

"Maybe she mixes up serious with responsible," she suggested.

Rhys's step faltered for a moment. "Why do you say that?"

She shrugged. "I can tell from the few things that you've told me that you are the reliable one. I've met Sebastian—he's happy-go-lucky, devil-may-care. You said that Christian is the wild one. And Elizabeth is the baby. That leaves you to care for everyone."

She fell silent after her explanation. Maybe she'd said too much. But somehow, she knew that was the truth—Rhys did care for others. His amnesia didn't affect that. He was a good person, a compassionate person. The kind of person who would save a stranger. She knew that firsthand.

After a few moments, she realized that he was still silent. His eyes had lost their excited glitter, and his mouth was set in a solemn line. He suddenly reminded her a lot of the man she'd met in the bar.

"I should have taken better care of them."

As soon as the words were out of his mouth, he wanted them back. He didn't even understand why he said them. He had done his best to care for his siblings since their parents' deaths.

But he should have done more. If he'd been stronger, he could have stopped everything that happened. He should have . . .

"Well, from what you've told me, it sounds like you've done a wonderful job," Jane's sweet voice said, pulling him back from wherever he'd been.

He blinked. "I hope so."

"It can't be easy to be the oldest. All the burdens fall on you."

That was true. Sometimes far too much burden.

He gazed down at Jane at his side. She offered him a

reassuring smile. He smiled back, glad that she was there. Maybe she'd help him. Help him cope with all the burdens.

They both focused on the sidewalk in front of them.

"Oh, look," Jane said suddenly, pointing to a cart selling hotdogs. "I have to get one."

He smiled, bewildered by why she would be so excited about a common barrow. But he nodded. "All right."

She let go of his hand and dashed up to the cart. The man with olive skin and a thick mustache didn't appear nearly as thrilled to wait on her as Jane was to order.

Rhys picked up his stride to join her.

"I'll have a hotdog with mustard and relish. Lots of mustard, please." She shot Rhys a proud sidelong glance as if she had done something amazing. "You always see people in movies—I mean, people always talk about ordering hotdogs from street vendors in New—er, London."

Rhys noticed that the barrow man raised an eyebrow, obviously surprised by that comment, too. Hotdogs? What an odd thing for Americans to find so fascinating. He didn't even know that England was famous for that particular product.

"What can I get you, buddy?" the man asked him as he prepared Jane's food.

Rhys breathed in deeply, and even though the smell of the hotdogs didn't appeal to him, he ordered one anyway—exactly the same as Jane's.

"My treat," Jane told him as she pulled money out of her coat pocket.

Rhys started to argue, but Jane smiled saucily and said, "Tough." She thrust a bill at the barrow man.

After the change had been given, and they both got their foil-wrapped meals, Jane led him over to a low concrete wall that ran the perimeter of a fountain.

They sat, their backs to the gushing water. Jane happily peeled open her food and bit into the yellow and green slathered concoction. Her eyes closed in bliss, and she moaned with complete satisfaction.

Rhys's body reacted immediately to the throaty sound. Hunger of his own ripped through him, his eyes fastened on her rapturous expression. Then his gaze strayed from her face to the glimpse of bare skin at the base of her throat.

Suddenly he wanted to taste her there. He had to taste her.

"Are you going to try it?"

He blinked, focusing back on her eyes. She lifted her hotdog and then gestured to the one he still held.

It took him a few moments to calm his raging desire, but finally he managed a nod. "Yes."

After a few more moments, he followed her earlier actions and unwrapped the foil. He hesitated, inspecting the unappetizing tube of meat. Then he took a bite.

He immediately grimaced, chewing slowly, fighting back a gag. How could she enjoy this? The meat tasted old and rancid, like the sausage had been improperly smoked.

He forced himself to swallow, even though every muscle in his body was ordering him to spit out the vile creation.

"Good Lord," he groaned, after he could speak. "That is absolutely disgusting."

She chuckled, having to finish chewing before she could ask, "You've never had a hotdog before?"

He shook his head. "No. Nor will I ever have one again."

She laughed again. Suddenly her eyes widened, and she grabbed the remainder of the horrible meal from his hands. "Oh, no! You probably aren't supposed to have them. Sebastian said you are allergic to a lot of foods."

"Yes, I remember you saying that," he said, giving her a wry look. "And I have no idea where he gets that information. Surely, I'd remember if I had these allergies. In this case, I don't believe I'm allergic—I simply think I dislike hotdogs. Intensely."

She studied him for a minute. Then relief softened her features. But the look was quickly replaced by another look that was almost impish. "Then I just have to eat yours, too."

He shuddered, then laughed. "By all means."

They sat there quietly. Jane happily munching. Rhys still feeling hungry, but certainly not for hotdogs. He was hungry for something out of his reach. Something he couldn't quite define.

He watched Jane. Maybe he was mixing up hunger with desire, although he didn't have to try to figure out what he desired. Jane. Definitely Jane. Too bad, for the time being, she was out of reach, too.

Jane finished, wadded up the wrappers and sighed. "That was great. Sorry you didn't enjoy it."

"Well, I enjoyed watching you. I have to respect a lady with a hearty appetite."

She blushed. "I don't think that is a compliment."

"It certainly is," he assured her, then leaned in to steal a quick kiss, despite the fact that it was just a frustrating torture. A sweet taste of what he couldn't have. Not for a little longer anyway.

She responded immediately, as she always did.

When they parted, she shivered.

He hoped it was desire that caused the tremble, but he asked, "Are you getting cold?"

She shook her head, but her voice didn't sound quite as definite. "I'm fine."

"Maybe we should try to find a place to get out of the night air for a while."

Jane shook her head again. "No, I'm having a wonderful time walking around, taking in all the sights. Just as you said I would."

"Are you sure?"

"Yes." She stood. "Plus, I'll warm up once we start walking again."

Rhys relented. "Where to, then?"

"Let's go to Central Park," she suggested with a wide grin.

He smiled indulgently. "You mean Hyde Park."

Her smile slipped slightly at her mistake. "Right."

"Don't worry," he told her. "You'll remember where you are soon enough."

She raised an eyebrow, but didn't say anything.

Chapter 14

Rhys took Jane's hand as they started down Fifth Avenue.

At first, she wondered if they were heading in the right direction, but she cast the thought aside. His confident stride made her think he knew exactly where he was going.

They reached an intersection and were waiting to cross the street when the rich, wonderful scent of coffee filled her nostrils. She looked around, noticing a coffee bar on the corner behind them. Several bundled-up patrons exited with steaming, white cups in their hands.

"Oow, I would love a hot cup of chai. How about you?"

Rhys followed her gaze. "I don't drink—chai. But let's get you one. Maybe it will warm you up."

She smiled, touched that he was still concerned she was cold. She just wasn't used to someone looking after her.

"Yes," she agreed, and they headed inside.

The place was packed, people lounging on overstuffed, purple, velvet chairs and sofas, sipping lattes and cappuccinos. Several read books or typed on laptops, but most of the patrons sat chatting, filling the room with a warm buzz that combined nicely with the pleasant scent of roasted coffee.

"Why don't you wait here," Rhys said, gesturing to the one vacant chair. "I'll order for you."

She glanced at the line waiting to order and the limited space at the registers. "Okay. I'll have a spiced chai. Tall."

Rhys frowned. "Spiced? Tall?"

She laughed. "It's the type of tea and the size."

"Oh. Right. Tall."

She nodded, grinning as she watched him head up to the long line, confusion still clear in his handsome features. She settled into the comfy chair and took in her surroundings. It was a neat place—sort of edgy bohemian, if there was such a thing. And the patrons looked very much like she pictured young New Yorkers—stylish even in their casual clothes. Hip, interesting.

She glanced down at her jeans, thick sweater and bulky parka. She looked like a Mainer—all she needed were the L.L. Bean boots and a hat with ear flaps.

Her gaze found Rhys again. He fit in here with his classy all black attire, right down to his chunky-soled shoes. And black looked fantastic on him. It brought out the shades of amber and gold in his dark hair and made his skin look warm and perfect.

Then she noticed the woman in front of him, a tall woman with exotic dark eyes and long, glossy dark brown hair. She kept turning to cast sidelong glances at him, and there was no missing the interest on her face.

Finally, she must have caught Rhys's attention, because she smiled openly at him and said something. Jane couldn't see Rhys's reaction, because his back was to her. But something that felt altogether too much like jealousy welled in Jane's belly.

She had no right to feel jealous. Did she?

Well, she had slept with him, but she had no way of knowing whether that was a common thing for Rhys. After all, he was an extraordinarily beautiful man, and he had to garner a lot of female attention.

Obviously, she thought bitterly as the woman laughed at something Rhys said.

Jane sank back in the chair, feeling even more unfashionable compared to the tall brunette. She glanced down at herself again. And as if the heavy, cumbersome coat wasn't bad enough, she noticed a small blotch of mustard on the dark green material.

She sat up and swiped at the splotch, looking around for napkins. She spotted them over by the door on a table with creamers, sweeteners and straws.

After waiting for a man to add nearly a dozen packets of sugar to his coffee, she finally got to the napkin dispenser. She grabbed a couple of the brown paper napkins and rubbed at the spot until it was only a faint discoloration on the material.

Barely noticeable, she told herself as she started back to the chair where she'd been sitting. The man with the very, very sweet coffee sat there, relaxed against the soft cushions.

She glanced back at Rhys, trying to decide if she should just go join him, when she noticed he was still talking to the brunette. Then Rhys glanced over at the chair where he'd left Jane. When he saw the man there, he quickly searched the room until he spotted Jane. Something flickered in his eyes when he located her, but she couldn't quite make out what it was.

He smiled, but then he turned back to the other woman.

Disappointment filled Jane. What had she expected him to do? Blow her a kiss? Yell across the room that Jane was his girlfriend? Or that he loved her?

She paused, her gaze fastened onto his back. Why had she even thought that? Love. She should laugh at such a crazy thought—but instead she felt sick. She couldn't be thinking that she actually wanted Rhys to be in love with her. Or that she could fall in love with him.

She was still staring at him, completely freaked out by that train of thought, when someone brushed against her.

"Sorry," a deep voice said, right beside her ear.

She started and turned to look up into a pair of eyes so pale they appeared closer to white than the blue she knew they must be.

"That's—okay," she managed.

The man gave her a small, closed-lip smile. "Waiting for someone?"

She nodded, overcome by uneasiness.

He smiled again. "Too bad." Then he inclined his head and left the coffee shop.

Jane watched him. He paused for a moment outside the doors, tugging up the collar of his jacket against the cold, and then he disappeared around the corner.

She blinked and shook her head. What had that been about?

Suddenly Rhys was at her side, his eyes searching her face, his expression concerned. "Are you all right?"

She nodded, startled by this intent behavior. "Yes. Why wouldn't I be?" *Other than I'm jealous of a woman merely talking to you.*

He studied her a moment longer. Then he shook his head, seeming almost bewildered. "I don't know—I just had the strangest sense . . ." He laughed, a low, self-deriding rumble. "Just imagining things, I guess."

He held out a lidded paper cup. "Here you go. Spiced chai. Tall."

"Thank you," she said, accepting the drink. The heat through the insulated paper felt comforting against her cold fingers.

"Do you want to drink it here or walk on to the park?"

"Let's keep walking." Between the strange man with the eerie eyes and the gorgeous brunette, Jane felt the need to get away from this place.

But before they could exit, the tall brunette walked over to Rhys. "It was very nice meeting you," she said. Her voice was sultry with the hint of an accent.

"Likewise." Even though he was polite, Jane noticed that no interest showed in his eyes.

The brunette cast a quick look at Jane, her eyes dropping for a fraction of a second to the faint mustard mark on her coat. Then she turned back to Rhys. She fished in the pocket of her fitted, leather jacket and pulled out a business card, holding out the small rectangle to him.

"If you ever want to get together."

Jane knew she was probably doing a fair impression of a beached cod, her mouth gaping open, her eyes wide with shock. But she could not believe the woman's audacity.

Jane quickly gathered her wits and moved closer to Rhys and linked her arm through his, silently letting this woman know that at least for tonight, Rhys was with her.

The woman ignored the hint. Not that Jane considered her actions a hint but rather more a flashing warning sign.

"Take it," the brunette said, waving the card at Rhys again.

Jane had certainly never been possessive of a man, but she was darned if she was going to let this woman openly proposition him as if she didn't even exist.

She reached forward and snatched the card out of the woman's hand.

"Hey," the brunette said, glaring at Jane.

"I'm sorry," Jane said, forcing as much politeness into her voice as she could muster. "I guess you didn't understand. But Rhys is mine." Oh, my! Had she actually said that?

Instead of looking contrite or even irritated, the woman actually looked unconvinced, until Rhys said to her, "She's quite right. I am completely hers."

The woman paled. She snatched her card back, spun and left the shop.

But instead of feeling triumphant, Jane felt slightly ill again.

"Are you all right?" Rhys asked, leaning forward to look into her eyes.

"Can we go?" She wanted to get out of there—suddenly the air seemed too warm, and the smell of coffee was too cloying.

"Sure." He continued to hold her arm as he led her to the doors.

As she breathed in the cold winter air, she realized something that was very, very frightening. She wanted Rhys to be hers—no matter their situation.

Christian stood in the shadows across the street, watching his brother and his mortal whore leave the trendy coffee bar. He'd known it was risky to approach the mortal with Rhys so close, but he couldn't seem to help himself. He liked the thrill of getting so close to her. Although he didn't understand why Rhys hadn't sensed him. Christian hadn't bothered to mask his energy. He hadn't cared if Rhys saw him. He'd wanted Rhys to see him.

He wanted Rhys afraid. The time was long past due for Rhys to understand the fear of losing someone he cared for, that she could be taken, snatched away. And even if returned, she would never be the same.

Under the guise of doing the right thing and of protecting his family, Rhys had taken Lilah and returned a woman only half there, a woman never fully Christian's again.

Christian watched as the couple disappeared down the bustling street, vanishing into the crowd.

"Now it's my turn to return the favor, big brother," Christian murmured under his breath.

Rhys glanced at Jane out of the corner of his eye. She hadn't spoken since they left the shop, since the incident with the forward woman. She hadn't even commented when they left the street to head into the park.

Of course, he had been quiet, too. Lost in his own thoughts.

Something had happened back there—something outside of the pushy, rude woman. He couldn't quite figure it out, what exactly it had been, but while he was ordering Jane's drink, he'd had the strangest sensation that she wasn't safe. That something bad was about to happen. But when he'd finally been able to go to her, she'd been fine. Nothing out of the ordinary, other than the brunette.

He glanced at Jane again, and he smiled slightly to himself. She'd definitely been irritated by the aggressive woman.

"So, I'm yours, am I?" he asked, breaking the silence, his voice teasing, although he quite liked the idea of Jane being possessive.

Jane immediately blushed. "I—I just couldn't believe that woman's audacity."

"So are you saying that you don't really want me?"

She didn't speak for a moment, keeping her attention focused on her feet. "I do want you."

Rhys caught her wrist to pull her to a halt. He turned her to face him. "Why do you say it as though you think you should be ashamed?"

Her wide eyes met his, and he did see shame there. "Rhys, how you feel right now? It's not real. It's—it's like we are both living in a fantasy world, and eventually reality is going to return. And I'm afraid of how you will feel when that happens."

He frowned, confused and also a little upset. How could she think this was fantasy?

"No," he said, shaking his head. "This is real. Now is real, and all the things I feel for you are very real."

She looked down at the cup of tea that she'd barely drunk since they left the coffee shop. She fiddled with the edge of the plastic lid.

"You don't know me," she said slowly. "Not really. And maybe—maybe once you do you won't want—you might decide I'm not what you want."

"You've said that before, after we made love. That I don't know you. And I suppose that is true, that we haven't had long together, to get to know everything about each other. But what I do know, I want."

Her eyes stared into his, almost pleading. "But you may not later—and I don't know if I can risk that."

"It isn't possible for me to stop wanting you. I've waited a long time to feel this way. I can't tell you how I know, but I do know this feeling will never leave my system. You will never leave it."

She continued to stare up at him. The shame had disappeared, but now it was exchanged for longing. She still didn't believe him, but she wanted to.

And she would.

He pulled her against him, his mouth finding hers. He intended for the kiss to be persuasive, a sweet lulling caress that would calm her doubts.

But as soon as he tasted the velvety texture of her lips, clinging hungrily to his, all thoughts of coaxing were gone.

He wanted her.

Need tore through his veins, urging him to deepen the kiss. She responded, opening to him, giving him access to the sweet moisture of her mouth.

Sweet moisture.

He groaned as her tongue touched his, a fleeting brush. A tiny taste.

Just a tiny taste.

He nipped at her bottom lip, the flesh fragile and sensitive. His teeth sank just a little harder into the pillowy softness. Pink and warm and so, so sweet.

Jane gasped, and Rhys immediately released her.

He stared down at her, his chest heaving, as he realized that his hunger for her had so easily spun out of control. By a mere kiss.

"I'm sorry," he breathed.

She shook her head, looking as dazed as he felt. "No, it was . . . " The tip of her tongue touched her lower lip, making it glisten in the lamplight. Red and shiny.

His stare locked there for several seconds before his stunned mind registered what he was looking at—she was bleeding.

"Jane," he said, alarm chilling the desire in his limbs. "Damn." He reached for her, his fingers nudging her chin up to get a better look at what he'd done.

Jane frowned. "What?"

"Your lip is bleeding. I must have bitten you."

She brought her hand up to touch her mouth. Her fingers looked very pale, small and elegant, brushing over the reddened skin.

She frowned down at her fingertips, then showed them to him with a reassuring smile. "Barely a nick."

He stared at the faint crimson smear on her fore and index fingers. Revulsion filled him. How had he lost control like that? He'd never intended to hurt her. Never.

"I'm fine," she told him. "Please stop looking at me like you've mortally injured me. I didn't even notice until you pointed it out."

"But you gasped."

She smiled again, this time sheepishly. Her cheeks reddened to nearly the same color as her lips. "Only because—because I was feeling—overcome."

He peered into her green eyes. The darkness of the night and the shadows of the trees surrounding them couldn't dull the vividness of their color.

But even though she gave him another encouraging smile, he couldn't let go of the irritation he felt with himself.

"Maybe we should go back."

She hesitated, and for a moment he thought that she was going to say something, but then she simply nodded, falling into step beside him.

On their quiet walk back to the club, Jane's mind raced. She felt confused, scared and exhilarated all at once. But Rhys had that effect on her, a way of making her feel more than she ever knew she could. He made her feel more alive. More aroused. More beautiful.

And that kiss. She released a shaky breath. That kiss had been like being tossed, head first, into a sea of unadulterated passion.

When he had tasted her, nipped her . . . She'd felt his desire throughout her entire body. She had felt him inside her as surely as she had when they had made love.

How could she feel all of that from just a kiss?

Granted, Rhys really knew how to kiss. Even now, her toes curled in her scuffed oxfords.

But her rational mind reminded her that she needed to try and remain distanced from him. She needed to remember that they didn't really know each other. That she needed to wait.

But her heart told her that between his sweetness, his wonderful smile and his gorgeous eyes, she was already lost. She was already crazy about him, and no amount of repeated warnings and logical reminders could keep her from this man.

The boom of bass brought her out of her reverie. She was surprised to see they were back at the club.

Now a long line of eccentric-looking patrons waited to get inside. Rhys didn't even look at them. He, too, seemed lost in his own thoughts, and from the serious look on his face, they didn't appear to be particularly nice ones.

They headed down the alley, and he knocked hard on the steel door. After a few moments, she heard the series of locks click, and Mick opened the door. He stood back to let them enter. The fluorescent light reflecting off his bald head was the only hint of animation on the huge man's features.

Rhys nodded his thanks at the man, but didn't speak either. He led her to the elevator.

As before he held the grate and waited for her to enter. She did, standing in the center of the elevator.

He dropped the grate and pushed the button marked with a four.

Jane turned slightly, so she could look at him, his lean, muscled body, his beautiful face.

She remembered what she'd thought about him, when she'd first seen him, sitting on that bar stool next to her. He was a heartbreaker.

He still could be, her head warned her. *And it could be your heart that he breaks.*

He suddenly turned his head. His eyes like pools of

molten amber locked with hers, pulling her into their heat.

It's too late, her heart told her. *You are already in too deep.*

"I want to sleep with you tonight," she said, and her heart gave a triumphant punch in the air.

Chapter 15

Rhys didn't quite believe he heard her correctly. But then she stepped toward him and touched his face. Her fingers caressed his jawline, tracing upward until they sank into his hair, gently brushing the long strands back from his cheek. The touch was both comforting and arousing all at once.

He closed his eyes and swallowed. Her gentle caress was exactly the touch he had been craving for so, so long. The grazing of her fingers over his skin, through his hair, loosened something coiled tight inside him. Something that he didn't even know was twisted, twisted so tight that it threatened to suffocate him.

"Jane, are you sure?" He didn't think he could handle it if she changed her mind again. "If you come to bed with me tonight, you are staying there. Every night."

Her hand paused, the pads of her fingers soft against his cheekbone. She stared into his eyes, her irises as green as new grass. "Yes. I'll stay as long as you want me."

Why did she still doubt him? Doubt his need for her? A need he knew he would have forever.

Forever.

The word echoed in his mind. Could he ask that of her? If he had it to offer . . .

Her fingers moved again, drawing his attention back to her eyes, her pale skin, her pink lips. She threaded her hand into his hair, cupping the back of his head, and drew him to her, rising up on her toes to meet him. Those beautiful lips brushed over his jaw, inching upward, tasting him, adoring him—until they were pressed fully to his.

He was lost.

No, he had been lost, and now he was found. He didn't understand where he'd been, but it didn't matter. In Jane's arms, he had sanctuary. He felt alive and whole, safe from the shadows and darkness . . .

Her tongue traced the seam of his lips, shy and fleeting, asking to taste him.

He moaned. Damn, her sweetness was enough to kill him. Death. Maybe this was what that mysterious entity felt like—like falling straight into heaven.

Yes, Jane was heaven. As close as he'd ever get.

He moved his hands up to cup her face, to hold her there, although she showed no signs of moving away.

Their lips continued to caress, velvet against velvet. Their breaths mingled, hot and moist. Their tongues touched, brief licks of fire.

Nothing but their mouths moved. Even their hands, holding each other, remained motionless as if neither one wanted anything to compete with the absoluteness of this kiss.

Rhys knew that the elevator had shuddered to a stop

long ago, but still he couldn't bring himself to release her. Afraid if he did, the moment would end. She would disappear.

But finally, Jane broke the kiss, looking up at him, her lids heavy with desire. "Oh, my."

He smiled. "I plan to make sure I hear that several more times tonight."

He brushed a thumb along the fullness of her lower lip and the tiny cut there from earlier, before he dropped his hands from her cheeks and turned to open the elevator.

Then he reached back and took her hand, her small, slender fingers linking between each of his.

They headed through the apartment straight to the hallway and their rooms.

Outside his bedroom, Rhys stopped and turned to face Jane. "Are you absolutely sure." He had to ask one more time, because if she said yes, he didn't plan to ever let her go again.

She nodded, a firm bob of her head, nothing like the uncertain shakes he'd seen before.

Relief filled his chest, and he opened the door, waiting for her to enter first.

Once she was inside the room, she stood there, her back to him as if she was uncertain what to do next.

He walked up behind her, circling his arm around her waist, although the thickness of her coat made it hard to tell exactly where he held her.

"Let's get rid of this," he murmured as he tugged at the zipper. The coat parted, and he slid the puffy armor off her shoulders and tossed it onto a chair in the corner. He took off his own jacket, also throwing it onto the chair.

His arms returned to her waist, only to discover the

sweater she had on underneath the coat was equally bulky, still disguising her curves. Slipping his hands under the heavy knit, he felt her heat, although through the thin cotton shirt she wore beneath the sweater.

"I'm glad we aren't playing strip poker," he murmured, leaning down to nuzzle her neck.

She tilted her head to give him better access.

"Why?" Her voice was a mixture of confusion and breathiness as he kissed the silky skin just below her jawline.

"Because we'd have to play into the wee hours of the night to get you out of all these clothes." He tugged at the shirt under the sweater.

"Oh. Yes," she breathed as he kissed her neck again. "No strip poker."

He smiled against her skin, breathing in her wonderful scent, flowery and warm.

Beneath the sweater, his hands skimmed up over her stomach, the crisp cotton smooth under his fingers. But not nearly as smooth as he knew the skin underneath was. He stopped just under the curve of her breasts.

"Should we take this sweater off?"

"Yes." Her voice trembled with need.

He slowly ran his hands up her sides, feeling the delicate ridges of her rib cage. She wiggled and laughed slightly when his hands reached her underarms. But she readily raised her arms, so he could peel the sweater off over her head. The article of clothing joined their coats.

He returned his hands to her waist, guiding her around to face him. She gazed up at him, her eyes full of desirous expectation.

He kissed her, promising her satisfaction, but then straightened again and began to work on the small buttons of her white cotton shirt, taking his time. Their anticipation mingled in the air around them as the flick of each button revealed more of her milky white skin.

Her shirt finally fell open to reveal lace, pale yellow like wispy sunlight, covering her breasts.

His fingers trembled as he cupped her. She even felt like sunshine, golden warmth heating his hands.

Another breathy gasp escaped her, and she pressed against his hands, willingly giving him what he wanted.

His thumbs rubbed over her nipples. They responded immediately, prodding the pads of his thumbs.

As he teased her breasts, his mouth found the side of her neck, trailing kisses downward over her chest until he reached the peak of one breast, straining against the filmy veil of sunbeams.

He pulled the beaded nipple into his mouth, suckling her, drinking in her warmth and the shudder of her reaction.

Her fingers dug into his shoulders, anchoring herself.

His mouth traveled across the shallow valley to her other breast. He grazed his teeth over the silky flesh, and her hands tangled in his hair, holding him closer. Begging for more.

He gave it to her, drawing her other nipple between his lips, abrading the hardened nub gently with his teeth.

She gasped. "Rhys," she whispered, his name a plea and a demand.

He lifted his head, staring down into her passion-hazed eyes, knowing his must look the same. He wanted all of her pale skin bared to him. His to touch. His to taste.

He nudged her shirt off her shoulders, baring her upper body, except for the bit of sun at her chest.

His hands then went to the button of her pants, his fingers brushing against the heat of her belly before he unfastened them.

He knelt before her, working the waistband down over the rounded curve of her hips until they were gathered at her ankles.

Hands on his shoulders, she balanced herself, toed off her shoes and stepped out of the pants.

Rhys looked up then, his eyes level with a triangle of lace, the same lemony color of the lace over her breasts. Another ray of sunshine.

He leaned forward and kissed her stomach just beneath her belly button.

Jane's fingers dug into the hard muscles of Rhys's shoulders, desire making her legs weak.

His lips felt hot, his breath moist, against her stomach. Then his tongue licked the edge of her panties, a slow sweep, rough and wet.

She gasped, gripping him tighter.

He smiled against her skin. "Do you like that?"

"Mmm-hmm," she managed as he tasted her again, this time where her panties touched her thigh.

To her disappointment, he gave her only a quick kiss where he'd just licked her, then stood. "I want to taste every inch of you, but not here in the middle of the floor. I want you stretched out in my bed. Under me."

She swallowed. Under him. Under that hard, lean body. That was exactly where she wanted to be, too.

She frowned, for the first time registering that she was almost naked, while he was still fully clad.

"Your skin is so smooth," he murmured as he pulled her closer, his hands stroking over her back.

"Yours is so covered," she grumbled.

He pulled back and smiled down at her. "So it is." He stepped back from her. "Would you like to rectify that?"

She nodded, desperately wanting to touch him, although her fingers trembled as she reached for the hem of his sweater. But she managed to push the soft material upward, exposing inch after inch of flat stomach and muscled chest.

Once she had the sweater up over his flat nipples and lightly haired chest, Rhys took it out of her grasp.

She watched mesmerized as muscles rippled throughout his torso and arms as he pulled the sweater over his head and tossed it onto a chair.

She stared at him, once more amazed that any mere mortal could be this beautiful. And more astounding, all this masculine beauty was hers.

Slowly, she reached for him. She attempted to work the button of his trousers, only to jump nervously when her knuckles brushed the heat of his belly. Trying again, her fingers felt alien and clumsy; her breath came in shallow puffs as she again touched the downy tautness of the stomach.

Finally, he caught her bumbling hands, bringing one up to his mouth, touching his lips to the knuckles that still burned from the fleeting brush against his belly.

"Why are you so nervous?" he asked, his voice low.

She took a deep breath, then met his eyes. "Do you have any idea how perfect you are? It's a little nerve-wracking."

He cocked an eyebrow, skepticism clear in his slight half smile. "Nerve-wracking? Me?"

"Yeah," she said, astounded that he honestly seemed to have no idea how beautiful he was. "Haven't you looked in the mirror lately?"

He frowned, grooves marking the perfection of his face. "I don't . . ." His frown deepened, his eyes growing cool, distant. And Jane suddenly wished she hadn't posed the question. Although she didn't understand why the question would cause him to look so aloof. Maybe the fact that he *was* a hunk, and he was now questioning his decision to be with a plain Jane—literally.

He blinked, his eyes refocusing on her. "I don't like mirrors."

She hadn't expected *that* response. But it was obvious from his voice, which was lower and huskier than usual, that the mere mention of them had irritated him. What a strange reaction.

But before she could ponder his response further, Jane suddenly found herself pulled tightly against his massive, hard chest, and his mouth seized hers.

Unlike the kiss in the elevator—or even in the park— this one was almost rough, a determined assault, but no less arousing. And in some ways, more arousing. This kiss claimed her, possessed her, and she felt it to the tips of her toes.

Jane's hands slid up his chest, feeling the roughened silk of his skin and hair. His muscles moved under her fingers—powerful, alive.

His teeth grazed her lower lip, and his tongue tasted the inside of her mouth.

She moaned, opening wider for him, her tongue touching his, encouraging him to continue his raid of her mouth.

Without taking his lips from hers, he lifted her into his arms, striding to the bed.

He broke the kiss, placing her in the center of the mattress. He stood over her, his eyes intense like smoldering coals.

"And you call me perfection," he murmured, reaching down to run the back of one of his fingers up the length of her calf. "All flawless pale skin and sunshine. All I want is to bury myself in your light."

She stared up at him, the need in his eyes and the husky hunger in his voice causing her heart to pound in her chest.

She watched as he flicked open the button of his pants, letting them slide down his narrow hips.

Her eyes widened as he stood before her completely nude. Although they had made love before, this was the first time she'd really had the opportunity to see him in his full glory. And he was indeed glorious.

His body was all sinewy muscle and golden skin like Michelangelo's *David* gilded. The hair that lightly covered his chest tapered into a thin line under his belly button, then spread into a thatch of burnt gold at his groin.

She stared at his penis, long and thick and very erect, jutting up against his flat stomach.

Okay, she breathed, maybe not quite like *David*.

Despite her awe and all the flattering thoughts that were whipping through her head, the first thing out of her mouth was, "You're not wearing underwear."

He grinned. "Very true, which now leaves you far too overdressed. Let's see what we can do about that, shall we?"

He joined her on the bed, sitting, facing her. He reached out both of his hands, stroking her shoulders, the touch both comforting and sensual. He trailed them down over her arms, finally catching her wrists, pulling her up toward him.

He kissed the sensitive spot just beneath her earlobe,

while his fingers found the clasp of her bra in the center of her back.

His tongue swirled and teased the skin of her neck, and his hands found her now bared breasts, teasing the nipples, squeezing them.

Electricity seemed to shoot from his fingers and his mouth, snaking through her limbs, her belly, centering between her legs.

She felt weak in his arms, unable to focus on anything aside of that snapping current in her veins. Gasping, she felt the gentle tug of his teeth on the skin of her throat.

Another violent jolt of pure blue electricity surged through her, and her head fell back as if she didn't have the energy to hold it upright any longer. Rhys overpowered her, his hands, his teeth, his lips—and the fierce sensations they were creating in her.

He pushed her back, following her down, his wonderful, solid weight pressing her into the mattress. His mouth moved from her neck to her lips while his hands continued to stroke her breasts.

She wrapped her hands around his back, tracing sinew and hot skin. His lips left her mouth and moved down her chest until he captured one of her pebbled nipples. He drew on the throbbing point, suckling her deep.

She gasped, the sound not quite a breath and not quite a moan—more a tortured, ecstatic sound somewhere in between.

He turned his attention to the other breast, while his hand caressed down her body. The air seemed to crackle around them.

She closed her eyes, fighting to keep control. He

hadn't even touched where all this electric current centered, and she was losing her mind.

"Rhys," she said, her voice ragged, strained. "I can't take any more. I need you."

He lifted his head from her breast, his eyes intent, his smile hungry. "You will have me, Janie. But not until I've had my fill of you. I want you too much to deny myself. I can't."

She jerked as his hand slipped under the elastic of her panties and a long finger parted the damp folds of her sex.

He watched her, his eyes burning. "You are so hot."

She moaned and bit her lip.

"And wet."

"Yes." Briefly, she thought maybe she should be mortified, but the thought zipped away on a sizzling wave of need as he slid the length of his finger inside her. Then his thumb found the nub at the top of her sex.

She writhed then. Good Lord, she was going to die.

"Do you want me inside you?"

She bobbed her head, adamant, demanding.

His finger plunged deep; his thumb stroked harder. "Then come for me."

She cried out, the sound desperate and broken. She strained against his hand.

He plunged his finger into her again and again. His thumb swirled and pressed. And she was certain that she was going to shatter apart. And just as she was sure that she'd die from this relentless torture—his mouth returned to her breast.

She felt the hard edge of his teeth grasping her nipple, the pressure firm, on the brink of pain. And then suddenly, the hint of pain turned into violent release as an orgasm ripped through her, splintering her into tiny pieces as shockwave after shockwave of rapture overtook her.

Chapter 16

Rhys lifted his mouth from her breast, licking his lips. He watched Jane as she panted in rapid, shallow breaths, the muscle of her body still clenched, still reacting to the intensity of her climax.

He licked his lips again, tasting the force of her release on them, sweet and warm in his mouth. The taste alone had brought him to the edge—but he'd held on, unwilling to come anywhere but inside her.

How did you taste her release? his mind questioned, the thought vague and distant but still there. How did he know it was the specific tang of Jane's passion on his tongue?

He didn't know. He didn't care. He just knew he'd drunk in the very essence of her—and she'd tasted just as he knew she would. Like all things good, all things pure.

Unable to stop himself, he slipped her underwear down her legs. She barely reacted, her eyes closed, her breath still labored.

He parted her thighs, looking at the lovely, moist

flesh there. He stroked her, her sex quivering under his fingertip.

She gasped, gazing up at him, passion weighting her lids and making her eyes a vivid green under her dark lashes.

"Can you still take me?" he asked, praying she wouldn't say no.

She smiled, tremulously. "Yes. Oh, yes."

He positioned himself and slowly buried himself deep inside her. Her heat surrounded him; her muscles embraced him, accepting him, welcoming him.

He kissed her then, taking her sweet moans and gasps in his mouth as he began to move inside her. She clung to him, moving with him, and he realized he had truly discovered heaven.

Jane woke to find herself draped over Rhys's chest, his arm flung around her back. Probably exactly how they had finally collapsed into exhausted sleep, worn out by their lovemaking.

She shifted off his chest, stretching. Her muscles complained and her limbs were heavy.

She looked over at Rhys. He slept as he always seemed to—dead to the world. His beautiful, thick hair fell around his head on the pillow. His dark lashes were long and slightly curled under his closed lids. He looked almost angelic in his sleep—certainly not of this world. An archangel fallen to earth.

She smiled to herself. This had to be a dream. She didn't know anything—anyone—could be this wonderful. She supposed she always expected making love to be nice and fun, but she hadn't been prepared for the reality of it.

Making love with Rhys was fun all right, but nice? No. It was amazing, breath-stealing, erotic beyond words and . . .

She stretched again, her muscles crying out. And very, very demanding.

She looked at him for a moment longer, then rolled over to slip out of the bed. She walked to the chair where their discarded clothes were tossed and grabbed Rhys's sweater. Tugging it over her head, she moved toward the bathroom.

Nature called, even as her exhausted body instructed her to crawl back into bed and curl up once again against Rhys.

The bathroom was dark and a little chilly. She flipped on the light and looked around. The chill in the air was nothing but exactly that—a draft, a normal temperature drop. Not the eerie, creeping cold she'd experienced the past two nights.

After going to the bathroom, she crossed to the sink to wash her hands. As she worked the soap between her palms, she frowned. There *was* something strange about this bathroom, all the same. Not creepy or frightening, just something different. She looked around, trying to decide what it was.

No mirrors, she suddenly realized. What bathroom didn't have a mirror? She was reminded of Rhys's earlier reaction.

I don't like mirrors.

Why on earth not? He couldn't look in a mirror and see anything less than physical perfection.

So what did Rhys see when he looked in a mirror? Maybe the flaw wasn't physical—maybe he saw the thing he was repressing. The cause of his curious amnesia.

She shook her head as she turned off the water faucet. Great, she could be his armchair shrink to go along with his quack physician. Rhys needed professional help— and she did mean that in the nicest way possible.

She wandered back into the bedroom. Rhys still slept in the same position, totally unaware that she'd gotten up. She crept up to him, gently lifting a lock of his silky hair. The strands slipped through her fingers back to the white pillow.

The symbolism wasn't lost on her. But she had to get him help, even if that meant ultimately losing him. She knew it, but another part of her liked things just as they were. She liked his sweet words. His promises of a future together. But she had to do the right thing.

Sighing, she left the edge of the bed and searched the floor for her panties. Finding them in a ball at the foot of the bed, she tugged them on, then looked at the clock on the nightstand. It read 3:58 P.M. She'd slept the day away just as she had since moving in with Rhys and Sebastian. It was amazing how quickly she'd fallen into their schedule.

But it was still early enough to try and contact a doctor—a specialist who, hopefully, could give some definitive reason for Rhys's memory loss.

She gazed back at Rhys for a moment, then sighed. She would do the right thing.

Once she was clad in a thick terry cloth robe, she headed to the kitchen to make some breakfast—or rather dinner—and look for a phone book.

She heated a mug of water in the state-of-the-art microwave, which looked as if it had never been used until she got here. She added two slices of bread to a toaster that looked equally unused. And as her bread toasted and her tea steeped, she searched the kitchen for a telephone book. Given the mostly empty state of the cupboards, she found the book rather easily.

Grabbing her toast and tea and the cordless phone, she headed into the dining room to look through the yellow pages.

How did a person go about finding a specialist in amnesia? She flipped to the Ps, looking under physicians. Did Rhys need a neurologist? Should she just make him an appointment with a general practitioner who would examine him and then suggest the next course of action? Or maybe she should talk to a psychiatrist, since there didn't seem to be anything wrong with him physically. Absolutely nothing wrong.

She chewed on her toast, debating over the names in black print on the yellow paper. That was all these doctors were—names. Should she just pick one?

She sighed, read through several of the names again, then picked one. Sabrina Harrison, MD. She supposed choosing a doctor based on the fact that they shared the same last name was as good a reason as any.

She picked up the telephone and began to dial the number when Sebastian strolled into the room.

"Hey, what are you doing?" He yawned and rubbed a hand over his bare chest.

"I . . ." She didn't know whether she should tell him. She didn't want him to be offended that she'd taken matters into her own hands. But something did need to be done for Rhys.

"Did you know that Rhys's memory loss is selective?"

Sebastian frowned as he pulled out a chair and joined her at the table. "It is?"

"You didn't notice that he's fine with a lot of things a

viscount from the nineteenth century wouldn't be? Lights, running water—that sort of thing?"

He considered what she said. "Now that you mention it—yeah, he is cool with that stuff."

"And," Jane hesitated for a second. "We went out last night and walked all around the city—and nothing upset him."

His relaxed posture suddenly grew straighter. "You weren't supposed to go out."

Jane felt a slight wave of guilt, but that was quickly smothered by indignation. "I know that. And I tried to stop him, but he was determined. Besides, he's fine— like I said, nothing shocked him or upset him."

"But he still doesn't remember what he is, right?"

She stared at him for a moment. *"What* he is?"

Sebastian waved a hand with impatience. "What. Who. I meant he doesn't realize that he's not a viscount, right?"

She shook her head, still confused by the wording of Sebastian's questions. "No—as of last night he still thinks he's a viscount."

"And you didn't notice anything strange while you were walking around, did you?"

Jane frowned. "You mean other than your brother thinking New York was London?"

"Right. But you didn't notice anyone odd around? Other than my brother."

Jane started to shake her head, then stopped. "There was this . . . No, it wasn't anything."

Sebastian leaned forward, his eyes intent. "What?"

"It was just this guy." She gave a slight laugh. "It was nothing. He was just odd—nothing scary or anything."

"You're sure?"

She nodded. Who would be around—watching them? Was this part of what Rhys was trying to forget? Was this part of what she'd forgotten? A tingle of uneasiness played over her skin.

But Sebastian sagged back against the chair, looking relieved.

"Is there something else I should know about?" Jane asked, again watching his reaction closely.

"No." He sat up again. "No. I just don't think it's a good idea for either of you to be out in the city right now. You're new here. Rhys isn't thinking clearly. I'd hate for you to end up in a bad part of the city or something."

She supposed his worries made sense. Although Rhys seemed to know his way around just fine. Another odd factor in his memory loss.

"You seemed almost relieved that Rhys is still experiencing memory loss." Why would Sebastian want Rhys to continue to believe he was someone else?

"No," Sebastian said immediately. "No. That isn't it. But I—I didn't want him to suddenly remember everything out on the streets. He could be confused and upset. I'd rather"—he sighed, looking shaken—"I'd rather he was here with me. So I can help him."

Jane eyed him suspiciously for a moment, then decided it was unfair not to believe Sebastian's words. Rhys was his brother, after all. He had every right to want to be there for him.

"I know you want to help him," she said, reaching out to pat his hand. "So do I. That's why I've decided to go ahead and call another doctor." She pointed to the phone book. "I know you have a family doc—"

"No!" Sebastian declared, reaching to snatch up the phone. "No," he repeated more calmly when he saw Jane's startled expression. "Dr.—No—is a very renowned physician. Rhys couldn't possibly do any better than him."

"Dr. No?"

"Yeah, he's Asian."

She regarded him closely for a moment, trying to decide if he was serious. He looked back at her with sincere eyes and a stony set to his jaw.

Finally she sighed. "I understand you want your doctor, a person you trust. But he hasn't come to examine Rhys yet. That doesn't seem very professional to me."

"Well, he is very busy. Because of how renowned he is. But I'll call him again. Now." Sebastian stood, waving the phone in determination. "Right now."

He headed to the kitchen, pausing to give the phone another resolute shake in the air, then closed the door behind him.

She stared at the door, then turned back to her breakfast, taking a bite of her toast. Sebastian had to be up to something. No one had all the answers like he did, even if they were very weird answers.

She finished her toast, and was taking a sip of tea, when Rhys walked into the room. His furrowed brow relaxed once he saw her—almost as if he was afraid she wouldn't be there.

Silly man.

"Good morning." She smiled.

He smiled back, and again, she was struck by the sheer beauty of his features. Her heart skipped against her breastbone.

"I was disappointed you weren't in bed with me when I woke," he said, sitting at the table across from her. "I had plans for you."

"You did?"

He nodded, his smile widening. "I did promise to taste you all over, and I know I missed a few places."

She stared at the sexy curve of his lips, then looked up to his eyes. They sparkled with desire and a hint of amusement.

Oh, he knew exactly what he was doing to her. Her skin tingled at every minute spot that those talented lips had touched.

"You are very bad," she told him, her eyes drifting back to his mouth, wondering exactly where he wanted to taste her now.

"Mmm-hmm," he agreed, the sound low and velvety.

She shifted in her chair, then shifted again. Finally, she crossed her legs.

"So what are you doing?" He reached over and pulled the thick phone book across the table toward him. His eyes skimmed over the columns of names before she could grab the book back and flip the pages closed.

"A physician?" He frowned up at her. "Are you feeling unwell?"

"No," she said, but didn't get to say anything more before Sebastian came back into the room, announcing as he entered, "I reached Dr. No. He'll come tonight."

Rhys looked at his brother and then to Jane. Both of their shocked expressions made it clear that he was not intended to hear about the doctor's visit.

"What's going on?" he asked.

Neither Jane nor Sebastian said anything for a moment. Then they spoke at the same time.

"It's—"

"I—"

They looked at each other, and both fell silent again.

"Jane." He reached out to grasp one of her hands. Her fingers were cold. "Is the doctor for you?"

Her eyes held his. Then she slowly started to shake her head. "N—"

"Yes," Sebastian said abruptly. He stepped farther into the room. "Yes. Since—since you mentioned she might be pregnant, Jane decided that she should see a physician. Just in case."

"Then why didn't you come to me?" Rhys asked her. Jealousy tightened his chest. Why would she go to Sebastian?

Jane opened her mouth to say something, but Sebastian cut her off before she could utter a sound.

"She didn't want you to worry."

Rhys frowned at his brother. He was acting very strange. All agitated and—shifty.

Something wasn't right here.

"Jane, do you mind if I talk to my brother alone for a moment?" Rhys asked.

She narrowed her eyes at Sebastian, but then stood. "No, not at all."

Rhys squeezed her fingers gently before releasing them and watching her leave the room. Once the door was shut behind her, Rhys turned back to his brother.

"What the hell is going on here?"

Sebastian tried to gather his wits and come up with a plausible story—quickly. He should have come up with a better lie, but his first thought had been that Jane was going to tell Rhys the truth. And he had to stop her. Rhys didn't need to know that the "doctor" was for him. He was afraid Rhys might remember he was about two centuries past needing medical attention.

"What do you mean?" Okay, he was definitely stalling. Stalling's good.

"Why did Jane come to you to help her find a physician?"

"For the very reason I said. She didn't want to worry you."

"Is there something I should be worried about?"

Sebastian hesitated again. "She—she's worried that she can't have children."

Rhys stared at him. "Why?" he finally asked.

"It runs in her family."

"Barrenness runs in her family?"

Sebastian nodded. "Her moth—no—her *sister* is barren."

"She doesn't have a sister."

Shit. "Oh, well, she must have said her mother's sister was barren. Yeah, that was it."

Rhys studied him, his eyes full of skepticism. "What does she expect this doctor to tell her? It's too soon to know if she's with child or not."

"I think she just wants to make sure she is healthy. As healthy as she can be to carry your—babe." Sebastian tried hard not to roll his eyes. Why was he doing this, again?

Rhys considered that. "I suppose if it makes her feel more relaxed, then it can certainly do no harm."

Sebastian nodded, relieved that he seemed to be accepting the story. But, man, he was only keeping this shit up for a few more days. If Rhys got his memory back after that, and he was too stupid to realize he needed Jane, that he could find happiness with her, then that was his own problem. Sebastian was sick of making up these cockamamie stories. He had far better things to do.

"Speaking of the possibility that she is already with child . . ."

Sebastian fought back a groan, knowing what was coming.

"Did you arrange the special license?"

"Yes. It's in the works."

Rhys nodded. "And you will get the vicar to come here to perform the ceremony as soon as it is ready?"

"Absolutely." Right after he found someone to pretend to be Dr. No. And again, why was he doing this?

The suspicion finally left Rhys's face, and he actually smiled. "Good. Now, please excuse me while I go join my betrothed."

"By all means," Sebastian said, then sneered at the closed door after his brother exited. Rhys better appreciate this once he got his memory back. It wasn't every brother who'd create fictional doctors and materialize "special licenses" just to get the guy laid.

Sebastian sighed. As Dickens wrote in *A Christmas Carol*, he was a martyr to his own generosity.

Jane paced around her room, wondering what Sebastian was telling Rhys. She could only imagine. And why on earth had he lied to Rhys and said the doctor was for her? As soon as he actually arrived, it wouldn't take Rhys long to figure out that the doctor was examining him.

Once again she wondered which one of the Young brothers was the crazy one.

She sighed. It didn't much matter how they got Rhys help, she supposed, as long as he did get it.

Again her resolve was laced with reluctance. She wanted him to get his memory back; she just desperately hoped he still wanted her afterward. That he wouldn't think she took advantage of the situation. That he wouldn't think she was awful and pathetic.

"You should have come to me," Rhys said from behind her.

She spun to look at him. He stood in the doorway, looking so tall and broad. And stern.

"I . . ." She had no idea what to say. What had Sebastian told him?

He pulled the door closed and strode into the room, stopping directly in front of her. "I'm to be your husband, not Sebastian. Your worries are my worries. Your problems are my problems. And we will work them out together."

She stared up at him, her heart thundering at the possession in his amber eyes. She didn't understand most of what he meant. But she still loved the protectiveness of his words. The idea that he would be there with her—no matter how difficult things in her life got.

"You won't go to him again?"

"No." She wouldn't. She hadn't. She blinked. This was all so confusing.

"You will only come to me?"

She nodded.

He kissed her then. The pressure of his mouth as possessive as his words had been. She submitted, loving the power there, and the yearning she tasted under all his dominance.

He broke off the kiss, his chest rising and falling with his need. "And you will only come for me."

Her passion-addled mind couldn't quite wrap around what he was telling her. Then he slid a hand under the fold of her robe and cupped her bare breast, his palm slightly rough and burning hot.

She gasped, the sound more a hiss through her teeth.

He leaned down, his breath caressing her skin and

stirring her hair like a warm breeze. "Tell me, Janie. Tell me no one else will ever touch you like this. No one else will ever know what it's like to be buried deep inside you."

Her breath hitched in her throat, and her heart threatened to hammer its way out of her chest. His demands were so thrilling, so arousing. And so, so easy for her to agree to.

"No one," she breathed, before she turned her head and captured his lips, kissing him with all the greed and hunger she felt for him, too.

His one hand continued to hold her breast, while the other slipped around her back and pulled her tight against him. Her hands sank into his hair, and they clung to each other, their bodies, their mouths, demanding things for each other that maybe neither of them could give when they finally fell back to earth. Back to real life.

But it didn't matter at this moment.

He finally broke his hold, but only to walk her backward across the room. When her heels bumped the rise of the step to her bed, he lifted her onto it. He followed her up, his mouth falling on hers, his kiss rough and hungry.

And then they were both falling, her soft mattress coming up to catch them.

He lifted his mouth from hers, and his hands found the belt at her waist, yanking it. He parted the robe, baring her body to him. He stared at her, and even though his unruly hair fell forward and shrouded part of his face, she could see his amber eyes glinting in the lamplight. Immediately she was reminded of that feral look she'd seen the first night she met him.

For a moment she was frightened. This Rhys seemed so different from the one who'd made love to her before. That Rhys was gentle and giving.

This one looked wild, starved. His eyes raked over her nakedness, as though he wanted to consume every inch of her, yet despite her uncertainty, she responded. Her nipples puckered into tight throbbing buds. Her vagina pulsed, and she could feel the moisture beading between her thighs. She wanted him. She wanted his possession.

He seemed to sense her submission, and he fell on her. His mouth sucked at her breast, pulling the nipple deep into his mouth, his teeth scraping against the throbbing flesh.

She cried out, the sensation almost too much, teetering somewhere between pleasure and pain. But still his aggressive touch aroused her madly as she writhed underneath him, her hands knotting in his hair, pulling him closer.

While his mouth tormented her breasts, his hand slipped between her thighs. Spreading her open, he stroked the dampness there. His fingers were as rough as his mouth, and just as excruciatingly exciting.

She wiggled against him, unsure what to do. How to please him.

"Just let me taste," he muttered against the curve of her breast, and for a moment she wasn't sure if the voice was truly his or a figment of her own arousal-hazed mind.

He moved down her body, his lips trailing wet kisses and little nips over her belly, heading lower and lower. Until he knelt between her spread thighs.

She whimpered and tried to close her legs. But he caught them, keeping them open.

"I want to look at you." His voice was low, almost gruff. "Open them wide, Janie."

A ragged breath escaped her as she looked at him kneeling there, his eyes burning like a ravenous beast, and she knew he wanted her as his meal.

She felt the heat of a blush scorch her cheeks, seeping down toward her chest. But then she also felt a matching heat between her thighs.

Her legs quivered, but she did as he asked, letting them fall open.

He groaned, his eyes fixing on the point at the apex of her thighs that begged for him. He touched her then, using both hands to spread her labia, exposing her.

"So beautiful," he murmured. "And mine. Mine alone."

She closed her eyes, overcome by his words, the hunger in his expression and her own spiraling need.

She felt his hair brush her inner thigh first, but that tickling sensation was quickly obliterated by the sweep of his tongue, fiery and rough, licking over her.

She gasped, then cried out as his tongue found her clitoris, lapping the hardened bud, circling it, finally sucking it with greedy lips.

She called out his name, begging him to—she didn't know what exactly. She just knew he was the only one who could give her the completion she needed.

Rhys closed his eyes, drinking in the flavor of Jane. Her hands twisted in his hair, and her hips bucked up against his mouth. She moaned his name over and over again, her head thrashing back and forth on the mattress.

His tongue left her clitoris and darted into the heat of her vagina, tasting her arousal, tasting the need and the thrill growing stronger in her very essence.

And as her passion spun, and she spiraled wildly toward the release, the fierce, frantic hunger in himself took complete control.

He had to taste her. Deeper, more fully than the juices of desire. He wanted to be one with her, to feel her life mingle with his. He had to satisfy this blinding hunger that tore at him.

He again lapped the rigid little nub at the top of her sex, and she cried out, pressing herself hard to his mouth. He felt his teeth sharp against his own lips, and he shifted his mouth, moving upward until he was kissing the curls covering her plump mound.

He opened his eyes, staring up at her, hoping that seeing her would help him focus, help him keep control. But it had the opposite effect. Her skin was creamy in the light, her breasts jiggling as she squirmed against his mouth. Her eyes closed, her mouth parted as she breathed in shallow puffs.

He closed his eyes.

God, he wanted her. For his very own. For eternity.

He heard her scream, the sound sharp, piercing. Then he felt her convulse under his mouth. Then the sweet, delicious flavor of her release swirled over his tongue. He drank in her climax deeply as his own orgasm met hers.

She cried out again and again as their orgasms united, and Rhys ceased to be and Jane ceased to be. They were one—their passion one.

Chapter 17

"Jane," Rhys said, his voice low, the natural huskiness replaced by an almost guttural quality.

She forced herself to open her eyes and found him watching her, his peculiar amber eyes fixed on hers. A frown creased his brow.

She breathed a deep gulp of air, trying to calm the intense waves of sensation that still surged through her.

She offered him a tremulous smile, even though she felt shaken to her core. What had just happened?

Somehow she felt as if she'd just given Rhys more than when they had full intercourse, which made no sense. He had given to her, pleasured her.

No, pleasuring didn't even begin to do justice to what he'd done to her. Yet, she felt as though she'd given him her soul with her powerful release. But at the same time she felt as if he'd given her his soul in return.

She closed her eyes again. She wasn't making any sense. She wasn't thinking straight. And a bone-deep exhaustion seemed to weigh heavily on her whole body.

She felt Rhys move, coming up to lie beside her. Still

she couldn't seem to gather the strength to open her eyes.

"Are you all right?" His voice was low, but not as harsh as moments earlier. And it was laced with concern.

She wearily turned her head, opening her eyes and offering him another small smile. "Yes, just exhausted—and very, very satisfied. I can't even move."

Her compliment didn't seem to reassure him. He reached out and touched her cheek, his fingers just a faint whisper over her skin.

"Your skin is so cold."

She smiled serenely. She didn't feel cold. She felt weak and a little light-headed and most definitely sated. Her body seemed to be floating on a cool cloud. It was lovely.

Her eyes drifted shut.

"Jane?"

She blinked, forcing her gaze to meet Rhys's. "Hmm?"

"I'm going to draw a bath for you. And while you relax and warm up, I'm going to get you something to eat."

"Okay," she agreed, but didn't really comprehend his words. She just wanted to sleep—to drift on this puffy cloud of satisfaction.

"I'll be right back," he assured her, although his voice seemed miles below her.

She nodded, or maybe she didn't. She continued to float.

Rhys scrutinized Jane. Other than the faint smile still lingering on her lips, she didn't look like a woman who'd just experienced sexual gratification.

The pallor of her skin matched the sheer curtains

framing the bed, white and translucent. He could see the pale blue traces of her veins under her eyes. Her lips, which always looked rosy, were now an unnatural color of muted mauve.

He watched her breathing as he had that morning. Her chest no longer rose and fell in a deep soothing rhythm, but rather in shallow, rapid starts.

God, what had he done? A rush of fear and anger rushed through him. Fear for her and anger at himself. He had caused this—whatever was wrong with her—although he couldn't quite figure out what he'd done. But he did know that as soon as he had touched his mouth to her and felt her reaction to him, everything was a blur. All he could remember was both of their passions swirling around him, spurring him on until they'd both shouted out their climaxes.

He closed her robe to protect her chilled skin. She was so pale, so fragile; she appeared like a porcelain doll tossed carelessly onto the bed.

Another wave of anger coursed through him.

What had he done?

He stared at her a moment longer, then started toward the bathroom. But at the last minute, he changed his mind. She was so exhausted; he didn't trust that she could actually sit up, alone, in the bathtub.

Besides, she was too pale. Food. She needed food.

He returned to the bed and carefully pulled the comforter over her as much as he could without disturbing her.

But she still opened her eyes to gaze up at him. She smiled again. "Hi."

"Hi. Are you comfortable?"

"Mmm-hmm. I feel—nice."

He smiled back, but his lips turned down as soon as her eyes fluttered shut again. She was responding to him. That was a good sign, but she still needed food.

He adjusted the blanket a bit. Then he headed to the kitchen.

Once in the narrow room, he stood there, looking around. What did Jane eat? He didn't know. He didn't even know what to prepare. Had he ever prepared any sort of meal? He didn't think so.

Damn his drunken stupidity for sending Cook on holiday.

Finally, he strode over to the refrigerator, yanking the door open. Surely he could make something.

He frowned at the meager selection of food on the shelves. Eggs, milk, orange juice and some cheese. Plus the bags of . . . What the hell was that stuff anyway?

He grabbed one of the pouches filled with dark liquid and the orange juice, then headed to the cupboards to see if there was anything there that he could fix Jane.

As he searched the cupboards, he unstopped the container of dark fluid and took a sip. He grimaced slightly as he swallowed. The drink tasted cold and stale, with a strange hint of chemicals under the salty flavor.

Jane had tasted so much sweeter.

He pushed that thought out of his head. He didn't have time to reflect fondly on his sex life at the moment. Jane needed food.

He browsed the cans on the shelves. Tuna—in a can? Bleh, he thought as he absently took another swig of the chilled red liquid.

He reached up and picked up another can wrapped in white paper. "Deviled Ham? Does she really eat this?"

He placed that back on the shelf and opted for something called peanut butter. He at least knew what butter was, and when he sniffed the creamy brown substance, it didn't smell too awful.

He considered the peanut butter again for a moment, trying to decide what she would eat it on. Crackers? Bread?

He spotted a loaf of bread on the counter. Bread it was.

After opening several drawers, he located a knife and began to prepare Jane's meal.

"What the hell did you do?" Sebastian said from right behind him.

Rhys started, smearing the gooey butter on his thumb. He turned to glare at his brother. "What the hell, Sebastian. Why are you lurking around like the dead?"

Sebastian smirked slightly. "It's what I do." But then his expression grew serious again. "Where's Jane? Is she okay?"

Rhys frowned. Was she okay? He wasn't quite sure. "She's in her bedroom. Resting."

Sebastian stared at him for a moment, then nodded as if he decided Rhys was telling him the truth. "What are you doing?" He gestured to the knife in Rhys's hand and the glob of peanut butter on his thumb.

"Jane is hungry. I was making her something to eat."

Sebastian nodded again, his expression looking even more relaxed. "Good. That's a good idea. That will definitely help."

"Help?" Did Sebastian know that something was wrong with Jane?

Sebastian waved a hand. "You know what I mean."

No, he didn't.

"Listen," Sebastian said. "I've got to go out for a while. You will be okay, right?"

"I'll be fine," Rhys said gruffly, suddenly annoyed with this conversation. Of course he'd be fine. And Jane would be fine, too. He had things under control. He was in control.

Sebastian studied him for a moment, then said, "Good. I'll be back in a bit. Make sure you drink plenty of that." He pointed to the pouch of liquid on the counter. "It's good for you."

Rhys didn't respond, but watched Sebastian until he disappeared out into the hallway which led to the elevator.

He stood there for several more seconds, even after Sebastian was gone. Why did he get the feeling Sebastian knew something he didn't?

"Great," Sebastian muttered as he pulled down the grate to the elevator. At this rate, he was going to have to get a doctor for real. And not for Rhys.

He'd smelled *the feeding* as soon as he'd walked into the kitchen. Rhys had reeked of residual bloodlust, and of Jane.

If Rhys got carried away, things could get dangerous very quickly. Fortunately, Sebastian had been able to sense Jane. And she was fine—a little on the dry side, but nothing that wouldn't repair itself with some food and rest.

Sebastian lifted the grate and stepped out onto the second floor and the back entrance of the nightclub.

He was just going to have to be more careful about Rhys getting enough blood. If he fed regularly, the bloodlust shouldn't be an issue. He just had to make sure Rhys was drinking the blood from the blood bank.

He reached the heavy steel door that led into back of the club. But right now, he had to find a Dr. No.

Rhys placed the plate and glass of orange juice on the nightstand, then sat down on the edge of Jane's bed.

She lay against the pillows in exactly the same position as when he left. One small hand rested on her stomach; the other was flung back next to her head. She looked so small, so delicate. And again he was disturbed by the pastiness of her skin.

You can't do this, his mind told him. *You don't deserve her, and she certainly doesn't deserve what you are doing.*

He closed his eyes, forcing those thoughts from his head. He wasn't doing anything aside from caring for her. He wanted to protect her, to hold her close to him, to make love to her. There wasn't anything wrong with that. It was the natural reaction of any normal man toward the woman he would soon marry.

A man. His brain locked on to that word. Normal. He wasn't norm . . .

He closed his eyes, willing these strange thoughts away. And when he opened his eyes again, he stared at Jane. Then gently, he brushed his index finger over the curve of her cheek. Her skin still felt cool, but he could detect a little pinkness returning to her lips.

He touched his hand to her brow. She would be okay, and from now on, he'd be more careful. Less demanding in his lovemaking. He'd take care of her.

"Jane? Janie, love, wake up."

She blinked up at him, another smile ready on her lips. "Mmm." She stretched, causing the covers to slip away from her, and her robe parted slightly, revealing the inner curve of one of her breasts.

Control, Rhys's mind warned him. He forced his eyes to her face, but her sweet smile and sleepy gaze didn't lessen the desire budding inside him one iota.

"I . . ." He frowned, trying to recall what he wanted to tell her. After a deep breath, he managed, "I brought you some food. I think you should try to eat it."

"I am hungry," she said, trying to brace her arms under her so she could sit up.

He placed a hand on her arm, stopping her. Then he twisted his body around so his back was against the headboard, and he pulled her up so she was situated between his legs and she could recline with her back against his chest.

He picked up the glass of orange juice. "Here, drink this."

She lifted her head slightly, placing her hand over his as they both guided the cup to her mouth.

She took several large swallows, before pushing the glass gently away.

He set it aside and reached for the plate. Placing it on her lap, he said, "I hope you like it. It's something called peanut butter."

"I love peanut butter," she said, but she didn't make a move to pick up the slathered bread.

He tore off a piece of the bread, his arms rubbing against her sides as he did so. Then he raised the tidbit to her lips. "Please, you need to eat this."

She dropped her head back against his chest, and from his taller angle he could see her eyes were closed again.

Panic tore through him. Had she passed out? Was she all right?

"Janie?"

"Why do you call me that?"

His relief was so sharp at hearing her speak that he didn't even hear her words. "What?"

"Janie. Why do you call me that?"

He frowned. He didn't even really notice that he did. The nickname just seemed natural to him.

"If you don't like it—"

"No," she interrupted him, her eyes still closed, a slight smile curving her lips. "I like it. I just wondered why you called me it."

He thought for a moment. "Jane doesn't seem to fit you. It's too ordinary, too plain."

Her smile widened, revealing a slight dimple in her right cheek. "That's me, Plain Jane."

"No," he said quickly. "There is absolutely nothing plain about you. You are so lovely and sweet and so, so desirable. How could you ever think otherwise? Especially after the way I lose total control in your arms? Good God, I want to make love to you every time I'm near you."

Her eyes opened, her gaze locking with his. "I . . . I hope you continue to feel that way for a while longer."

"I will feel that way for a bit longer than a while. I hope you are prepared for forever." He leaned forward and pressed his lips to hers—needing her to believe him. Needing to know she felt the same.

Jane tilted her head back, accepting his wonderful, persuasive kiss. Forever. That wouldn't be long enough to be with this man.

Even as tired as she was, her body began to hum again. His desire mingled with hers—drawing her need out, around him. It was as though their yearning was completely linked, tied to each other's until she couldn't tell where they ended. They were one. How could a kiss make her feel so encompassed, so possessed?

But that overwhelming possession was as revitalizing as any type of nourishment or any amount of sleep.

Too soon, as seemed to be Rhys's way, he broke off their kiss and told her. "You still need to eat."

She shook her head. It was truly uncanny how he seemed able to read her thoughts.

But she didn't question it. Instead, she obediently opened her mouth and allowed him to pop a piece of peanut butter bread inside.

She chewed slowly but didn't really taste it. Instead she watched as he ripped another piece off the slice and held to her lips. A bit of peanut butter was smeared on his fingers, and as she took the next bite, she flicked her tongue against the pad of his thumb, savoring the sweet, roasted flavor mingled with the taste of his skin.

She couldn't miss the slight hiss of Rhys's breath near her ear, and his reaction made her feel powerful and so, so aroused.

Rhys continued to feed her, and she continued to eat with relishing brushes of her tongue and her lips against his fingers.

All too soon, the food was gone.

She twisted so she could look up at him. His eyes were hooded and his breathing a little uneven.

"Your color looks much better." His voice was low and had taken on that husky tone that seemed to stroke over her skin.

"I feel great. Not even tired." She wiggled against him so her hip rubbed along his groin.

He lifted an eyebrow and gave her a slow, sexy grin. "Is that so?"

She shifted again, and this time felt his penis, rock hard and ready.

Her own breathing hitched. She was insatiable. Then she looked at him. His gorgeous features, his muscled chest, that sexy smile. If she was going to be insatiable, this was the man with whom to be it.

She shifted again, but he placed his hands on her hips, stopping her movement.

"Sweetheart, I'd like nothing more than to make love to you. But I think you need more time to rest."

"I feel great," she insisted.

"How about this?" His fingers caressed her waist through the thick terry cloth of her robe. "I'll get you a little more juice, and if you drink it all, then we'll talk about making love."

"Talk about it, huh?"

"Talking can be pretty exciting." He wagged his eyebrows.

Her heart hopped in her chest. She had no doubt talking about sex with Rhys would be more than exciting. Talking about the weather was pretty darn thrilling with this man.

But she sighed as if she had to think about his offer. Yeah, right. "Okay, I'll drink the juice."

He gave her a quick kiss, then slid out from behind her.

"Rest. I'll be right back."

She nodded and watched him leave, his back and his tight little derrière just as gorgeous as the rest of him.

She fell back against the mattress and stared at the sheer canopy over her bed, a ridiculously happy smile on her lips.

She knew she should be acting wiser about the whole situation. That she should be preparing herself for the eventuality of Rhys getting his memory back. But right this minute, she couldn't seem to stay focused on that. In an odd way, they both seemed to be repressing things they didn't want to think about.

She sighed, not feeling sad precisely. She felt far too good to feel upset. But her happiness was diminished a little.

She rolled over onto her side, moving her hands up to rest them under her cheek. But as she did so, she brushed her breast, and pain prickled her skin. Not sharp pain, but rather an annoying stinging like a paper cut.

She frowned and pushed aside her robe, looking down at the swell of her left breast. At first she didn't see anything, although the faint stinging continued. Then she noticed the marks. Two spots, deep pink. She almost missed them because they blended with the color of her areola.

But as she studied them closer, there was no denying the marks were there.

She brushed her finger over them, trying to decide what they could be. They looked like puncture wounds—but puncture wounds that were mostly healed.

She couldn't imagine she would miss an injury like that—especially long enough for them to heal. She inspected the marks a bit more.

Vaguely, she recalled Rhys biting her there last night. But there was no way that nip could have created such an abrasion. His bite hadn't been painful. In fact, it had been amazingly, overwhelmingly erotic.

Plus, even if it had been possible for his bite to create

those marks, they would be fresh, not nearly healed as these appeared.

She shrugged and closed her robe, trying to simply dismiss it. But in the back of her mind, she knew something was strange about the marks.

"Very strange," she repeated out loud. That seemed to be the norm here.

Just then, Rhys stuck his head in the doorway. Gone was the sexy smile. Now his normally full, sculpted lips were compressed into a straight line.

"Sebastian says there is a doctor here."

Even though Jane knew she should finally be relieved that Sebastian had gotten the doctor here, apprehension filled her chest.

She forced a smile. "Good. I'll get dressed."

Rhys nodded and hesitated as though he wanted to say something else. Then he nodded again. "I'll wait for you in the living room."

She watched as he closed the door, and still she remained on the bed. Suddenly she wished Sebastian hadn't gotten the doctor to come. After this evening, she wanted just a few more perfect days with Rhys.

She knew he was centurially challenged. She knew he couldn't continue on that way, but a few more days, that couldn't hurt.

Her conscience warred with what she wanted and what she knew was right. But she desperately wanted to keep feeling all the things Rhys made her feel—attractive, exciting and so cared for. Those sensations were too novel, too wonderful, to lose just yet.

No, she couldn't be selfish. Rhys needed help. And she couldn't stand in the way of that.

She rummaged through her suitcase, finding a pair

of jeans and a sweatshirt. She tugged them on, then rushed to be with Rhys. She wanted to be there to see how he was going to react when he realized that the doctor was there to see him.

Somehow, she didn't think he'd respond well. He'd gone to great lengths to forget something, and she didn't think he'd want anyone to force him to remember. She just hoped he'd be okay when he did.

When she reached the living room, Rhys was waiting by himself. "Where are Sebastian and the doctor?"

He gestured toward the library. "Sebastian is waiting with him in there."

She nodded, but neither of them moved. Then Jane realized he was waiting for her to go first. After all, he believed the doctor was here to see her.

She gave him a smile that she knew didn't hide her nervousness, and she went to the library door. She cast one more glance at him. He smiled back, his amber eyes filled with warmth.

She prayed that when this was all done, he'd still look at her that way.

Taking a deep breath, she turned the knob and opened the door.

Sebastian looked over from where he stood in front of the unlit fireplace. "There you are. Let me introduce you to the esteemed Dr. No." He waved his arm like he was a model revealing a new product.

Jane followed his gesture until she spotted the figure seated on the sofa, a drink in his hand.

The diminutive man stood and saluted her with his glass, then gave her a slow, wide grin that could only be described as lecherous.

Chapter 18

That was Dr. No?

Jane scrutinized the man as he rose and crossed toward her. He appeared to be in his thirties with brown hair cut closely to his head. His black pants hung loosely on his thin body, and the blue material of his shirt shimmered in the lamplight. But it wasn't his age or his size or his clothing that surprised her. It was his ears. Or rather the piercings in his ears.

No, piercings didn't quite do them justice—he had *holes* in his ears as if the regular earring holes had been stretched to ten times their original size. Then the expanded holes were kept open by metal rims.

That almost overshadowed the fact that he didn't look remotely Asian.

Suddenly Jane realized she had been staring at him far too long. He wagged his eyebrows and gave her another lascivious smile, apparently unbothered by her rudeness. Stepping forward, he extended his hand.

"Yeah, that's me, Dr. No."

Jane accepted his hand and tried to keep her gaze from wandering back to his ears.

"Thank you for coming," she managed, and received yet another lecherous grin.

"I couldn't resist. When Sebastian explained the situation, I had to see it for myself."

Jane frowned. Those were hardly the words of a concerned family physician. She cast a worried look to Sebastian.

Sebastian stepped forward and clapped the doctor on the back. "Dav—Dr. No is always interested in new cases."

"Sebastian," Rhys said slowly, and for the first time, Jane noticed that he was in the doorway, staring at the doctor with an equally stunned expression. "Can I talk to you in the living room?"

Rhys nodded at the doctor, his amber gaze going once more to his ears before he looked to his brother, who had joined him at the door.

"We will just be a minute," Rhys said as he nudged Sebastian toward the door. He paused and looked back to her. "Just stay right here."

Jane nodded and then, through the doctor's ear holes, watched the two brothers disappear into the living room.

"So Rhys has gone nuttier than a Nutter Butter, eh?"

Jane blinked at the man. Was that his technical take on Rhys's ailment? "He's a little confused. And I think he does need professional help." Even though she knew it was a little rude, she did emphasize the word "professional."

"Well, I'll tell you, from what I've heard from Sebastian, he's needed help for a long time. He's one uptight dude. Actually he seems happier now than I've ever

seen him—not that I know him that well. But I'd say amnesia seems to be workin' for him."

She knew she was gaping at this man, but she couldn't
believe her ears. This was the much sought-after physician Sebastian swore by.

"Or maybe it's you that has him all mellowed out."
Dr. No nudged her, wiggling his eyebrows knowingly.

She stepped back from him. Well, it was certainly no
mystery now why this guy would just diagnose Rhys over
the phone. That had to be how he did most of his
exams.

But she gave him the benefit of the doubt and asked,
"Don't you think he needs to go to the hospital? Or see
a specialist? A psychiatrist maybe?"

"Ahh, psychiatrists. I went to one of those once. Rhys
would do better with a bottle of Jack Daniels and a prostitute. The booze will get him talkin', and a prostitute
will listen to his problems for a whole lot cheaper. Plus
he'd get a blow job while she listened. That's the only
way to get psychiatric help." He nodded as if he'd actually offered her a good solution.

She stared at him for a moment, then edged toward
the door. "Will you excuse me for a moment?"

He nodded and flopped down into one of the chairs,
crossing his blue suede sneakers on the coffee table.

She glanced at him once more, then reached for the
doorknob. But it slipped out of her grasp.

Both brothers came back into the room. Rhys looked
annoyed. And Sebastian looked tense.

"Jane. Can I talk to you?" It might have been posed
as a question, but the look in Rhys's eyes stated there
was no room for debate. Not that she wanted to, she was
more than happy to leave Dr. No's leering looks and of-
fensive comments.

Once they were in the living room and the door was shut, Rhys turned to her. "I don't want you being examined by that man."

"Me neither," she agreed heartily, even though she knew Dr. No wasn't here to see her.

"Good. Now—"

The door swung open, and Sebastian stuck his head in the room. "Dr. No says he's done with Jane. But he wants to see you, Rhys."

Rhys cast a concerned look to Jane. "He did an examination already?"

Jane immediately shook her head. "No. He just asked me a few questions and offered his"—she gave Sebastian a disapproving glare—"professional advice."

Rhys looked relieved. Sebastian looked unimpressed.

"Now he wants to talk with you," Sebastian told Rhys again.

Rhys gave his brother a puzzled look. "Why?"

"He has some advice for you, too."

Rhys hesitated, then walked toward the library. He paused in the doorway. "You are all right, aren't you?"

Jane nodded. "Fine."

Sebastian started to follow Rhys back into the living room, but Jane called out to him. "Wait, Sebastian, may I talk to you?"

She could have sworn he rolled his eyes, but then he smiled so broadly she wasn't sure she'd seen his expression correctly. "Sure."

Rhys disappeared into the library, and Sebastian stepped into the living room.

"That is your renowned doctor?" Jane questioned in an emphatic whisper.

"Don't let his looks throw you. He's the best." The

best DJ that the nightclub had ever hired. Also the newest, which he hoped would prevent Rhys from recognizing him and trying to get the DJ to "ready a carriage." Or whatever other nonsense Rhys came up with.

"He seems to think Rhys's amnesia is a positive thing."

"Well, that's good, right? At least he doesn't think it's a bad thing."

Jane shook her head, shock clear in her green eyes. "Sebastian, this is crazy. How can amnesia be anything but bad? Your brother needs help, and no one seems to care."

Sebastian gritted his teeth. No one cared! If he didn't care, he wouldn't be inventing doctors. He wouldn't be trying his damnedest to keep Jane with him. He wouldn't be trying to protect him. "I do care, Jane. But I have to admit, I like Rhys better now. He isn't hurting. He isn't mourning our sister, Elizabeth, who died a long time ago—but, he can't seem to let her go. And he isn't beating himself up over our brother, Christian, with whom he hasn't spoken in years."

Sebastian snapped his mouth shut. He hadn't intended to tell Jane about their other siblings. When the time came for her to hear the truth about them, he thought that was Rhys's responsibility.

But maybe she did need to know. She was in deep— she needed to understand the Rhys who would very likely return when his memory did.

Jane stared at him, her eyes growing damp like emeralds glistening at the bottom of a lake. "I—I didn't know."

"How could you? Rhys doesn't even know now."

"Right. And you think that is why he has this amnesia?"

Sebastian nodded. "In part, yes."

"Oh, Rhys." Her voice was filled with so much sympathy, so much despair.

Sebastian stared at her, at the tears in her eyes and the pain clear in her features, and for the first time wondered if he'd taken this all too far.

"Please excuse me," she murmured and headed down the hallway, without waiting for his response.

"Sure," he answered anyway. Until this moment, he'd only thought to give Rhys what he wanted—Jane. Not once had he considered that he was toying with her life, too. Playing with her future, her emotions.

She loved Rhys. Her love scented the air and swirled through the room in her wake.

God, he hoped he was doing the right thing for both of them.

Jane fled to her room. Her pain for Rhys and the tears she was trying to hold at bay strangled her. How had she gotten into this mess?

But now she finally understood what Rhys was repressing. And she also understood that cold man she'd met back at the bar. The one who had been so distant. So cool. He'd been a man who had been hurting. The smiling, kind, gentle Rhys that she knew now was free of that pain. Able to laugh.

Suddenly, she felt so selfish. Here, she'd been worrying about what would happen to *her* when he got his memory back. She hadn't fully thought out what might happen to him.

But she didn't believe what Sebastian was suggesting, that Rhys could continue to go on living in a fantasy world. Even though his delusions allowed him to live free of old heartaches, they were still delusions. Eventually he would remember.

Or would he? Her own father was a prime example of someone who had lived in his fantasy world forever. But she didn't want that for Rhys.

She knew firsthand that a fantasy world was very limiting. Her father had worked hard to keep out anything that might interfere with his beliefs. He'd had to cut himself off. And in doing so, he'd cut Jane off, too.

But even though she had been distanced from her father, she'd still had to live in his parameters. She'd had to go along with her father's delusions, because she didn't know what else to do. A need to protect him and herself had made her separate them from the outside world. And in the end, all she'd managed to do was lose everything that was real and normal.

She didn't want that for Rhys. She wanted him to have a real life.

He needed to confront his old wounds. Wouldn't that be the only way for them to heal?

Yes, it was the only way. She truly believed that. But just like Sebastian she ached for Rhys. To remember was going to be like losing everyone again. Elizabeth. Christian.

This was terrible. She just didn't know what to do. She didn't know how to help him.

She sank into one of the wing-back chairs, dropped her head into her hands.

"Jane?"

Her head shot up, and she blinked through her tears to see Rhys standing in the center of the room.

He watched her, his amber eyes dark with worry.

"Rhys," she said, her voice sounding raw. "I'm so sorry. So sorry."

He crossed to her and knelt down. He caught her hands, stroking his thumbs back and forth across the backs of them.

"You have no reason to be sorry," he assured her.

She stared at him. She had so many reasons to be sorry for both of them. For all the pain, for the loss, for allowing a relationship between them, when she knew it was wrong.

"Darling, if there are no children, then there are no children. I want you more than I could even consider wanting an heir."

Jane blinked at him. "What?"

"If you are barren, it is what was meant to be."

She stared at him, his words permeating the anguish that had surrounded her. Barren? Heir?

She gritted her teeth, fighting back the irritation that welled in her chest. Of course, this was another of Sebastian's little stories. Another of his helpful lies, designed to protect his brother.

She couldn't even think what to say. She couldn't sort out all the emotions and thoughts battling inside her. She needed time to think. Time to decide what was best for both Rhys and herself.

"Rhys." She pulled a hand from his hold and touched it to his cheek. "I really just want to rest."

He nodded, and before she realized what he was doing, he lifted her up in his arms.

"Rhys! I can walk."

He smiled down at her. "I know you can walk, but you've had a grueling day. I want to pamper you."

He strode to the bed, setting her down in the center. His fingers moved to the button of her jeans.

She caught his fingers. "Rhys," she said slowly, uncertain how to say no to him now. After all the times she had adamantly said yes.

"Love, I'm not some rutting beast," he said with a slight smile, although she could see the hurt in his eyes. "I just wanted to make you more comfortable."

She suddenly felt guilty. She had no reason to mistrust him. He'd never pressured her. She was the one who was taking from him.

Deftly, he removed her jeans, then plumped the pillows and tucked the covers over her.

"Do you want me to stay?" he asked quietly, as he brushed a lock of hair from her cheek.

She shook her head. "I think I need to be alone." Having him so close clouded her judgment, and she needed to think about what was right for him.

He nodded, resignation in the gesture as if he'd known her answer already.

He kissed her forehead, and her eyes grew teary at the sweetness of his touch. How could she lose this? How could she walk away from something she'd craved her whole life?

He turned off the lamp and started to leave the room. In the doorway, he stopped, his tall form silhouetted against the hall light. "Janie, everything will be fine."

She closed her eyes. She hoped so.

Jane had no idea how she could have fallen asleep, not with all the worries she had on her mind. But she had.

She opened her eyes and looked at the alarm clock. The numbers glowed eleven thirty-one A.M.

She let her eyes drift closed, exhaustion still enveloping her. Given her new sleep schedule, this was far too early to get up anyway.

She started to doze off again, when something prickled over her skin. Her eyes snapped open, and she lay perfectly still.

The prickling intensified until she was covered with goose bumps, and her hair felt as if it were standing on end.

She closed her eyes. Not again.

But just as she told herself that she had to be imagining the sensation, a heavy weight pinned her down to the bed.

She willed herself to stay calm. It was a dream. It had to be a dream. She was still sound asleep, and whatever this was couldn't hurt her.

Her heart thundered in her ears, but she forced herself not to struggle, even though everything within her said to fight.

Vaguely, over the thrum of blood rushing through her veins, she heard the creak of the bed as the "thing" pressed her harder into the mattress. Again, her instincts told her to fight, to flee.

But she lay perfectly still, trying to overcome her terror to comprehend what held her. She realized after several moments the "thing" did seem to have a form. It was a body, she could sense that. Yet, when she moved her hand to touch it, she encountered nothing.

Suddenly, the form began touching her. She shivered as cold fingers stroked over her legs, then her arms.

She began to struggle then, unable to control the fear consuming her.

But the shadow fingers caught her wrists and pinned them to her sides, and for the first time she heard breathing, low and steady.

She tried to shift her head away from the sound, but it moved closer.

Then she heard it. A voice low and guttural—unnatural in its deepness. Whispering against her ear.

"Hello, Janie."

Chapter 19

Rhys awoke and was out of bed in a single movement.

Jane.

She was in danger. He didn't question how he knew it. He simply knew it. Fear scented the air like a strong, cloying cologne. Jane's fear.

Even though he was aware that his body was still bone-weary, almost as if there was some external force weighing down on him, his movements were fast, if not quite as agile as usual. He rushed for her room. The doorknob turned easily in his hand. For some reason, he'd half expected it not to.

Jane lay in the center of her bed, her arms down at her sides, her legs out straight and her eyes wide. Terror gleamed in their green depths. She appeared to be restrained in that position, held by some unseen force.

Rhys paused for only a second as an acrid scent swirled around him, strong and foul. But he forced himself to ignore the scent and raced to the bedside.

As he reached out to touch Jane, the overpowering

smell began to evaporate. She jerked toward him as if she'd been struggling and the bonds had finally been released. She scrambled toward him, flinging her arms around him, her hands touching his face, his hair, as if she didn't quite dare believe he was real.

"Shh," he whispered, touching her, too. Relief flooded him. She was fine. She was safe. He'd made it in time. In time for what, he couldn't say. But it didn't matter. He made it.

"Did—did you see it?" Her voice shook, and her eyes still looked wild.

"No," he told her, but he had felt something.

"Rhys, I tried to convince myself it was a dream. Some crazy nightmare that I was having. But tonight, I know, whatever it is, it's real."

He stared at her for a moment, his attention on her, but also focusing on what had been there. The smell was completely gone; only Jane's fear remained.

"You're sleeping with me."

She nodded, crawling out of the bed. He wrapped an arm around her and led her out of the room. She shivered against him, and her skin felt icy under his hands.

Once they were in his room, under the covers, her body pulled tightly to his, she finally asked, "Did you feel anything? A presence? Something?"

He started to nod, but then stopped. What good would it do to tell her what he'd experienced? He didn't even understand it himself. Instead he breathed in the fresh scent of her hair, of her skin. Whatever he'd sensed was gone. Jane was safe. That was all that mattered.

"I think you must have had a very vivid dream." He rubbed his hand up and down over her back, hoping the caress would calm her.

She was silent for a few moments. Disappointment that he didn't believe her radiated from her skin.

He did believe her. He just didn't want to. He didn't want to think about what that smell meant, what it symbolized. He wouldn't.

"Do you believe in ghosts?"

His hand paused. "Ghosts?"

She nodded, her short hair tickling his chin. "Yes. I never did. Even growing up in a funeral parlor. Maybe because of growing up in one. Maybe because of my father. But now . . . Now I don't know."

"Janie, it wasn't a ghost," he assured her. Again, he didn't question how he knew that.

She lifted her head, and even though there was no light in the room, Rhys could see the bright green of her eyes. "So you don't believe in some sort of existence after death?"

Oh, he believed. He knew.

But instead of telling her that, he kissed her. Savoring the life he tasted there. And the goodness.

"I think you had a very bad nightmare," he told her after they parted.

She let out a slow breath. "It seemed so real."

"Some nightmares are very real." He knew his words were an understatement.

"How did you know I needed you?" Her voice was growing calmer, quieter, and he realized his touch was lulling her into a drowsy state.

But her innocent question made him feel agitated, uncomfortable. Another question that he knew the answer to, but the answer shouldn't make sense. He was a viscount. A man who ran several estates, had the luxury of a reasonable fortune, and who enjoyed a good fox hunt. He was a normal fellow, about to be blessed with a marriage to a truly remarkable woman. He shouldn't be able to sense her fear, feel and taste and smell it in the air.

"I must have heard you cry out," he finally said, realizing it was the only logical answer.

She snuggled closer to him, and she managed to say through a yawn, "I don't remember crying out."

She hadn't cried out, not verbally. But she had been calling to him. And he'd heard her loud and clear.

"It called me Janie," she mumbled, just before she drifted off into a tranquil slumber, but the soft words left Rhys's body cold.

He knew the name Rhys had given her. It didn't mean anything. She had a nightmare.

A nightmare they shared.

Christian lay on his makeshift bed, his body completely drained to the point he couldn't even lift a finger. He'd be lucky if he could even rouse tonight to feed. But the crippling exhaustion was well worth it. His outer body journey had shown him much, plus it had just been fun.

His powers were growing stronger. Very few middling vampires could actually leave their physical form and travel in the daylight.

He was still weak, and couldn't sustain the travel, but he had done well enough. He'd scared his brother and his little mortal.

He closed his eyes. And he'd learned something else interesting. Rhys still had no idea who or what had been in the room.

Avenging Lilah's death was really going to be painfully simple.

* * *

"Now you're the one who is freezing," Jane murmured against Rhys's ear as she snuggled closer to him, her chest pressed to his back, her head on the pillow next to his.

"I'm fine," he said, although he knew his voice sounded nearly as cool as his skin felt. A voice in his head kept repeating that he needed to pull away, distance himself from her.

But she didn't seem to notice his detached reaction as she snaked her arms around him, splaying her small hands on his chest. Her leg looped over his as if she could act as his own personal blanket.

He closed his eyes, willing himself not to respond.

Her fingers brushed over the coarse hair on his chest. Her thumbs inadvertently, or maybe not so inadvertently, rubbed over his flat nipples until they hardened. Warm breaths stirred his hair.

He didn't have to let her go. He could take care of her. Keep her safe. He could.

She moved behind him, levering herself up to nibble his ear, then to press sweet, hot kisses along the column of his neck. Then along his jawline.

His reaction was immediate, his cock engorging against his stomach. He rolled over, pinning her under him, kissing her, his mouth telling her how much he needed her. Even if he shouldn't.

"How do you do that?" she murmured against his lips.

"Do what?"

"Make me forget everything."

He chuckled dryly. "I was wondering the same thing about you."

She touched her fingers to his face. "Are you forgetting something?"

Her question startled him. It was too probing, too accurate.

He shifted away from her, a look between a frown and irritation on his flawless features. "Weren't we originally discussing you forgetting, not me?"

"Yes. But don't—don't you suppose there are things you are forgetting, too."

Rhys sat up, his first reaction to pull away. But then his emotions calmed. He had no reason to be upset by her words. After all, the answer was very simple. If he was forgetting anything, it was only to be with her, to protect her.

"I would imagine we all forget things that are unpleasant. It's a way of dealing."

She sat up, too, and rested her head on his shoulder, her hand brushing lightly over the tense muscles of his back.

"Just remember—no matter what, you can always have me."

Her soft words were like bolts of lightning. He couldn't imagine anything more awe-inspiring, but with so much potential to damage him, and more importantly, her.

No, everything was fine. The strange events in Jane's room were . . .

It was nothing.

He leaned over and kissed her.

"Since that is settled, I think we should take a bath." He rose from the bed. "Stay here while I draw the water."

Jane watched as he strode into his bathroom, unable to stop herself, even though her mind whirled. A totally muddled mind couldn't stop her from appreciating him, his long muscular legs, firm bottom and broad shoulders. Beautiful . . .

But she could not believe what she'd said!

No matter what, you can always have me.

She fell back against the mattress, her heart still jumping against her rib cage. It seemed as though the overactive organ had made the decision her brain should have. What had happened to last night, and trying to do what was best for both of them? What had happened to being rational?

She'd always considered herself a sensible person. Sensible to the point of dull. But since she walked into that seedy bar on Christmas Eve, the person she knew had totally disappeared. And all because of a pretty face.

No. Rhys certainly did have a pretty—everything. But she was drawn to everything about him. The way he laughed. The way he made her feel beautiful. The way he made her feel protected and cared for.

She closed her eyes, listening to Rhys start the water.

The interesting thing was Rhys seemed to know he was repressing something. He didn't know what, but when she mentioned forgetting, he'd gotten distinctly uncomfortable.

Maybe he was close to remembering. And he would need her, need her affection to help him deal with all those repressed memories.

At least that was her hope.

But she knew the truth now. She couldn't walk away. She couldn't stop being with him. It was too late.

He had this ability to make her believe. Believe they would be together forever. That they were destined to be. And she wanted to believe. She wanted him. Just as she had from the moment she saw him in the bar. She knew, as surely as she knew her own name, she'd always want him.

"The water is ready," Rhys said, poking his head out the doorway, a lopsided grin on his wide lips.

She smiled back. *Please, please let us be destined to be.*

Rhys watched with anticipation as Jane slipped out from under the covers and walked toward him, her expression a combination of excitement laced with shyness.

"How can you possibly be shy around me?" he asked as he caught her hands, walking backward, pulling her into the bathroom.

She blushed, the steam in the air making her skin look dewy like rose petals at dawn.

He frowned. What did he know about rose petals at dawn? When had he last seen a dawn or admired rose petals? Certainly not while he could.

He closed his eyes briefly. He had no reason to think like that. Not when he had Jane. Here. Now. She had managed to give him back all the things he'd lost.

He gazed down at her. She continued to hold his hands, her fingers delicate and warm in his.

He leaned forward and captured her mouth, and as he hoped all other thoughts except Jane were banished. Her sweet taste. Those delightful, timid brushes of her tongue against his. Her lovely scent swirling around him, cocooning him, protecting him from things he did want to think about.

She made him feel safe. As safe as he would keep her.

Jane wrapped her arms around Rhys's neck. Desire and longing churned with a sudden feeling of security that seemed to encompass her as tangibly as his strong arms.

You make me feel safe.

The words bounced through her head as clearly as if they had been spoken, but they were quickly drowned under the heat and hunger created by his lips molding to hers. His lips played over hers, their tongues mingled, and she was lost in the lovely sensation of him.

But to her dismay, he pulled away far too soon.

She groaned, not able to hide her disappointment. She loved Rhys's kisses.

"I'm supposed to be giving you a bath," he said, his voice husky and his eyes rich with the invitation to all sorts of decadent delights.

She did love his kisses, but she loved his hands on her just as much. This seemed to be a win/win proposition.

He grinned then, and she had the strange impression that he knew what she was thinking.

He pulled her toward the tub, which was the same deep-set style as the tub in her bath. The water lapped the rim, and steam curled off its surface. Towels and a washcloth rested on the edge.

And she was about to get the chance to see if the luxurious tub was indeed big enough for two.

Unless, he didn't intend to join her in the bath.

Self-consciousness swept over her at the idea of being the focus of all his attention, even though she desperately wanted to accept his offer.

Let me bathe you, Janie.

Again, the words were clear in her head. But they weren't her words. It seemed as if Rhys had gently whispered them in her ear.

She turned her gaze from the water to him. He stood, silent, watching her, waiting for her response.

She nodded, unable to speak. Her mind too muddled, her body too aroused by the intimate words echoing in her head as if he knew her fears, her desires, without her saying a word. There was something infinitely thrilling about that—even if it was only her own imagination.

He lifted her sweatshirt up over her head, leaving her standing in front of him in a pale blue bra and panties.

Warm summer days, and clear blue skies.

Again Rhys's husky voice tickled in her ears and caused tingles to dance over her skin. Yet, he still gazed at her, silent.

"I love these," he whispered as he reached out to finger the lace covering her breasts. "As blue as cloudless skies."

She breathed in sharply, startled by both his words and aroused beyond belief by them.

His hands cupped her breasts, kneading them, stroking them, before they left to slip around her back. His mouth returned to hers as he unfastened the clasp at the center of her back and the scrap of lace fluttered to the floor.

"The water is getting cold," he said against her lips.

She didn't care about the water. She just wanted him to continue touching her.

"I will keep touching, darling," he promised, responding to the words she knew she hadn't said aloud.

Then his hands ran down her body, the pads of his fingers leaving sizzling trails of heat over her sides and belly, moving to her undies, and all other thoughts were lost.

He nudged her panties down over her hips, and they slipped down her legs. He lifted her out of them and placed her in the tub.

Warm water lapped around her feet and ankles, stopping just above her knees. But the wet heat seemed to curl upward to lap all the way up her legs until a matching moisture pooled between her thighs.

She shivered.

Rhys followed her into the tub, standing in front of her, facing her.

Her eyes roamed over him, his achingly beautiful face, his lean muscles, his throbbing, thick erection. The embodiment of power and beauty. Like a god rising from the sea.

The birth of Venus.

She blinked, her gaze lifting back to his face. He watched her, his eyes hot with hunger.

He picked up a washcloth from the edge of the tub, wetting the cloth. Then he brought it to her chest, stroking out over her shoulders. Water beaded on her skin, down her arms, over her aching breasts, along the slight curve of her belly.

She trembled, the water going from hot to cold as it teased over her skin, oversensitizing her nerve endings.

"Does that feel good?" he whispered as he repeated the wonderful torture, as more water trickled hot to cold over her aroused flesh.

"Yes. Oh, yes."

She closed her eyes, her body naturally swaying toward his. She wanted his hands on her, to satisfy the yearning inside her.

More water seeped down her body. Fire, then ice.

Open your eyes. Watch me. Watch me love you.

She obeyed the voice in her head, her body too stimulated, too hungry, to care whose voice was whirling through her mind. She just knew she needed to respond to it.

She watched as Rhys lowered his head to lick a drop of water that clung to her erect nipple.

Like rain on a plump pink raspberry.

His tongue curled around the hardened bud, and her legs no longer seemed capable of holding her. His arm came out to catch her, pulling her tight to his muscular chest.

"Perhaps you should finish the rest of your bath seated." A smug grin curved his lips.

He should be proud. Surely no one made love like this man.

He turned her away from him and eased himself down into the hot water. Then he reached up to grip her hips and guided her down between his legs.

The water lapped over her breasts, teasing her, and her sex pulsed and ached against the surrounding heat. But again, she knew the water was a very, very insubstantial lover to the man pressed firmly to her back.

As if to prove that fact, his hands came around her to cup her breasts.

He caressed her, the water creating a pulling friction as he gently twisted his fingers around the distended nipples.

Then he reached forward, his chest rubbing against her back, his chest hair both silky and rough all at once. He grabbed a bar of soap from the built-in soap dish. Lather bubbled through his long fingers as he twirled the bar around and around in his hands.

The soap slipped through his hands, danced through the water and disappeared somewhere underneath their twined limbs. But her attention was promptly brought back to Rhys as his soapy hands shaped to her breasts, massaging her in slow, slick sweeps, causing her heart rate and her breathing patterns to completely go haywire.

"Does that feel good," he murmured in her ear, or

maybe he didn't. Maybe it was his sinful voice resonating in her head.

Either way, it felt wonderful.

She moaned, letting her head fall back against his chest as his hands continued their slippery kneading.

Then one hand left her breast to glide down her belly.

Watch, Jane. Watch me touching you.

She managed to lift her head, although she felt weak with need, barely able to focus on anything other than his hands, his fingers.

Look, darling.

And on his voice.

She opened her eyes, blinking down to where he touched. Suddenly she was mesmerized by the sight of large hands moving over her, the way his long, masculine fingers looked against her pale skin. One hand still lingered at her breast, teasing the swollen nipple, while his other hand brushed over the curls at the junction of her thighs. The tiny curls undulated in the water, inviting him to touch her.

He did, just a light, tantalizing brush over the curls. Then another, touching her a little firmer, but still not parting her, not finding that one spot that pleaded to be touched.

When he caressed her a third time, tracing the folds of her labia, she began to writhe, desperate for his full touch.

Patience, Jane.

"I can't," she muttered to him, to the voice echoing through her mind. "Please touch me."

His pleased laugh rumbled against her back, as stimulating to her as everything about Rhys.

But he did relent, parting her, touching her with repeated light strokes. The continual swish of warm water, the fleeting brush of his slightly callused finger. More water. Another faintly harder massage of his finger. And the steady build of her arousal, being nudged forward with each sweep, each swish. Until she reached down and caught his hand, pushing it tight against herself.

His other hand moved down to hold hers as if he was trying to memorize what she wanted, the exact pressure, the exact speed.

I want to know everything about you.

She gasped, the idea of that so erotic, so wonderful. Pressing harder against his hand, she guided him. His other hand tightened on hers, following her motions.

I want you to know everything about me.

She moaned, her raw need echoing off the tile walls. She stopped knowing whether her hand guided him or he guided her. She just knew his touch was perfect.

Her bottom lifted slightly as the first waves of release lapped over her. Flooding her, drowning her.

"Rhys," she cried. Or maybe she only called out to him in her mind, she didn't know.

Gradually the pounding swells of her climax rippled slowly through her, fading to gentle waves. Then a sensation replaced her satisfaction, one that was far more overwhelming, far more beautiful and rare and true.

I want you to stay with me forever.

Love encompassed her, filled her.

She let her head drop back against Rhys's chest. Yes. "Yes."

She wanted forever, too. She loved him.

Chapter 20

Rhys poured himself another scotch. He downed half the fiery liquid in one swallow.

He was a coward.

He sat here, in the library, while Jane still lounged in the tub, her gorgeous skin pink from the warm water, her body so responsive to his.

She'd given him exactly what he wanted from her. She had opened to him. They had bonded in a way he knew he never could with another woman.

But after she'd found her release, he'd fled. She didn't know he'd fled. He told her to enjoy the rest of her bath, and he'd return with some food for them.

But once he'd left her presence, what was the eloquent word Sebastian had used when Jane first arrived? Oh, yes. He'd freaked.

Whatever had just happened between Jane and himself went beyond mere sex. Even great sex. He'd known her thoughts. She had known his. And somehow he'd controlled the whole experience.

How could that be? Was that even possible?

"What are you doing in here?" Sebastian asked as he strode into the room. He headed to the bar to retrieve a glass, then joined Rhys, dropping down into the chair across from him.

"I don't suppose it dawned on you to ask if I wanted company?"

"*Moi?*" Sebastian reached over the table and pulled the crystal decanter toward himself. "Of course you want my company."

Rhys grunted, then took another sip of his drink.

Sebastian stopped pouring, the decanter still in his hand. He narrowed his eyes, studying Rhys. "Are you back?"

Rhys frowned at his brother. "Where have I been?"

"You tell me."

Rhys set down his glass with more force than necessary. "Sebastian, sometimes you make me weary."

Sebastian raised a noncommittal eyebrow to that and finished filling his glass.

Both brothers drank silently, until Rhys finally asked, "Do you believe in ghosts—the occult?"

Sebastian, who had been about to take a sip of his scotch, paused. "Why do you ask?"

Rhys shook his head. He didn't know if he wanted to share the odd events of the past few hours with his brother. Sebastian would likely just think him mad. And there was nothing worse than someone as frivolous as his little brother thinking *him* mad.

"You can't ask a question like that and not tell me why."

Rhys took another sip of the amber liquid. Oh, what the hell. Perhaps he was mad.

"Jane has felt a presence in her bedroom. I thought she was just having vivid nightmares. Until this last time." He hesitated. "I felt something in her room, too."

Sebastian sat forward in his chair, his knees bumping the coffee table. But he didn't seem to notice; he was too intent on Rhys. "You felt it."

Rhys nodded. "And . . ." How did he tell Sebastian this? The ghost thing was strange enough. "I also felt Jane's fear."

Sebastian didn't look particularly shocked. Instead he almost appeared as though he expected Rhys to say that.

"That isn't possible," Rhys stated, hoping his own determination would garner Sebastian's agreement. But of course not.

Sebastian shrugged. "If it happened, it must be possible."

"No." Rhys didn't want to hear that. He wanted Sebastian to verify it was impossible. That it all had to be a figment of his imagination.

Just like what had happened in the tub. He hadn't heard Jane's thoughts. He hadn't been able to send her his.

All just strange coincidences. All just imagination.

"Maybe you are out of the ordinary," Sebastian suggested, his voice casual, his eyes not. "Maybe you can sense things like emotions. Presences."

Rhys shook his head. "No. Those things don't exist. And I've never experienced anything like that before. Why should it appear now?"

"Maybe you have experienced them before."

"No," Rhys insisted.

"What did the presence feel like?"

Rhys didn't want to think about it. He never should have brought this up. He'd nearly convinced himself it was all a strange nightmare anyway.

Then the bathtub. What was that? Not a nightmare. A fantasy. A dream. A perfect moment.

But still filled with the same type of "knowing."

"The presence . . . It was more a scent in the air. Sour and tainted."

Sebastian nodded, and there was still no surprise on his face.

"Did it intend harm to you or Jane?"

"It was around Jane."

"And you saved her."

This time.

"Rhys, I know you don't want to, but I think you need to pay attention to these signs."

Rhys stared at his brother. "Why?"

Sebastian polished off the rest of his drink, set the empty glass on the table, then stood. "Unfortunately, I think you are the only one who knows."

Rhys watched as Sebastian left the room.

He did know. But God, he didn't want to.

Jane rested her head on the edge of the tub, soaking in the heat of the water and her new knowledge. She had been almost relieved when Rhys offered to go get them some food. Her realization that she was head over heels in love with him was too startling. She needed a moment alone to digest it.

Although now, in retrospect, she supposed it wasn't a real surprise. She'd been falling in love with him from the moment he saved her life. Maybe even earlier. It was almost silly that she hadn't given her emotions that name sooner. Her love for him was the most natural thing in the world, really.

The best reason for her to stay, which was all she'd wanted to do. No matter how much she told herself otherwise. The best reason to become intimate with him. The best reason to explain why she felt so connected to him.

What was the saying? Sometimes you can't see the forest for the trees?

She grinned to herself, fishing through the slowly cooling water for the soap. She lathered her hands like Rhys had, but she didn't massage the bubbles over herself with the same slow, arousing strokes. Strokes and caresses that had been designed to show her how much he treasured her, cared for her.

He hadn't used the word love either. But after what had just happened, she didn't doubt he felt the same. She couldn't. Love had swirled around them, the emotion a palpable thing in the air. Like the water that now covered her body, virtually unseen, but all around her.

She finished washing her arms, then her legs. Then she stood, letting the water sluice down over her.

She suddenly didn't feel unsure, or afraid. She knew her feelings for Rhys. And she knew his.

There really was no logical explanation why this time, opposed to all the other times Rhys had made love to her, she felt so joined with him. But she had.

The other times she'd felt satisfaction, so much satisfaction her toes curled against the slick porcelain just thinking about it. And she'd also felt connected to him as though they were one.

But this time . . . She reached for one of the thick,

white towels. This time she'd felt *him*. What he felt as he held her. As he touched her.

She wrapped the towel around herself and stepped out of the tub. She turned, flipped the stopper, and the water gurgled down the drain.

She padded out into his bedroom. The room was empty, and she considered going to find him.

Then a much better idea struck her. She hurried out into the hallway. She didn't want Rhys to beat her back to his room.

She quickly ran to her room, crossing to her nightstand. The necklace that Rhys had given her Christmas night still lay on the table, the jewels twinkling in the light.

She picked it up, touching the center stone that reminded her so much of Rhys's unusual eyes. Then she put it around her neck, fumbling slightly with the clasp as nerves and her anticipation caused her fingers to shake.

Once the necklace fastened and the pendant nestled between her breasts, she dashed back to Rhys's room, relieved to see he hadn't returned.

She sat on the edge of the bed and waited.

Rhys left the library, knowing what he had to do, even if he didn't fully understand why. Things weren't that clear in his head. It was as if he would just realize why odd things were happening, and his mind would lose its place. Like a song where he could begin to hum the tune, but the title was just out of his reach.

But he knew he had to talk to Jane.

He reached his bedroom, the door was ajar, but he

couldn't see her. But he didn't need to see her to know she was there. He could smell her flowery scent warm on her flawless skin.

He closed his eyes tight, willing the thoughts, the senses, to go away. He was Rhys Young, the fifth Viscount of Rothmere. He was . . .

He swallowed and pushed open the door. He hesitated for just a fraction of a second, then stepped into the room.

Jane sat on the bed, but she rose when he entered. Her tiny, perfect body was wrapped in a towel. Her hair, still damp from the bath, clung to her cheeks.

"Hi," she said. "You—you forgot the food."

He looked down at his hands. That's right, he was supposed to be getting food.

She took a step toward him, her toes sinking into the thick pile of the dark carpet. "I wasn't hungry anyway."

He closed his eyes again. Damn, he *was* starving.

When he opened his eyes, Jane stood just an arm's length away from him. His gaze roamed from her wide eyes to her full mouth, then to the pale skin of her shoulders, her neck, her chest.

He was ravenous.

"I enjoyed my bath," she said softly, her eyes holding his.

He nodded, unable to speak. He knew he had to, but to say what?

"And I want to make you feel the same way." She came to stand directly in front of him.

He watched as her dainty fingers moved to the front of his shirt. She worked each small button through its hole until the shirt fell open. Then her hands left his shirt to rub up over his chest.

A hitched breath escaped his lips as her fingers

paused at his nipples, teasing them like he'd done to her. Then her hands continued upward, her fingers and palms shaping the muscles of his shoulders as she nudged his shirt off.

He let the garment fall to the floor.

She stroked down his arms, then back up again, her hands contouring the shape of every muscle. Her inquisitive fingers wandered back down his chest over his stomach to the top of his trousers.

He thought for a fraction of a second to stop her. To tell her . . .

The button of his pants popped free. Then she slowly worked down the zipper. Once they were open, she caught the waistband and pushed them down his hips. His erect penis bobbed free, then pulled up against his stomach, rock-hard, throbbing.

Jane knelt to slip the pants off over his bare feet, but instead of rising again when the pants were cast aside, she remained on her knees.

As if in slow motion, she reached out to touch his erection, her fingers, light and cool, brushing the sensitive underside, shaping over the head.

"You're soft and hard at the same time."

He swallowed as she touched him again, this time curling her fingers around the girth.

"And you are hot," she murmured. Her fingertips reached the rounded top and the glistening bead at the tip. "And wet."

She smiled up at him. "Not so different than me, after all."

He felt his chest tighten. *So different, Janie. So very different.*

She rose up slightly, the towel parting so he could see the bare curve of her thigh and hip.

He watched as she leaned forward and brushed her lips against him. Then again. And again. Each kiss getting braver, more daring, until her tongue flicked out to taste him. To drive him mad.

He remained perfectly still, the lucid scraps of his brain telling him he shouldn't react.

Then her tongue lapped across the bulbous head, circling it, then flicking over the top again.

He swallowed, trying to keep control. The hands at his sides trembled.

Her lips parted, and he was surrounded by searing heat. And that swirling tongue.

Then his hands were in her hair, pulling her closer.

She didn't resist, but slipped those full, beautiful lips over him, savoring him, devouring him.

His head fell back, his eyes closed. He couldn't think, couldn't comprehend anything but the feeling of Jane loving him. Her mouth slid up and down. Her tongue traced the column of nerve endings that ran up the center of his cock, then curled over the head. Her hands stroked the rest of his length, which she couldn't take into her small mouth. Her other hand touched his stomach, his thighs, his testicles.

Light burst behind his closed lids. Pale light. Bright yellow light. Oranges, and pinks, then back to clear, warm light. She was giving him all her light. All her sunrises, all her sunsets.

His penis pulsed against her tongue, under her lips. His testicles pulled tight against his body. And he felt heat spiral through him, the heat of her mouth, then the heat of the light. The light she was giving him.

But just as his muscles tensed and he was about to

come, he pulled back, dropping his hands from Jane's hair to her arms, lifting her to her feet.

"Jane, I have to be inside you." His voice was low, rough, demanding.

She stared up at him, her lips rosy from rubbing over him and damp. And for the first time since Rhys met her, he couldn't read her expression. Fear ripped through him, intensifying the need pulsating in his veins.

Then she stepped back and unknotted the towel, letting the white cloth fall away from her.

Her pale skin glowed like pearls in the lamplight. Her small, round breasts creamy and topped with raspberry nipples. Shapely legs and dark curls at the apex of pale thighs, soft, inviting. She stole his breath, all sense, reason. She was his only thought. Janie. Beautiful.

Then his gaze finally centered on the jewel glinting between her perfect breasts. Topaz and diamonds twinkled against her skin.

The necklace.

"I wore it for you, because I am the very person it was intended for. Like you said."

Rhys's gaze jumped back to hers. She wore a small, unsure smile. But in her green eyes, he saw courage and knowing.

She took a step toward him, but she didn't need to take any more. He closed the small gap between them, pulling her tight against him, his mouth finding hers.

He walked her backward, until the backs of her legs hit the edge of the bed. She lost her balance and sat heavily on the mattress.

A laugh started in her throat, but he caught her shoulders, pushing her down on the bed.

She stared up at him, her eyes wide. He knew he must look wild, half-crazed. He was.

The sight of that necklace. Of her body splayed out before him. This was his woman. His.

His hand slipped between her thighs, massaging her with rough, greedy strokes. She didn't reject his possessive touch, writhing against his hands. She was ready for him. His finger slid into her wet vagina easily.

He moved his hands to her knees, spreading her wide, and he entered her, impaling her to his hilt with one thrust.

She cried out, the sound one of shock, but also pleasure. Her muscles embraced him. Her arms held him.

And they began to move, coming together, drawing apart. Their craving to touch each other, feel each other, uncontrollable, hungry.

She arched under him, her breasts thrusting upward, her vagina constricting around him.

He watched her. The pleasure on her face. The sinuous movements of her body. The emotion darkening her eyes.

And just as her muscles pulsed around him with her release, he felt them. Their lengthening. The sharp pierce of them against his lips. The tang of blood on his tongue.

Under him, Jane clenched her eyes shut and arched up against him, her body begging for release, crying out to him for it.

He threw back his own head, his teeth bared.

"I love you, Rhys! I love you."

He stopped for a fraction of a second, her words shaking him to the core. But then her confession, like the necklace, served only to intensify his hunger, to make him insane with need to have her.

He fell forward, his canines plunging into the fragile skin of her neck at the same time his cock filled her to her womb.

She screamed out, a keen filled with devastating ecstasy.

And as he drank in her bliss, her release, he joined her in their unnatural rapture.

Chapter 21

What had he done?

Rhys stared down at Jane. She slept; he knew she slept. But it wasn't an ordinary sleep. Not the drowsy half-awake/half-dozing state created by demanding sex.

Her skin blended with the whiteness of his sheets, and her hair clung to her face in a cold sweat. She looked frail, ill.

And he'd done that to her.

His gaze dropped to the twin marks on the side of her neck. The wounds still seeped a tiny bit of blood. The redness stood out violently against her white skin.

He shoved off the bed, backing away from her. Away from what he'd done. But the puncture wounds mocked him. The crimson blood hurt his eyes.

This is what you are. This is what you do. What made you believe you could ever change that?

He stared at her a moment longer. Then he quickly covered her chilled body with a blanket. He started to move away from the bed again, but hesitated. His eyes moved back to his marks on her. He leaned forward to lick the wound, which would instantly heal it. But he stopped.

Maybe he should let her see what he was. What he could do to her. Not that she would understand.

He moved away from her, pacing back and forth at the foot of the bed. How could she understand? He didn't.

He paused to look at her once more. Her sweet face. Her generous lips. The crescent of her dark lashes against her cheeks as she slept.

He had to get out of here.

He had to think.

He pulled on his clothes and left the room.

By the time he reached the living room, he was trembling. Rage and self-hatred coursed through him, merging with the warmth of Jane's blood in his veins. Even in his anger, he could still feel her, taste her. Her sweetness served only to make him more furious.

He was a monster.

His glass and the decanter of scotch still sat on the library's coffee table where he'd left them. He poured himself a full glass and downed it. The burning of the liquor on his tongue and throat didn't even remove the flavor of Jane.

He fell into one of the overstuffed chairs and stared blankly into the unlit fireplace.

How could he have been so foolish? So stupid and naïve to think that he could just go back? That he could just return to the man he once was? Hadn't two hundred years taught him there was no going back?

He refilled his glass, this time taking only one large gulp before setting it onto the table.

The man in the alley. Christian. Lilah's death. It was all there now. And while the shock of it all, the horror, made him understand why he'd wanted to forget, how had he? And how had he allowed Jane to become involved in all this?

He dropped his head onto the back of the chair and closed his eyes. Jane. He'd left her at her rundown hotel. He had let her go. Even though, from the moment she walked into that bar, he'd wanted her. But he *had* let her go.

So how had she come back to him? That much he truly didn't remember. And why had she stayed after she woke up with him that first night?

And who had found him after Christian's attack?

He lifted his head, his eyes coming open.

Of course. Sebastian.

Rhys didn't have any trouble finding his little brother. Now that his memory was fully intact, Rhys knew exactly what club Sebastian was going to, and it definitely wasn't White's.

He found Sebastian on the dance floor of Carfax Abbey, surrounded by vampires and vampire-wannabes. Rhys simply stood behind him, until Sebastian sensed him there.

"Rhys." Sebastian peered at him through the haze of red neon and flashing lights. "What are you doing here? Are you—are you—"

"Yeah," Rhys said flatly. "I'm back. We need to talk."

Sebastian nodded, then turned to shout over the pounding techno to the mortals and immortals to tell them that he had to go. Several of the ladies actually groaned with disappointment.

But Sebastian didn't linger to console them. He followed Rhys through the doorway that led to the back hallway and the freight elevator.

Once they were inside, creaking up toward the apartment level, Rhys glanced at Sebastian. "So was there any reason that you decided not to tell me that I was acting like the world's biggest jackass?"

"I wouldn't say jackass. Although all the 'Ready the carriage' stuff got a bit annoying."

Rhys turned, glaring at his brother. "Why didn't you stop me? Make me listen to the truth?"

"You wouldn't have heard it. You wanted to forget. And I wanted that for you."

Rhys reached for the grate as the elevator shuddered to a stop. He threw it up with more force than was necessary, the metallic sound thundering through the hallway.

"Why?" Rhys asked as he stepped into the hallway, striding angrily toward the apartment. "Why, when the truth was going to come back eventually?"

"Because you wanted Jane."

Rhys came to a halt, turning back to Sebastian. "What?"

"You wanted Jane. That's why you repressed what you were. You wouldn't have her otherwise."

Sebastian had never struck Rhys as particularly insightful; he was generally too self-indulgent for that. Yet he had somehow deduced Rhys's deepest yearning.

Still, the realization that his baby brother might be something more than a vain hedonist twit didn't make Rhys any happier.

"So did you convince her to stay?"

Sebastian nodded, a smug grin on his face. "Yep. Told her that the doctor told me you needed to be supervised at all times, and I was too busy at the nightclub to do it myself."

"And she offered to stay?"

"No, not really. I had to bribe her, and remind her that you saved her life." Sebastian grinned again, proud. "I bribed her with a lot of money."

Money? Rhys never would have taken Jane as a woman who would take a bribe.

"Of course, after you two knocked boots, she told me she couldn't accept the money. She said it made the situation feel cheap." Sebastian shook his head, clearly amazed by that level of integrity. "You two really are made for each other."

Rhys ignored the last statement.

"Then why did she stay after that?"

"You." Sebastian gave him a "duh" expression. "Well, and I did offer her a legitimate job at the nightclub. As our accountant. But she only took that because she is a little desperate for a job, which I was counting on."

Rhys stared at his brother. Jane was going to work at the nightclub? No.

"Pretty ingenious, huh?"

Rhys grabbed the lapels of Sebastian's designer suit coat and shoved him against the wall, pinning him there.

"I'll take that as a no," Sebastian rasped, his breath knocked out of him.

"Do you have any idea what you've done? What I've done?"

Sebastian shrugged off Rhys's hold. Rhys let him. "Yes. I gave you the chance to be with the woman you love. Because you couldn't do it yourself. And this is the thanks I get?" He pointed to the wrinkles in his coat, raising an eyebrow at Rhys. Then he straightened the mussed garment.

Rhys stared at him for a moment, then stated, "I don't love her."

"Do I smell smoke?"

The question was so random, it took a few seconds for Rhys to understand that Sebastian was referring to a children's rhyme about lying.

"How old are you?"

"Two hundred and eight, and still young."

"I give up," Rhys muttered and headed into the apartment. He walked directly to the library and to the decanter of scotch. He knew he wouldn't find any answers there; he already knew what he had to do. But it might make him calmer until the time came to talk to Jane. Right now she needed to sleep. To recover from what he'd done.

Unfortunately, Sebastian followed him.

"Listen, I did what I thought was right," he told Rhys. "What I *know* was right."

Rhys topped off his glass, then went to the window, his back to his brother. He leaned a shoulder on the window frame, took a sip of his drink and looked out at the city skyline. Somehow it had seemed prettier when he'd thought it was London.

Or maybe it had just been prettier through Jane's eyes.

He closed his own.

"You know, I liked you better when you were repressing," Sebastian said flatly.

Me, too, Rhys immediately thought, but he opened his eyes, still not turning back to Sebastian. "That person doesn't exist."

Sebastian was quiet for a moment. Rhys heard him shift in his chair.

"He does exist, otherwise he never could have reappeared. Maybe it is your love for Jane. Maybe you were just tired of brooding. God knows *I'm* tired of your brooding. But the Rhys that you've been for the past few days was the old Rhys."

Rhys turned to look at him.

Sebastian stared back for a moment; then he modified, "Except you were happier these past days than you ever were—even alive."

Jane.

They both knew it was Jane who'd managed that feat.

"You found me in the alley?"

Sebastian nodded. "You'd been attacked. By a vampire, from the looks of the wounds."

Yes. Definitely by a vampire. "And Jane was there?"

"Yes. She was unconscious, and she had a memory hex cast on her. Which verified you must have been attacked by a vampire."

"It was a vampire," Rhys told him, his voice devoid of any emotion. How did one feel about his own brother trying to kill him. He still didn't know.

Sebastian sat forward in his chair. "You remember the attack?"

"Yes."

"Was it a random attack? A rogue vampire?"

Rhys laughed, the sound humorless, brittle. "No. Definitely not random."

"Who, then?"

Rhys left the window, not sure where he was walking, just feeling the need to move. He paced back and forth in front of the fireplace.

He wished there was a fire burning. He felt very cold, very empty.

"Who, Rhys?"

Rhys stopped, staring into his glass. Finally he garnered the strength to say it. To hear the truth out loud. "Christian."

Silence filled the room for a full second, before Sebastian stood. "Christian? Are you sure?"

"Yeah." Rhys laughed again, still no amusement in the sound. "I'm pretty sure."

"Why? How? Christian isn't any more powerful than you."

"You'd be surprised what blind rage can do."

"But why? Why now?"

Rhys didn't mind saying this out loud. He'd waited a very long time to be able to say this very thing. "Lilah is dead. Walked out into the sunlight."

Sebastian's hazel eyes widened. Then his lips split into a huge and still amazed grin. "Really? The bitch is finally gone?"

Rhys nodded, joining him for a split second in the joy. But his slight smile faded. "Christian came to tell me. Then to kill me."

"Well, ding dong." Sebastian was clearly stunned. "I wouldn't have ever guessed Christian. I'd been asking around at the club if there was any word in the community about a rogue vampire and other attacks. This explains why no one had heard anything."

Rhys stared at his brother for a moment. Even though Sebastian often had odd ways of showing his concern, he did care. Despite Rhys's annoyance with his heavy-handed meddling and silly comments, he did appreciate that Sebastian had always been there. Was essentially the brother he'd known in life.

"So what are we going to do?"

Rhys frowned. "We aren't going to do anything. If Christian comes to me, I'll deal with it. And I need to get Jane to leave."

"What? Why?"

"It's been Christian that has been coming to Jane. And she has to go for her own safety."

"Wouldn't she be safer with us? With us to protect her?"

But who was going to protect Jane from him? Rhys wondered. "No. She will be safer if she just cuts ties with us altogether."

Sebastian shook his head. "She loves you, Rhys. Are you prepared to break her heart?"

Rhys's chest tightened. "A broken heart will heal."

"Rhys—"

"This is what has to be done. Jane isn't safe. She needs to leave."

Sebastian nodded, although Rhys knew he didn't agree. Then he stood, heading to the door. He paused with his hand on the doorknob and looked back at Rhys.

"You are sending away the best thing that has ever happened to you."

Rhys didn't respond, and finally Sebastian just shook his head again, clearly disgusted with him. The door slammed, accenting his irritation.

Rhys stared at the closed door, then crossed back to the window. The sky was starting to turn the vibrant indigo color that it often did as sunrise slowly arrived. A couple more hours and he'd have to scurry for his bed. To hide. Hide from daylight and life.

Jane couldn't live like that. She'd been surrounded by death long enough. She needed to live, to love.

His chest tightened again at the thought of some other man holding her, making love to her.

He took a sip of his drink, then rested his forehead on the icy windowpane. But he had to let her go. For good this time.

Christian was a real threat. Rhys didn't even want to contemplate what Christian could do to Jane.

Rhys didn't want to contemplate what *he* could do to Jane. What he'd already done.

Jane had to leave, even if Sebastian was right. Because Sebastian was right.

Rhys would let her go because he loved her.

Chapter 22

Jane sat up, blinking around her, trying to get her bearings. She was still in Rhys's bed, although he wasn't next to her.

She glanced at the digital clock. Three forty-eight P.M. She must have slept half the night and nearly all the day away. Lazybones.

She stretched, but she had to admit all that sleep had made her feel great. Beyond great. Her whole body hummed with energy. She felt as if she could jump up and run ten miles. Or at the very least, find Rhys and make love for a good, long time.

She crawled out of bed, realizing she was nude. She searched around on the floor for something to put on and finally gave up and wrapped the towel from last night around herself.

She headed to her room to get dressed. Then she'd find Rhys. He never roused before she did—at least not to get out of bed. And she'd never noticed if he came to bed in the first place, although she *had* slept like the dead. All of Rhys's sleep habits must be rubbing off on her.

Then again, she'd absolutely had to sleep after that last bout of lovemaking. Rhys was incredible. She didn't need to be experienced in intimacy to know that what Rhys did to her not many lovers could. He was great in bed, but she knew it was the fact that she loved him that made it all the more amazing.

She hummed to herself as she flipped on the light to her bedroom and searched through her suitcase for something nice to wear.

Maybe she should unpack, she decided as she rooted through her clothes once more to find a pair of panties. It was practical. And she wasn't even going to continue fooling herself that she was leaving.

She started to put what was left of her clean clothes in the bureau. As she worked, she wondered again where Rhys could be.

He hadn't gotten out of bed before nightfall since she arrived. A sudden sense of unease came over her. What if he'd gone outside? The sun had to be low at this time, but its rays could still damage his allergy sensitive skin.

She paused. No, she had the feeling, although she couldn't say why, that Rhys was in the apartment. His presence was just—there.

She pushed in the drawer to the bureau and turned to gather the clothes she'd chosen to wear tonight.

In the bathroom, she rushed through her morning ritual, anxious to find Rhys.

After she was dressed and had just added the final touches to her makeup, she stood back and studied herself in the mirror. She didn't look too bad. The style of her top, which wrapped around her and tied on the side, gave the impression that she had fuller cleavage. And the deep green of the velvet brought out her eyes. She couldn't see her skirt, but she knew the ruffling hemline fluttered when she walked and made her look feminine.

She had strappy heels that went with the outfit, but she decided to forgo them. She liked walking barefoot, and she was wearing the outfit only for Rhys, not to go out.

She plucked at her hair, arranging the pieces in a more hip style. Not too bad. The faint steam clouding the mirror made her reflection look softer. Then she touched the necklace that she still wore.

She smiled, lifting it to admire the stone again, but as she did, the chain rubbed against a painful spot on her neck.

"Ouch," she muttered, dropping the pendant back against her chest. She leaned forward to examine the soreness.

Two marks, angry red wounds, marred the side of her throat. She tilted her head, trying to see them better. Then she wiped her hand over the mist-covered glass. But it didn't help. Her reflection was still blurred.

She squinted and did her best to see the marks again. They appeared to be similar to the ones she'd noticed the other day on her breast. Although these weren't as healed.

She rummaged through her toiletry bag until she found a bandage. She peeled off the backs and positioned it as best she could over the small wounds.

It kind of ruined the sexy effect she was going for, but it looked a bit better than the red marks. Or at least she hoped it did. Why hadn't the steam on the mirror evaporated?

She shook her head and left the room to find Rhys. He was in the library. She knew it as soon as she reached the living room, and wondered for a second at her certainty.

Shaking her head, she chuckled to herself. Oh, yeah, she was *so* in tune with him that she could just *sense* where he was in the apartment. More likely it was just the most reasonable guess, since it was his favorite room.

She pushed open the library door and blinked. The room was pitch dark. She'd never seen it this dark. Even at night, the city lights shining through the two huge windows cast faint light in the room.

But as her eyes adjusted to the darkness, she realized that heavy custom blinds covered the windows. She'd never even noticed them before.

She stepped farther into the room, brushing a hand along the wall, searching for a light switch, but before she could find one, a table lamp flicked on.

Jane jumped, her hand coming up to her chest. "Rhys! You startled me."

He sat in one of the large, comfy chairs, his clothes rumpled, his feet up on the coffee table. From the look of him, he'd been up all night. His eyes shadowed, dark.

"Have you been up all night?"

"Day," he corrected.

She wandered over to the chair across from him and perched on the edge, her hands on her knees. Again another rush of uneasiness came over her.

"Do you not feel well?" She hoped that was what was causing the apathetic look in his eyes.

He didn't answer for a moment. "Jane."

Just by the way he said her name—that one, single syllable—she knew. Funny, she should know so much from a tiny, little word. Her own name.

"You've gotten your memory back." Not a question, just absolute certainty.

He nodded, and neither of them looked pleased.

"Yes, last night."

"Are—are you okay?"

He shrugged as if it didn't matter one way or the other. "I'm . . . I'm as I've always been."

She didn't know what he meant by that. "Are you hurting over the loss of Elizabeth?"

"You know about her?" His question was sharp, his eyes narrowed.

"Yes."

"Sebastian?"

She nodded, then straightened the ruffle of her skirt, unable to look at his hard eyes.

"He's been busy."

Her head came up. "He was trying to protect you, and he told me about Elizabeth and Christian to help me understand what was happening with you."

"And did you understand?"

She tilted her head, her heart aching for this cold, hurting man. "Of course. Loss is a terrible thing, and I certainly do know about that. And I know how much you love your family. How responsible you feel for them. And no one could blame you for just wanting to forget."

He studied her again, those eyes of his like amber. Hard and ancient, but so beautiful.

"Don't make me sound noble."

She stood, moving over to the sofa so she could be closer to him. "Rhys, you can't continue to beat yourself up over Christian. And you can't change that Elizabeth is gone."

A muscle in his jaw ticked as if he was clenching his teeth. "Do you know anything about my fight with Christian? Do you know how Elizabeth died?"

"No, but—"

"Then you shouldn't assume that I couldn't have prevented either."

"I know you, Rhys. If you could have, you would." She pressed her hand to the knee closest to her, needing to touch him, comfort him.

He immediately stood up, moving to the fireplace. He remained with his back to her as if he couldn't bear to look at her.

She closed her eyes briefly. Uneasiness jelled to fear in her belly.

"Jane."

She'd once loved to hear her name on his lips; now she hated it.

"I made a mistake."

She closed her eyes again as every fear she'd had since she'd first touched him, kissed him, came to life in front of her.

"I'm not the person you have come to care about. I'm not even remotely like the person you think you know. And I—don't want a relationship with you."

Pain ripped through her chest, but somehow it immediately transformed to anger. "You could at least look at me when you are telling me this."

The muscles in his back bunched under his shirt as he gripped the mantel, but he did turn to look at her.

For a brief moment, she thought she saw pain there, pain that matched her own, but it quickly disappeared behind an emotionless mask.

"Jane, I'm sorry that I'm hurting you."

She nodded, keeping her back straight, her jaw high, even though she wanted to dissolve into tears. But she wouldn't cry. She'd prepared herself for this. Right?

But then there had been last night.

"Are you doing this because I said I loved you?"

Rhys immediately shook his head. "No. I'm doing this because I know we aren't right for each other, and it is simply better if things just end now. Before we get too involved."

"So making love, saying I love you, that isn't too involved." She bit the inside of her lips. She wasn't going to fight this. She might not know much about men, but she did know she couldn't make one of them love her if he didn't.

But he did. She felt it. She knew it.

"So who is right for you, Rhys?" Her voice didn't sound like her own. It was as cold as his amber eyes.

"Jane. I don't want to go into this. Our relationship never should have started. It should have ended that first night, when I left you at your hotel."

"But it didn't."

"No. It didn't. And I am very, very sorry for that."

"Why? Because you don't care about me? Or because you care too much?"

Rhys stared at Jane. This wasn't going how he'd anticipated. He'd expected tears. He'd expected her to plead for them to have a new start.

He'd never expected this cool poise. Jane had always been a little self-conscious, a little unsure. But now she sat before him, her green eyes determined, her chin held high like a fairy queen. Tiny and fragile, but so regal.

She had never looked more beautiful.

Then his gaze dropped to the bandage placed diagonally over his mark. He had to make her leave. She would be fine. And much safer if she cut all ties to him.

"Listen, Jane, I don't know how to make this any clearer. I'm sorry that you believe yourself in love with me, but the fact is, I do not love you. And I'm not interested in a relationship."

She flinched, just slightly, at his straightforward words, but then her chin popped right back up, her jaw set.

"I don't believe you."

Damn, he wanted to kiss her. To pull her into his arms. To hold her forever.

But instead, he pushed all his desires aside like he had for hundreds of years. This couldn't be about what he wanted. He had to keep Jane safe.

"Jane," he said, his voice low, but he filled each word with patronizing pity. "Stop this. You are just embarrassing yourself and me."

This time she couldn't quite keep that small chin aloft. She still stared at him with those relentlessly green eyes, but he could tell his words had finally hit their mark. Finally made her doubt him.

He turned back to the empty fireplace, so he wouldn't have to see her pain. "I'm sorry that things turned out this way. But I'm sure you can see that I'm not who you thought I was. And you are not the kind of woman I'd be interested in."

There was silence behind him, and he wanted to turn around. He wanted to go to her. But he remained still, his hands gripping the mantelpiece as if he had to anchor himself to something not to be drawn to her.

"Just tell me one thing." Her voice was quiet, and although she kept her composure, he could tell she was broken. He could feel it, like a painful, gnawing ache in his chest.

"What?"

"Why did you want me in the first place?"

He closed his eyes, the pain so agonizing he couldn't pull in the breath to speak.

"Because you were there."

He heard her rise and walk toward the door, then the faint rattle of the doorknob under her hand.

He allowed himself to glance in her direction.

She paused, just briefly, and he thought, hoped, she would look at him. But she didn't. With her back still iron-rod straight, she walked out of the room. The door swung shut behind her.

Rhys looked around, unsure what to do now. Then he wandered back over to the table to take a drink from the scotch that had been his constant companion. Instead of bringing the glass to his lips, he just stared into its golden depths.

He tried to pull in a breath, but the ache only intensified, tightening in his chest until he felt strangled by it.

He'd always believed he didn't have a heart. That no vampire really did—not like a mortal.

He cursed loudly, then spun and threw his glass into the fireplace. The crystal shattered into thousands of tiny, splintery pieces.

Just like his nonexistent heart.

Chapter 23

Jane didn't quite recall how she got to her bedroom. Or how her unsteady legs managed to hold her, but once she was inside, with the door shut, she collapsed on the bed.

She stared blankly at her hands folded in her lap, knotted together to keep them from shaking.

She sat that way, for how long she didn't know, feeling nothing. Or maybe conscious of everything at once, each emotion blotting out the other until she just felt empty.

But gradually, one emotion rose to the forefront. Pain. A horrible, heart-wrenching ache that seemed to cripple her.

She took in a deep breath to suppress the hurt, but when she exhaled, a broken sob escaped her. The pitiful sound shattered her fragile hold.

She lifted her trembling hands to her face and cried. She cried over Rhys's cold, emotionless words. She cried because she knew he was giving up something that was real and true. And she cried for herself, because she was right back where she always seemed to end up. Alone.

No. She swiped at her tears angrily. Angry with herself for feeling so hopeless. She couldn't make Rhys change his mind, but she wouldn't give up. She wouldn't let this ruin her.

"You can find love again," she vowed out loud, to the room, to herself. But even before the words faded, she knew she'd never find anything like what she had with Rhys. She knew she wouldn't ever feel the same way about another man.

You're being overdramatic, her mind told her. But her heart assured her she wasn't. She'd shared a connection with Rhys that came only once in a lifetime.

Maybe this was what her father and mother had shared. Maybe theirs was a love so deep, her father couldn't recover from it being severed. Jane had always believed that her father could have let go if he'd wanted to. If Jane was important enough to him. But maybe he just couldn't.

She rose, her pain suddenly laced with agitation. She couldn't deal with that. She couldn't live the rest of her life still longing for something that was out of reach. She'd done that with her father. She'd done that with the normalcy of being a kid. She couldn't keep wanting.

She had to get out. To be surrounded by people, by noise. She needed to know there was still plenty of life out there for her.

She looked for her coat, pausing to decide if she should put on warmer clothes, but she didn't want to take the time. She needed to leave now.

Where was her darn coat? She checked several places

but couldn't find it, her search becoming more desperate with each unsuccessful location.

Finally, she stopped rummaging through the room, remembering that the parka was in Rhys's room, in the chair where he'd thrown it, when she'd agreed to make love with him again.

She hesitated. She didn't want to run into Rhys. At least not until she'd had time to think and compose herself. But she wasn't going to be able to do that here. Surrounded by everything Rhys.

She straightened her spine and headed for his room. The door was still open. And Rhys wasn't in there. She didn't pause to wonder how she could tell that; it was just instinctive, something she knew.

She darted in and found the coat. She paused long enough to tug the thick parka on. As she pulled up the zipper, her knuckles brushed against the hard, cool topaz at her chest.

The pendant suddenly felt heavy around her neck, and she fumbled to get the small clasp undone. Once the necklace was off, she held it in front of her, the pendant twirling back and forth. The jewel winked at her in the lamplight as if to say that everything the necklace had come to mean to her was a colossal joke.

She placed the necklace on Rhys's nightstand and then left. She didn't slow down until she reached the freight elevator. She struggled with the large metal gate, but finally got it down. She pressed ground level.

The gate was even more difficult to get open, and just when she was starting to get a little worried, that she might be stuck on the stupid elevator, Mick appeared.

He easily lifted the grid for her.

"Thank you," she murmured, feeling silly and annoyed. She needed to be stronger. Physically and mentally.

Mick nodded. His usual silent self.

This time, she was too consumed with her own problems to find his stillness unnerving. She headed right to the metal back door and began turning the various locks. Finally she shoved the door open and breathed in the cold winter air.

"Be careful out there," Mick said, and for the first time, she realized he was right behind her.

She glanced over her shoulder at the huge man. "I will."

He nodded and reached over her head to hold the door open for her.

She slipped out into the alley, glancing back at Mick.

He nodded again, and she gave him a tentative smile back. Funny she should feel a strange affinity to the man now. Now that she'd be leaving.

She turned back toward the street, her heels clicking on the concrete as she hurried into the bustling city.

Rhys knew he shouldn't, but he couldn't seem to stop himself. He had to check on Jane, make sure she was okay.

He paused outside her closed bedroom door, but she wasn't there. He concentrated; he couldn't feel her anywhere in the apartment. Her scent still drifted in the air, but it had faded to only a faint hint like the smell of roses drifting away on a breeze. Soon it would be gone altogether.

Was she gone? Already?

He placed his hand on the doorknob, holding it for

a second before making up his mind. Finally he opened the door and peered inside.

Relief overcame him. Her suitcase still sat beside the bureau. She hadn't left for good. He knew he shouldn't be happy. That the goal was to get her out of here as soon as he could. To put distance between her and Christian. And himself. But he wasn't ready for her to be gone quite yet.

But she was gone. At least for a while.

His first instinct was to follow her. To see where she was going. To make sure she was safe. But he headed in the direction of his bedroom instead. He was going to have to let her go soon enough, and he wouldn't be able to follow her then.

But what if Christian is out there watching her?

Rhys spun on his heels, striding toward the elevator.

Once he was downstairs, he went directly to Mick, where he sat in his office watching several monitors, the images from different security cameras around the club.

"Did Jane leave this way?"

Mick nodded.

"Do you know which way she went?"

Mick nodded again.

"Follow her."

Mick rose, reaching for his jacket on the back of his chair.

"Just make sure she is safe."

"What am I looking for?"

Mick had worked for Rhys and Sebastian long enough to know that Rhys wouldn't send him after her unless there was a very real threat.

"Christian."

Mick's eyes widened just slightly, the only sign that he was startled by Rhys's announcement. But he didn't waste time heading for the door.

Rhys watched the giant disappear outside. Mick seemed to understand much quicker than Rhys what kind of threat Christian could pose.

"Excuse me, do you have the time?"

Jane turned from the bookstore window, where she was half-heartedly browsing the new titles in the window.

She blinked, looking into pale, pale blue eyes. Eyes she'd seen before. She instantly recognized him as the man from the coffee bar.

She hesitated, uneasiness stealing her voice.

The man smiled. A warm smile. A friendly smile. And she immediately wondered at her nervousness. Just wary given her bad experiences on the streets of New York.

She laughed self-consciously as she realized she was staring. But it was hard not to look at those eyes.

"I don't have a watch."

"Sorry to bother you then." He didn't leave, but rather moved beside her to look at the books.

She pretended to browse them again, uncertain why she didn't just walk away.

"Have you read *Interview With a Vampire?*"

She glanced at him. "No. Is it good?"

"Very."

She nodded, unsure what to say.

He frowned at her then. The lines across his brow somehow adding to the beauty of his face rather than detracting from it. "Do I know you?"

She quickly shook her head, then laughed again. "Well, you bumped into me once. Literally."

Recognition dawned in his pale eyes. "Oh, yes. I think I used a rather bad pick-up line on you?"

"Did you?"

He shrugged. "If you don't remember it that way, then neither do I."

She couldn't help but smile at his glib charm. She glanced back at the books, not really seeing them.

"I know this is rather forward. And it's really going to sound like a pick-up line now, but would you be interested in joining me for something to eat? There is a great café across the street." He gestured to a restaurant on the other side of the busy road.

Jane started to say no, but something about the man made her waver. Maybe it was the shape of his lips or the tilt of his eyes; something in his appearance looked so familiar. Outside of meeting him in the coffee shop.

What the heck, she decided. It felt nice to have the attention of this very attractive man, especially after the awful evening she'd had thus far. A little conversation would be a good distraction. Good for her ego.

She cast another look over to the restaurant he'd suggested. The building's façade was very quaint, decorated like a Parisian café. And it buzzed with patrons.

Not a dark alley. Or a seedy bar. She certainly would be safe enough there.

"Actually, I am a little hungry."

He grinned, obviously very pleased. "Great." He held out his hand, a nicely shaped hand with a broad palm and long, blunt-tipped fingers. "I'm Chris."

She smiled, touching her fingers to his. "Jane."

He gave her hand a polite shake and then immediately released it.

Certainly nothing inappropriate about that.

She followed him as he wove the way through the crowded sidewalk to the corner, and then they crossed to the restaurant.

But once they were seated in a softly lit corner, Jane began to question her decision. The restaurant radiated romance, from the soft French music to the flickering candles on the cloth-covered tables.

She shifted slightly, fiddling with the clasp of her purse.

Chris's hand came out to cover hers. "You don't have to be nervous. I just want some company."

She stared into his eyes, then nodded. "Sorry, it's just this seems like the type of place you'd take a romantic date, not an acquaintance."

He glanced around. "Yes. But I get the feeling you could use a little romance tonight."

She laughed at that. The sound was grim, even to her own ears. "That obvious, huh?"

He moved his hand from hers and gave her a sympathetic smile. "Sad eyes. I'm a sucker for them. I think that must be what I noticed about you back in the coffee bar."

She frowned. "Really? Sad eyes?"

He nodded. "So why are they sad?"

She didn't speak for a moment, not sure she wanted to talk about Rhys to a total stranger. How could she tell *anyone* about Rhys? The whole story was just too strange.

She picked up her napkin, placing the linen on her lap, smoothing it over her black skirt.

"I've recently just—broken up with this guy."

"Really?"

"Yes. He had been—ill. And once he got—better, he

decided we shouldn't be together. He decided that I wasn't the right woman for him."

Christian listened impatiently to her halting story. The only thing that really interested him was that Rhys had been "ill."

"What sort of illness did he have?"

She toyed with her purse again, and he fought back the urge to still her hand, tightly, violently.

Instead he tilted his head with feigned concern.

"He had some type of amnesia."

Christian paused, then fought back a smile. Leave it to his maudlin brother to be overcome with memory loss. Poor Rhys, unable to accept himself. To accept his vampirism.

The whole thing was so trite.

Of course, if he'd known this earlier, he could have put Rhys out of his misery, and dear, dear brother would have never even known what hit him.

No, where was the fun in that? He studied Jane. This was much better . . . and it was going to be a lot more effective.

"But you still have feelings for him? After he has acted so callous?"

She nodded. "Yes."

Much to Christian's annoyance, the waiter appeared, rambling off a long list of specials in an appalling attempt at French. When he was finally done, Christian ordered two glasses of merlot.

"I'm sorry," he said after the waiter left. "That was presumptuous of me to order for you."

"No, that's fine. I don't drink much, so I wouldn't even begin to know which wine to order. Thank you."

He smiled, although he really wanted to roll his eyes. Leave it to Rhys to fall for little Miss Polly Sunshine.

"Do you think this man still cares for you?"

She thought it over and finally admitted, "I do. But I don't think I will get him to acknowledge that fact."

But he still cared. That was all that mattered to Christian. Losing her would hurt Rhys—ruin him. Rhys would, of course, be distressed if Christian hurt any mortal to get to him. But Christian didn't want distress—he wanted devastation. He wanted Rhys to suffer with this for eternity.

Christian gritted his teeth. Just like he ached over Lilah.

The wine arrived, and Christian took a sip. Ugh. A mediocre vintage to say the least. He set the glass aside.

"The thing about Rhys—that's his name—is that he's very noble, and I think he's breaking things off with me in some misguided attempt to protect me. Although I'm not sure from what."

She sighed and took another sip of wine. "Or maybe not. Maybe I just don't want to believe all the hurtful things he said."

Christian pretended to listen, but his mind stuck on one thing she'd said. *Rhys is noble.*

That one statement made him want to bare his teeth. Make him growl like a wild animal. Rhys, noble. What a crock of shit.

"Sometimes people can be very deceiving," he said quietly. "I know that firsthand."

Suddenly he decided that it was important that this vapid little innocent really know the man she thought so noble. The man she was going to lose her life for.

"I was deeply in love once, too," he told her. "Lilah was my whole existence. All I wanted in the world. And like anyone madly in love, I wanted her to meet my family."

Jane nodded, her eyes intent on him.

"And like any younger brother, I greatly admired my older brother, and especially wanted his approval."

"Of course," she murmured.

"So I asked him to attend a party that Lilah was hosting. Lilah was an accomplished hostess. She loved to throw lavish parties. Elegant parties. And my brother agreed to come.

"That night, my brother not only met my beloved, but decided that Lilah was so magnificent, he had to have her for himself."

"Oh, Chris." She reached out to touch him, but he pulled back before her hand could come in contact with his. He didn't want her sympathy. That wasn't why he was telling her this. He wanted her to know the true nature of the man she loved.

"He forced himself on her. Afterward, she did come back to me, but she was never the same. How could she be after what he'd done to her?"

Jane's green eyes shimmered with tears. "Chris, that is awful. I'm so sorry."

He regarded her, his expression grateful for her compassion, his insides stone-cold.

He forced a smile. "So you see, we both know what it is like to lose someone we loved."

Jane picked at the soup she'd ordered.

She couldn't possibly eat after Chris's story, even though he tried to keep the mood lighter and put her at ease.

How could one brother do something that horrendous to another brother? And that poor woman.

"I guess my story has ruined the atmosphere, hasn't

it?" he said regretfully, gesturing to her nearly untouched meal.

"I wasn't all that hungry," she assured him.

"Well, let me get the check. And then I can walk you home."

She started to turn down his offer. She didn't have a home at the moment. But then she decided she did have to go back to Rhys's apartment. It was getting late, and she didn't have her stuff. Plus, she wanted to talk to Sebastian and thank him for all his help. And also tell him she couldn't take the nightclub job after all.

One more night with Rhys wouldn't kill her. And tomorrow she would scour the city for a place to live.

"Yes, I'd love you to walk me home. If you don't mind?"

"I don't mind at all."

Chapter 24

Rhys had never been a big fan of the nightclub. Even though he owned part of the business, Sebastian really ran the place. Rhys had no interest in mingling with other vampires. Or, even worse, mortals who were enamored with the idea of being a creature of the night. And since that was who the club catered to, he generally avoided it at all costs.

But tonight was different. He wanted to be surrounded by reminders of who he was. He couldn't sit in the apartment with memories of Jane all around him, yet her scent, her warmth, already beginning to fade.

So here he sat on the balcony level of the club, enveloped in flashing lights, loud music and goths. He leaned back in his chair, propped his feet on the railing and surveyed the dance floor below him. The crowd gyrated and flailed to the pounding music. He watched them with disinterest and took another sip of his scotch.

Where was she? Where was Mick? He should have followed her himself.

"Where's Jane?" Sebastian pulled out the chair next to him, straddling it, resting his arms across the back.

"I don't know," Rhys gritted out, not wanting his brother's company at the moment.

"You told her you don't want her, didn't you?"

"Yes."

Sebastian shook his head, disgust clear on his face. "You know, I told myself if you got your memory back, *and* you were still too stupid to realize you need Jane . . . I told myself I wouldn't say anything."

"Feel free to stick with that plan," Rhys said dryly.

"Oh, shut up. And stop being a fool. Both about yourself and Jane."

"How is it foolish to want her to be safe? To not want her to know what I really am?"

"She will accept what you are."

Rhys shot him a wry glance.

"Well, she will eventually."

Rhys snorted at that.

"Do you think she's really going to be safe with Christian out there?" Sebastian pointed out.

Rhys stared blankly at the mob below them. If he could convince Christian that Jane meant nothing to him, and he got her away from here, she'd be safe.

He'd been too rash tonight. Too determined to make Jane believe he didn't care about her. That had been very careless on his part. He needed to be sure Christian didn't realize there was any connection between them before he made her go.

He just hoped Mick had found her.

Where was he?

As if Rhys's thoughts had called him, Mick appeared next to his chair.

"I couldn't find her."

"What?" Fear curdled in Rhys's stomach.

Mick shook his head. "I followed her trail for a while. And it just vanished."

Rhys swore to himself. How could he be so stupid? Why hadn't he thought this out? He'd been so resolute about ending things; he should have been more careful.

He stood. He had to find her. If Christian hurt her . . . No, he had to believe that somewhere deep inside the cruel vampire was the brother he'd once loved.

He started to push past Mick, but the hulking man caught his arm.

"Shit," Sebastian muttered from behind him.

Rhys didn't even need to look at his brother or follow both men's gazes. The scent of flowers laced with something foul had already reached his nose.

But he did look, immediately spotting Jane in the crowd. And right beside her was Christian, his arm looped through hers.

Their eyes met. Pale blue clashing with hazel.

"It's strange," Jane shouted, gaping around her in amazement as she tugged off her coat. "I lived above this place, but this is the first time I've actually been in here."

"Really?" Even though Chris responded, she could tell he was distracted.

It was hard not to be with all the flashing lights and loud music. And the people . . . A guy with artificially black hair, heavy eye makeup and a three-piece suit walked past her. She frowned at the odd combination.

Suddenly, Chris's hand clasped hers, and he pulled her toward the dance floor.

"Oh, no," she protested, laughing.

But he didn't seem to hear.

Next thing she knew, she was in the middle of a sea of writhing bodies, and Chris held her tight against the full length of his tall, lean body.

She tried to pull away, but he grasped her closer, the arms around her back like steel bands.

"Chris!"

He grinned down at her, and sudden uneasiness seized her.

"Don't you like to dance?"

She didn't know what to say. He wasn't acting at all like the man she'd just spent the evening with. Even his features looked different, harsher, the bones of his face more pronounced.

One of his hands slid down her back to grip her bottom, the touch rough, designed to show possession. Power.

"Do you think he likes to watch us dance?"

For a moment, she didn't understand what Chris meant. Then she felt "him," a warmth on her skin unrelated to the sweaty heat of the gyrating mob, or Chris's shocking familiarity.

She looked around, spotting Rhys standing at the railing of the upper level. His eyes bore into her.

"That's Rhys," she stated, but then she realized Chris already knew.

He smiled again. "Yes. I know." He leaned forward, his lips brushing her ear, his voice low and silky and frightening. "Maybe I should have done a better job introducing myself. I'm Christian Young. Rhys's brother."

She tried to pull away, his words frightening her even more, although she couldn't say why. But he held her fast, his grip unbreakable. Then his tongue traced the shape of her ear.

"Don't forget to ask Rhys about Lilah."

His words barely seemed to register in her ears before he was gone. Disappearing into the sea of bodies.

She staggered, both startled by his sudden release and relieved.

Christian.

She started to leave the dance floor, her legs still shaky, her spinning mind made dizzier, more disoriented, by the swaying bodies all around her.

Then she saw Rhys.

He descended the curved metal staircase from the upper level, never taking his eyes off her, and she gave up trying to make her wobbly legs work. She just stood among the dancers, keeping her gaze locked with his, as if he were the beacon in a violent storm.

When he stepped onto the dance floor, she lost sight of him among the crowd. Then suddenly, he was right in front of her. They stared at each other, motionless in a sea of writhing bodies. Without a word, he grabbed her hand and pulled her away from the confusion. She followed, unable and unwilling to do otherwise.

His long strides took them into a darkened corner of the club. He swung her in front of him and walked her backward until she was trapped between the wall and the hardness of his body. His amber eyes blazed down at her with anger, desire and fear.

Jane's lungs seized to a halt.

"Did he hurt you?"

She shook her head, still unable to inhale. She felt as trapped by Rhys's intense stare as by the weight of his large, hard body.

"Are you sure?"

"I'm fine," she managed in a breathy voice, amazed that with all the confusion and all the questions whirling in her mind, her body still reacted so readily to his touch.

She started to open her mouth to speak, to try and stay focused on what just happened, but Rhys didn't give her the chance.

He shifted her hands over her head, pinning them there with one hand as his mouth came down on hers, fierce, desperate.

Despite her confusion, she couldn't stop herself from responding. She met his kiss with the same desperate urgency, sucking on his lips and tongue. His free hand touched her everywhere, the strokes as frantic as his kiss, as if he didn't truly believe she was all right, or maybe that she was even real.

He pulled his lips away from hers and began to stream open-mouthed kisses along her jawline, her neck, her chest. She leaned her head back against the wall and closed her eyes, helpless under his frenzied onslaught.

Fingers tugged at the tie at the side of her shirt, and the material loosened. He peeled the shirt open, his mouth finding her nipple through the lace of her bra, sucking hard. His hand stroked her other breast, her stomach, her back.

She pressed against him as much as her restricted position would allow. She needed to touch him, too. To calm him, to reassure him.

"Rhys," she murmured, her voice pleading, filled with longing.

His mouth returned, plundering her soft lips as he held his body close to hers, her breasts flat against his chest and his knee between her legs.

His touch was rough and exciting. She couldn't stop

herself from rubbing against him, her nipples rasping the lace and cotton, her mound pressing silk and soft denim.

His knee nudged her legs open wider, and his hand touched her through her panties. Then the panties were pushed aside, and callused fingers tormented her, circling her, filling her.

She panted, her need for him, sharp, violent, seeming to match the pounding beat of the music that surrounded them.

His hands left her, and she bucked against him, demanding him back.

He returned, the thick head of his penis replacing his fingers, rubbing along her wet, swollen flesh. He used his legs to spread her knees wider as he positioned himself.

In one powerful stroke, he entered her, filling her completely, his body, his hands, his penis pinning her to the wall. His mouth held her mouth captive.

He drove into her, deep, with his erection, with his tongue. One thrust. Another. And another. Pulsating music, flashing lights, and pounding, relentless desire, until spasm after spasm of violent release overtook her.

She cried out, the sound lost in his mouth, and her body fell limp under his.

Rhys stared down at Jane, unable to believe what he'd just done. Taken her, against the nightclub wall. In the dim corner and with the angle of his body, no one passing by would know he was buried deep inside her. But he knew. And he knew why he'd lost control.

The sight of Jane in Christian's arms had nearly destroyed him. He'd been furious, blind rage tearing through him that Christian dared touch her.

Then his rage had turned to fear when Christian had

lowered his head to whisper something in her ear. His mouth so near the tender skin of her neck. Sheer terror had gripped Rhys as he realized Christian might kill her right there. Right on the dance floor. Right in front of him.

But when he got to Jane and looked in her wide, green eyes, he had to hold her. Had to love her and make sure that she was all right. That she was still his.

But now with her collapsed against him, her eyes closed, her face a study in satisfaction, he couldn't believe he'd let things get so out of hand.

He gently lowered her arms, afraid they might be stiff from the angle he'd had them in.

She opened her eyes then and gave him the sweetest smile. Not looking in the least like a woman who'd just been taken roughly against a wall.

He kept his body close to hers, shielding her from any passersby as he straightened her clothing, then his own.

She leaned on the wall, watching him. Not saying a word, although he knew she must have questions. About what they'd just done. About Christian.

Once they were presentable, he took her hand and led her to the back entrance. The large bouncer that guarded the door simply stepped aside as they approached, and they exited the lights and the music.

The hallway was deafeningly quiet in comparison, but still neither spoke as they got on the elevator. Nor did they talk once they were inside the apartment.

It wasn't until they were in the library and Rhys had poured them both a drink that Jane finally spoke.

And Rhys wasn't at all prepared for her first words.

"Tell me about Lilah."

Chapter 25

Rhys's first reaction was to ignore her request. What could he tell her?

Oh, yes, Lilah. She was the evil bitch who crossed me and my brothers over to vampirism. She's dead now, though.

"Was Lilah Christian's girlfriend?"

Rhys almost smiled at that title. Christian's girlfriend. It sounded so sweet. So innocent. So normal. Christian's relationship with Lilah had been none of those things.

"Lilah was the woman, and I use that term loosely, that destroyed Christian's life. Quite literally," he muttered.

Jane stared at the glass in her hands, rolling it slowly between her palms.

"He said you . . . took advantage of her."

Rhys snorted. "Yes, he would say that."

"Did you? Is that what this feud with Christian is about?" She still didn't look at him.

He closed his eyes briefly. Why did it hurt that she might believe Christian's words? What did it matter? If it convinced her to run, then let her believe the worst.

He couldn't.

"Our feud is definitely about Lilah," he told her. "But the events didn't happen the way he recalls them."

She glanced up at him, her hands pausing on her glass. "Then how did they happen?"

He didn't say anything for a few moments. How could he tell the story when all the facts were exactly what made it unbelievable? Why was he even considering trying to tell her? He should just tell her he had done all the horrible things Christian said. And more. And convince her to run.

But his mouth didn't listen to the reasoning of his mind.

"We were living in England when Christian met Lilah."

Jane stared at Rhys, waiting for him to continue.

"Christian decided to move to London. We had a row house there. I preferred our country home, but he hated rural life. He hated the quiet and the slow pace. He craved excitement. I didn't want him to go; being the oldest, I felt responsible for him."

Jane knew that about Rhys—that he'd feel as though he had to watch out for his rebellious brother.

"He hadn't been in London very long when all communication stopped. Christian wasn't exactly the most dependable person, so at first, I didn't really worry about it. But after two months without a letter, I decided I'd better go see him."

Jane considered his words. A letter? Not a call or an e-mail? That seemed odd. The average person didn't generally correspond with letters these days, much less a wild young man. But she didn't say anything.

"The row house was lavish. Our parents had left us well provided for, and Christian fell into the life of the idle rich. When I got to the house, the place was in complete disarray, from parties and other decadence. Much of the staff was gone."

Again she wondered at his wording. It was as if he was telling her a story in the very same way that "Rhys the viscount" would have.

"Christian didn't even look like himself. He was pale, unkempt, his eyes wild. And I knew then he was mixed up with something."

"Drugs?" she asked.

Rhys laughed humorlessly. "You could say that. Lilah was definitely a drug to Christian."

"How so? What did she do?"

"She controlled him. He did whatever she said."

Jane frowned at the barely contained hatred in his voice. "Christian said you became obsessed with her, too."

He raised an eyebrow at that, another humorless chuckle escaping him. "When I met Lilah, I will admit, I was immediately drawn to her beauty. She was very beautiful." He admitted that as though he'd rather not. "But it didn't take me long to see beyond that illusion of beauty to what lurked under the surface."

Jane couldn't hide her confusion. "What lurked under the surface?"

His eyes suddenly found hers, and his gaze seemed a little disoriented, as though he'd been back with Lilah, seeing—what?

He rubbed a hand over his face. She noticed that his hands seemed unsteady.

"She wasn't a nice person," he said finally, but Jane knew that description stopped far short of whatever he was remembering.

Jane wanted to ask more, but didn't. She didn't think Rhys would tell her. Instead she told him what Christian had implied. "Christian made it sound like you . . . attacked her."

He shook his head, Christian's belief still injuring him. "No. I didn't attack her. But . . ." He turned away from her then. "We did have sex."

Rhys, no.

His admission staggered her. Disbelief, disappointment and jealousy jumbled inside her. Rhys wouldn't do that. He wouldn't ever hurt his brother. No.

"It was one incident," his voice was low, shaken. "And I was sick with myself at my weakness. I should have been able to deny her. To stop it."

Jane blinked at him. At his broad back and slumped shoulders. She couldn't see the man who'd cheated with his brother's lover. Or even the cold man who had pushed her away earlier today.

She just saw a man who had carried too much weight on his shoulders for too long. She saw Rhys, and she knew he ached over things in his past—enough to try to erase them from his memories.

And she also knew, without a doubt, that he wasn't telling the whole story. He wasn't weak. He never would have touched his brother's lover, much less slept with her. What had really happened?

She rose off the sofa and crossed to him. She slipped her arms around his stomach and pressed her cheek to his back, wanting to take away his pain. Wanting to carry a little of his burden.

He stiffened under her embrace, but he didn't pull away.

"What did Lilah do to force *you*?"

He remained perfectly still. Her hands brushed over the clenched muscles of his belly. Her cheek nuzzled the tenseness of his spine.

"What really happened?" she whispered.

Rhys remained motionless, though his entire body felt weak. Weak with relief and humbled by her trust. Jane didn't believe Christian. She didn't believe he would intentionally hurt his brother that way. She didn't believe he would ever force himself on a woman. Even after the way he'd just taken her, rough and half-crazed, against the wall, she still didn't believe him capable of violence.

But he was capable of extreme violence. He could kill if necessary. He'd kill to protect her.

He turned then in her arms, staring down at her open, trusting face. He could kill for her, but he wouldn't let her die for him. She had to leave. Even without the threat of Christian, she wasn't safe. He wanted her too much.

"What happened doesn't matter. It's over now. Christian will forever believe what he believes, and I will go on without my brother. That's just how things are."

She shook her head, her goodness making her assume all things could be fixed. All rifts mended. All pains healed.

He knew they couldn't.

And he wasn't going to allow her to become another loss he couldn't overcome. Another "if only" that he couldn't go back and change.

"Can't you talk to him? Tell him the truth?"

He laughed, the sound bitter, but his fingers on her cheek were gentle. "I've tried. Over and over. But he doesn't want to hear the truth. He believed Lilah. He will keep believing her. That is why you have to leave here."

She frowned, not following his reasoning.

"Christian is dangerous. And I'm afraid he could try to hurt you to get back at me. You have to leave."

She stared up at him, then smiled as though she thought he was acting like nothing more than a worried mother hen.

"I'm not scared of Christian."

Her words sounded confident, but he could sense apprehension, a subtle tang in the air.

He touched her cheek again, savoring the silky softness of her skin. Committing it to memory. Jane leaving would cause him pain, but as long as he knew she was out there somewhere, alive and safe, then he could bear it.

"I'm going to give you some money," he told her.

She shook her head, but he continued, "And I'm going to have Mick take you somewhere safe. Where would you like to go? You can go anywhere. London? Paris? Somewhere tropical, warm." He softened his voice, coaxing her.

She shook her head again. "I don't want to go anywhere if it means leaving you."

Rhys pulled away from her, irritation rising in his chest. Didn't she understand he was trying to protect her?

"I told you earlier. I do not want to be *with* you." The words came out rough, angry.

She remained silent for a moment, then said softly, "So that's why you made love to me right in the middle of the nightclub? Why I felt the desperation in your desire?"

He stared into her eyes, his frustration rising. But she didn't flinch under his cold glare.

Instead, she stepped forward and reached for his hands. Her small thumbs brushed back and forth across his broad palms, the caresses sweet, soothing.

"Rhys, you are in love with me. I know it. So instead of trying to figure out where you can send me where I'll be safe, why don't we figure out how I can stay right here and be safe."

"Jane—"

"What will either of us gain if I leave? We both end up alone."

"Yes," he agreed, his voice wry. "But you end up alive."

"If he wanted to do anything to me, he could have done it tonight." Her voice was calm, reasonable, but he knew she was unnerved by the idea that anyone would want to hurt her.

"Just answer this," she finally said, "and I'll consider going."

He waited, unsure he wanted to hear her question, but willing to answer if it would protect her.

"If I do go, and I never see you again, what would be the one thing, years from now, you would wish you'd told me?"

He raised an eyebrow. He'd have been amused if he wasn't so worried, so frustrated. He had to give her credit; she was persistent.

But he didn't respond immediately. Not in an attempt to hurt her, or convince her that he didn't care about her. He just couldn't say the words.

When was the last time he'd said them? Elizabeth? Yes, it had to have been to Elizabeth. Two hundred years was a long, long time to insulate himself, to attempt to remain numb. But Jane made him feel. And just like blood and heat returning to a frostbitten appendage, it hurt like hell.

He took a deep breath, afraid. Afraid to say something he would have once said so readily. Or at least he hoped he'd said it readily. To Elizabeth. And his parents. Even Sebastian and Christian.

And he had to say the words now. Even if it was only this once.

"I would wish," he said slowly, "that I told you that I love you."

She smiled, not the triumphant grin he'd expected, but a small, tremulous smile. Her eyes glistened.

"Thank you."

He nodded, but couldn't seem to respond any further.

She sniffed, then started to release his hands.

He clasped them before she could break the contact, and he pulled her toward him. Wrapping his arms around her, he cradled her against his body.

Now that the thaw had started, a flood followed, and he couldn't seem to control the emotion that poured through him.

"I love you, Janie," he murmured against her ear. "I love you more than I've ever loved anyone."

She hugged him back, her arms tight around his neck.

"Then that solves it," she said against his ear, her voice hoarse with emotion.

Finally. Finally she'd do as he asked. Because he loved her.

"I'm staying right here."

Chapter 26

Rhys set Jane away from him and glowered down at her.

"You are leaving." His voice boomed off the bookshelves and the ceiling, but she didn't back down.

"No. I love you, and I'm staying right here."

He narrowed his eyes at her. Then, as if he didn't know what else to do, he strode over to the window.

She watched him for a minute, then followed. Her arms wrapped around his torso. "We can't lose this."

"I can't lose you."

"You won't."

"I can't watch you every minute. And you'll never be safe with Christian out there."

Jane knew he was looking out over the city, wondering where his brother was right now.

"It will be okay," she assured him, even though she knew she couldn't guarantee that. But her mind couldn't wrap around the idea Christian would really want to hurt her.

"Please, Jane. Just go."

She shook her head, then pressed her cheek against his back. "I've been alone for too long. I can't leave you. I can't."

The muscles in his back relaxed, but she knew it wasn't relief that loosened them. It was defeat. She'd worn him down, at least for tonight.

She didn't feel any satisfaction in her victory.

"Come on," she said, lacing her fingers through the hand that hung at his side, tugging his immoveable body.

He glanced at her. "Where?"

"Let's go to bed. We can worry about Christian tomorrow."

He hesitated, casting another look out at the city. Then he allowed himself to be led out of the room.

Once in bed, they simply held each other, neither wanting anything more than to feel their bodies close together. To know that the other one was there.

As the night turned to day, Rhys gradually fell into his usual deep sleep, but Jane couldn't rest. There were too many questions. She tried to guess what had really happened with Lilah. She couldn't figure it out, but she knew there was more that Rhys wasn't saying.

And was Christian the only reason that Rhys had pushed her away in the first place? Or was there something more she was missing?

Finally, after only managing to doze off and on, she gave up on sleep and instead went to find food. She had to be safe in the apartment. With all the locks and Mick and the other security people in the nightclub, she had to be living in one of the safest apartments in the city.

The marble floor was cold as she padded barefoot

around the kitchen. She filled a coffee mug with water and then stuck it in the microwave to heat for her tea. Then she went to the cupboard to decide on what to eat.

She felt hungry, but nothing sounded appealing. Cereal? No. Toast? No.

She opened the fridge. She could make a sandwich. But that didn't sound very appetizing either. Her gaze landed on Rhys's protein drink. She started to reach for the pouch, then stopped. No, the dark liquid looked disgusting.

Ah, what the heck, a sip wouldn't kill her. Plenty of things looked gross and tasted great. Like steamed clams or creamed spinach.

She picked up the bag and popped the cap. She sniffed it, recalling that the scent had been rather unappealing. This time the smell didn't seem quite as bad.

She went to the cupboard and took down another mug. She sloshed a little of the viscous liquid into the heavy white cup. Gingerly, she raised the mug to her lips and took a small sip.

Grimacing, she swished the drink around her tongue. Then her face relaxed, and she shrugged. Not bad, really. It actually tasted rather good.

Forgoing her tea, she filled the mug with more of the protein drink and then headed to the library. Maybe a little reading would relax her, and she'd be able to sleep.

She didn't really feel in the mood to read, her mind still racing, but she grabbed a book off the shelf anyway and settled on the sofa.

She flipped open the cover, reading the title page. *"The Truth about Vampires and Werewolves."*

She closed the cover to look at the front. *"The Facts*

and the Fiction: A Study of the Behaviors of Preternatural Creatures."

Not exactly the type of reading she had in mind to calm her nerves. She started to place it on the table, then stopped. A word on the back cover just happened to catch her eye.

Mirrors.

Not a remarkable word. But one that did give her pause. She flipped the book open again, looking in the index.

Sure enough, there was a whole section on mirrors.

Turning to the selected pages, she scanned the paragraphs.

Historically, vampires have avoided mirrors, because they do not cast a reflection as humans do. Their reflections appear see-through, much like a ghost or spirit. This was once seen as an indication of the loss of their soul. However, current studies have revealed that the phenomenon is very likely the result of simple changes in the vampire's ionic makeup.

Was that why Rhys didn't have mirrors in his bathroom? He was afraid he was a vampire?

She laughed at herself. Not likely.

She turned back to the index. Crosses. Garlic.

She turned to the garlic section.

Garlic was once considered a potent deterrent against vampires, although now it is recognized that garlic in large quantities will deter just about any creature, preternatural or otherwise.

She shook her head, smiling. This was definitely an interesting book. And maybe garlic was just the thing to send Christian packing.

She scanned a few more pages.

Biting . . .

While a werewolf's bite is both undesirable in that it is the primary way to spread lycanthropy, and it is also extremely painful, the vampire's bite needs to neither spread vampirism nor be unpleasant. In fact, a vampire bite can be quite enjoyable, often leading to sexual gratification for both the partner and the vampire.

But conversely, a vampire can use its bite to cross a human over to vampirism, to injure the human or in some circumstances kill.

As Jane read, the small marks on her neck began to sting as if reacting to what she read. She went back to the index to look up hypochondria.

Nope, neither vampires nor werewolves seemed to suffer from that malady.

But her fingers did stray to the wound. She had to admit they did look like vampire bites. At least the ones in the movies.

She returned to reading about bites, learning that vampire bites varied based on the alignment of the vampire's teeth. And that braces can in fact help poorly aligned bites.

She laughed out loud and checked the author of the book.

Dr. Kurtland Fowler—not a very vampiry name.

Count Fowler. That just sounded silly.

But despite her doubts about the author, she continued to read, skipping around to topics that caught her interest.

But her amusement waned as she read one particular entry. Avoidance of sunlight.

She, of course, knew from old vampire movies that they couldn't go out in the sun, but something about Dr. Fowler's comments struck her.

The avoidance of sunlight is only applicable to vampires. The original concept of why vampires could not go out into the sunlight was based around the idea that the sun symbolizes life. Because vampires do not adhere to the same rules of biology as humans, and are often mistaken for dead, the assumption was made that vampires are intolerant to sunlight because they are inherently evil. Thus they were forced to cling to shadows and the darkness of night.

When, in fact, the sun intolerance is far less dramatic. The aversion is a metabolic issue that does not allow the proper absorbtion of vitamin D. The reaction is violent and often deadly. As of yet, no treatment has been found.

Vampires are also extremely sensitive to gamma rays, which have a sedative effect on them, causing the vampire to sleep very deeply in daylight hours.

She stared at the words. This sounded like Rhys. A violent allergy to the sun, and she had never met a deeper sleeper.

She stared at the words a moment longer, then snapped the book shut. She tossed it in the chair next to the sofa, suddenly unsettled, both by the book and by the direction of her thoughts.

Rhys—a vampire. That was just crazy.

Obviously, the return of Rhys's memory, his confusing behavior toward her and the idea that Christian might want to hurt her were allowing her imagination to get away with her.

Still, a lot of the things she'd read did seem similar to things that had happened. Rhys mentioning he disliked mirrors. The strange marks she had noticed on her body. And Rhys's sun allergy. Was that too many parallels to be considered a coincidence?

She glanced back at the book where it lay, the corner barely visible over the arm of the chair.

She shifted against the cushions, pulling her legs up underneath her. She was being silly. Vampires—there was no such thing. She didn't believe in supernatural stuff.

Or did she? She definitely believed there was something strange going on in the bedroom she'd been given. As much as she wanted to believe she'd imagined or dreamed the eerie chills that woke her, she couldn't. An entity, or something, had been there. A ghost. A spirit. She didn't know what to call it. But she did believe it was real.

So if that could be real, why couldn't a vampire?

She couldn't believe she was actually considering this. But her gaze strayed back to the book as if it were calling her.

She settled back into the soft sofa, determined to push all these ridiculous thoughts from her mind.

She looked out the window. The sun was low over the city, the sky a deep pink streaked with wisps of pale purple clouds. She rested her head on the puffy cushions, admiring the beautiful colors of the sky, feeling tired but still unable to calm her mind.

She forced herself to close her eyes, but within seconds, they were open again, first looking back at the sunset, then returning to the book.

She sat up. She would scan the index one last time, and when she saw that there were no other entries that could apply to Rhys, she'd drop these crazy notions about vampires and ghosts. And there wouldn't be any more connections. Because she was being silly.

She leaned over and retrieved the book. Sitting cross-legged, she rested the book in her lap.

"Thanks, Dr. Fowler. Like I didn't have enough on my mind," she muttered to the cover. Then she, almost reluctantly, opened to the back.

Crosses 49–52, 112, 176–181
Curses 2–4, 280, 291

Nothing so far. She flipped ahead.

Holy water 53

She turned several more pages.

Seeds 12, 45–46, 142, 167, 202, 310–313

Seeds? She almost looked at that, just because she didn't know seeds played such a big role in vampire or werewolf lore. But she didn't. Seeds definitely didn't apply to Rhys.

Then the hair on the back of her neck stood up.

Shape shifting.

That topic alone didn't cause her chill. It was the sub-topics listed underneath. Bats. Cold spots. Fog. Mist.

This wasn't about Rhys. But it did describe the thing she'd felt in her bedroom. She hesitated, then thumbed to the right page.

Vampires, because of their ability to manipulate the meta-physical, can shape-shift. Unlike werewolves, or any were-creature for that matter, which can only shift into the animal they were infected by, the vampire can shift into many different forms. Shadows, fog and cold air are the most common shifts used by vampires. These particular changes are believed to have come into vogue, over the traditional bat, simply because they were the most effective methods to escape marauding villagers.

Cold air. Fog. That was exactly what she'd felt in her room. Another coincidence?

What if she was being visited by a vampire? And maybe Rhys was a vampire, too. That was how he knew what was happening. He said he heard her cry out, but she knew she hadn't. She'd been too paralyzed with fear to scream.

"Vampires," she said out loud, her mind still toying with the idea.

"I'm surprised you guessed," a deep voice said from behind her, causing Jane to squeal and scramble to her feet. She spun around to see Christian, leaning a hip on the back of the sofa, his arms crossed over his chest as if he'd been standing there for a while. A mocking smile curved his lips.

"You are a smart girl."

Jane backed away from him, tripping on the book, which had fallen to the floor when she jumped up. She caught herself on the arm of the chair and kept moving backward.

"H—how did you get in here?"

He strolled around the sofa, stopping to pick up the book.

He opened it, absently flipping through the pages. "I came in as a shadow. It tends to be less noticeable than the cold air, as you can attest to. And fog—now that's hardly discreet, is it?"

Jane stared at him, dizziness coming over her. This couldn't be real. She didn't want this to be real.

Christian continued to saunter around the room, not appearing to pay attention to her, but browsing through the book.

"Vampires are believed to be the first creatures to rise out of the primordial ooze," Christian read aloud. His lip curled upward with disgust. "Primordial ooze. It just sounds unpleasant, doesn't it?"

She didn't respond.

He turned a few more pages, then placed the book on the piano and sighed. "So did you ask Rhys about Lilah?"

The question was asked so casually, so conversationally, that it took her a moment to comprehend it.

He gave her an impatient look.

"Yes."

"And he denied everything I said, didn't he?"

"No—not exactly."

He started to walk toward her. "Really? What did he say?"

She tried to back away farther, but her shoulder hit the marble molding around the fireplace.

He stopped just an arm's length from her. "Tell me."

"He said that he did—he was intimate with her. But that he didn't force her."

Christian rolled his eyes. "The same old story."

Jane glanced at the door. She couldn't make it from this angle. He'd grab her as soon as she tried to get past him. Could she outrun a shadow, anyway?

"But Rhys couldn't tell you much of the story, could he? Since he was still hiding the whole vampire aspect."

He didn't wait for her to respond. "So he couldn't tell you about the fact that he wasn't with Lilah just the once. He was with her many times. It is true that they only had intercourse that once, but vampires don't have to have intercourse to be intimate. A vampire's bite is every bit as intimate as sex. And Rhys bit her many times."

Jane glanced at the door again, inching slightly in that direction.

Christian noticed, moving closer, until she was nearly pinned to the wall. She stared up at him, and he smiled, a cold smile that didn't reach his frosty eyes.

"Does it bother you that Rhys bit Lilah? Just like he bit you?" He brushed a finger over the bandage still on her neck.

Rhys bit her? Yes. She suddenly knew it was true.

"Did you like his bite?" His voice was low. His finger

still touched her neck, trailing from the bandage to her bare skin.

She shuddered, his touch making her skin crawl. She didn't answer.

"What do you think? Would you like it if I bit you?"

Panic rose in her belly, in her chest.

"Rhys wouldn't like it if I bit you," he said softly, not looking in her eyes, but at the spot where his finger drew a little circle against the side of her neck. "He wouldn't like it one bit."

She swallowed, trying to remain calm. "I think you've been asking the wrong questions."

His finger paused, and his eyes met hers. He smiled sardonically. "And what questions should I be asking?"

She swallowed again. "Maybe you should be asking if it was Lilah who liked Rhys biting her."

His smile disappeared, and his eyes narrowed into a frigid glare. "You didn't know Lilah. She was madly in love with me. She'd never have gone to Rhys willingly."

"But I do know Rhys. And he'd never hurt his brother. He loves you, and misses you. He aches to have his family back."

Christian laughed, the sound cold, hard. "You don't know anything about this." He leaned closer. "And you don't need to. But you are going to help me show my brother how I've felt all these years. How I still feel."

She gaped up at him. Fear strangled her. What did he mean? What was he going to do?

He touched a hand to her hair, running his fingers through the strands, gentle, almost tender. "Rhys needs to understand what he's done."

Suddenly, his fingers yanked her hair hard, snapping her head back at a painful angle until her neck was fully exposed.

She whimpered.

"And killing you, Janie, is the best way I can think of to make my point."

Before she could speak or cry out, his teeth sank deep into her neck. She didn't feel any pleasure—only pain and mind-numbing fear.

Chapter 27

Blinding terror gripped Rhys. He struggled out of bed, the fear so strong his limbs were weak with it.

He shoved the fear aside and concentrated. Jane was in the library. She was in pain. She was scared.

He fumbled with his pants, then raced toward the room where he knew she was—and he knew, too, who else was with her.

Don't let this be happening, his mind begged.

As he raced down the hallway, he heard Sebastian's door open, and he heard Sebastian following behind him.

Please, please, let her be okay. Please.

At first, Christian didn't recognize it. He sucked in the initial warm gush of Jane's blood, and the flavor filled his mouth. Sweet and delicate. But the more he drank of her, the stronger it got.

Suddenly, he wasn't just tasting her blood. He was

feeling her. Her emotions were his, her thoughts. His knees started to buckle under the power of it.

He caught himself, bracing a hand on the wall behind her, refusing to stop. This was the revenge he'd waited for. Longed for. He wouldn't stop.

But her emotions bombarded him. Pain, fear, but much, much stronger than either of those was something that was unfamiliar. The "thing" he tasted as soon as he bit her. A feeling he couldn't understand. But he responded to it. Helpless to do otherwise.

Suddenly the nebulous emotion shaped in his head. Took a form. Found a name. It echoed through his mind.

Love.

He could feel Jane's love throughout him like wave after wave of warmth, all around him, curling over his skin. The love she felt for Rhys. A fated love. A true love.

How could this be unfamiliar? He'd loved Lilah. Lilah had loved him. Why didn't he immediately recognize the taste of it on his tongue?

Because he'd never tasted this in Lilah's blood, his mind told him. Even as he denied it again, he knew it was true. He'd never tasted sweetness or caring. He'd never felt warmth that encircled him. Held him.

Just greedy hunger. Constant craving. Had he somehow mistaken that for love?

He stopped feeding and looked down at Jane. Now barely conscious, she hung limply in his arms. But even in her unaware state, he could still sense that her connection with Rhys was intact. Calling to him.

Christian had never felt that with Lilah. Lilah had never reached out. Never connected to him. And he'd never been able to reach her. Not like this.

He shook his head angrily and repositioned his fangs

over Jane's neck. He could have had this with Lilah. It was Rhys who had ruined that. He was the one who'd destroyed everything.

But even as he returned his teeth to Jane's throat, he knew it wasn't true. Lilah hadn't ever, ever felt like this.

Christian lifted his head again, staring at the woman in his arms. His brother's love. His brother's mate. But now, she looked like a broken angel in his embrace.

A wretched sound escaped him. What had he done? What had he spent years believing?

He scooped Jane up into his arms and crossed to the sofa. He laid her among the cushions, unsure what to do. Confused without the rage that had driven him for years.

Then the door slammed open, and Rhys charged into the room. His eyes were wild as he searched for Jane, barely registering Christian at all.

He found her, running to her. Kneeling beside her. His hands shook as he touched her hair, her face, her neck.

He stared at his hand, now covered with Jane's blood. He saw the jagged wound oozing just below her right ear.

He rose then and spun toward Christian.

"What have you done?" His voice was low and filled with rage. "What have you done?"

He charged at Christian.

Christian accepted the blow, which knocked him hard against the bookshelves behind him. Several books fell to the ground around him.

Rhys hit him again. This time, Christian fell to the hardwood floor. His lip was bleeding, his nose broken. But he didn't feel the pain.

Rhys reached for him again, hauling him to his feet.

Fury burned in his eyes, and Christian knew that Rhys intended to kill him. Just as he'd once intended to kill Rhys. Only this time, Christian knew the killing would be justified.

Rhys wanted his death for the right reasons.

Rhys pinned him against the bookshelves and stared at him.

"Lilah had sex with me. She charmed me. Hypnotized me. And when I realized what I'd done I was sick with guilt. Sick that I couldn't stop her," he growled, his fangs already elongated. "And those times I went to her, to bite her, I only sought retribution from her for ruining my family. For killing my baby sister."

Christian didn't speak. What could he say now? He had been so obsessed with Lilah, he'd blinded himself to the truth. He'd refused to believe. But now that he'd felt real love, pure love, he knew he'd never known that emotion before.

Rhys bared his teeth, moving in for the attack, when Sebastian's voice stopped him.

"Rhys, Jane is dying."

Rhys released Christian, turning toward Jane.

Sebastian stood over her, his eyes bleak, his face drawn. "She's barely breathing. I don't think she's going to make it."

"No!" Rhys roared, striding over to her.

"No," he repeated as he knelt beside her, stroking her hair.

Sebastian watched Rhys, feeling helpless, angry.

Christian remained against the wall, also watching Rhys. But Sebastian couldn't see any of the bitterness or the hatred that had been a part of Christian's features for so long.

He looked devastated. Sick.

Sebastian had no doubt that Christian was simply going to stand there and allow Rhys's attack. Sebastian didn't know what changed Christian, what brought back the brother who'd disappeared when Lilah had arrived. But he was there, leaning against the bookshelves, tormented by what he'd done.

Christian was no longer the monster Lilah had created.

Christian's eyes locked with his. They stared at each other for a few moments. Then Sebastian nodded at him. A nod designed to tell Christian he understood. Or at least he would try.

Christian didn't react. He simply looked back at Rhys, kneeling beside Jane. Then with disgust and self-hatred burning in his eyes, Christian dissolved into shadows.

Sebastian returned to Rhys. He was the one who needed him right now.

"How is she?" Sebastian asked, but he already knew. Jane's breathing was so faint, even with his keen senses he could barely register the tiny breaths.

Rhys didn't answer. He just kept touching her. His fingers trembling as he stroked her face, her hair.

"You have to try and cross her over," Sebastian said.

"No."

"Are you just going to let her die?" Sebastian's tone was terse, but he didn't care. They couldn't just let her die without doing something.

"It won't work," Rhys said, still not looking away from her. "She can't give her consent."

Sebastian knew that what Rhys was saying was likely true. Mortals could not cross over without accepting the dark gift, as it was so quaintly called.

"Rhys," he said softly, placing a hand on his brother's shoulder, "she's going to die anyway. You need to try."

Rhys's head dropped, and he didn't say anything. Finally he stood and gently lifted Jane into his arms.

His swift steps took him from the room, and Sebastian didn't follow. Rhys needed to deal with this his own way.

Sebastian just hoped it was the right way.

Rhys carried Jane into his bedroom, placing her in the center of his bed. With great care, he arranged her in a position that made her appear as if she were only sleeping. Then he lay down beside her.

He tried to detect the rise and fall of her chest, the minute beat of her heart. He could, just barely, and he half feared it was only because he wanted to see it.

Tenderly, he touched her hair. The silken locks curled at the ends and twined around his fingers. He leaned forward to kiss her forehead.

When he moved back, he saw that her face had gone from pasty white to nearly gray. He closed his eyes, fighting with his indecision. He couldn't let her go. But if he couldn't cross her over, he couldn't bear to be the one to kill her.

He opened his eyes, feeling wetness roll down his cheeks. She looked so small, so fragile, lying beside him.

He hadn't been able to protect her. He had failed. Again, he'd failed.

Pulling her lifeless body to his chest, he hugged her tightly and buried his head into the crook of her neck.

"I'm sorry," he mumbled against her chilled skin. "Oh, Janie, I'm so sorry."

Letting out a strangled cry of agony, he reared back his head and sank his fangs into her jugular.

He drank until her breathing ceased and her heart stopped beating. Then with her body still cradled in his arms, he leaned back against the headboard. He looked down at her, her face a perfect, beautiful mask. Lifeless, empty. His tears rolled down his cheeks onto hers.

"Please come back to me," he pleaded in a whisper. "Please come back."

"Wake up, sleepyhead."

Jane's voice penetrated the darkness encompassing Rhys. He opened his eyes to find her leaning over him, a big smile on her full lips.

He immediately sat up, running his hands over her cheeks, her shoulders, her arms, making sure she was all right.

She laughed, the sound sweet and beautiful to his ears.

"I'm fine. In fact, I feel great."

He stared at her, still unable to believe that she was here, that she had crossed over. He'd held her until the sun, high in the sky, had forced him to sleep. But he'd fully expected to awaken to find her dead.

"I can't believe it."

"Believe what?"

He paused. Maybe she didn't realize what had happened. Would she understand? Or would she hate him for crossing her over?

"Janie, last night—Christian attacked you."

She nodded. "Yes, I remember."

"You do?"

She nodded.

"Do you remember what Christian is?"

"Yes. I put it together last night. You have this fascinating book written by a man named Dr. Kurtland Fowler, and I started to see a lot of connections between you and the vampires he described. Although I don't think I really believed it until Christian appeared."

He stared at her, dumbfounded. "You are taking this very calmly."

"Well . . ." She considered that. "You've bitten me while we were making love, right?"

He nodded, sheepishly.

She smiled at his expression. "It was very nice," she assured him.

He raised an eyebrow at the word nice.

"I think from those bites, I was already crossing over."

Rhys shook his head. "It's not possible. A mortal has to give consent."

She shrugged. "Well, you crossed me over last night."

She had a point.

"Why do you think that?" he asked.

"The bathtub," she said with a small, knowing smile. "I could hear your thoughts. And as a mere mortal, I shouldn't have been able to do that."

That was true. He could often read hers, but not vice versa.

She suddenly leapt off the bed and headed toward the door.

"Where are you going?"

"To consult Dr. Fowler," she called back from the hallway.

Rhys shook his head, falling back against the pillows. He didn't have the strength to follow her yet. He was still too shaken, still too relieved that she'd made it. She'd crossed over.

But Jane was back within minutes, a book in hand. She crawled onto the bed. She sat down beside him and began searching through the index.

"Here we go," she said.

"Crossing over is the term used when a vampire brings a mortal over to vampirism. Generally, the vampire has to obtain the mortal's consent to achieve this goal. But in rare instances"—she turned and gave Rhys a significant look—"in rare instances, when the vampire and mortal are soul mates, consent does not need to be given, and the crossing over will begin from the first bite the vampire gives his mate."

She snapped the book closed, giving him a smug look.

He couldn't help smiling. "Proud of yourself, aren't you?"

"Yes."

He sat forward and kissed her, her lips clinging sweetly to his.

"So you aren't upset?" he asked seriously.

"Upset? Why?"

"You're a vampire."

She shrugged. "It sure beats dead."

He knew she meant the comment to be funny, but guilt weighed heavily in his chest. "Jane, you've been surrounded by death your whole life. Are you sure you won't come to resent this—a state between life and death."

She touched a hand to his cheek. "Yes, I did grow up surrounded by death. I know more about it than I want to. And I also know that whatever we are, it's not dead. I feel like I didn't start living until I met you. How can I ever resent an eternity with you? I love you."

He pulled her against him, his lips nibbling her neck, now healed and perfect.

She turned her head and captured his lips, kissing him back with a possessiveness he reveled in.

But after a few moments, she pulled away. "What— what happened to Christian?"

Rhys looked down at her, mixed emotions roiling through him. "He disappeared. But I don't think he'll be back."

She nodded. "Good. I was afraid you killed him."

That wasn't the response he'd expected. Christian had tried to kill her, nearly did. He couldn't imagine her having any sympathy for him. But she did. It was there in her expressive green eyes.

"I didn't seduce Lilah." He felt the need for her to know that. "She used her powers on me, controlling me. I was so repulsed the next morning with what I did. I'd never hurt Christian that way."

Jane listened, waiting for him to continue, knowing that he needed to.

"She seemed to become obsessed with me, probably because I'd refused her. She wasn't used to that. And she wasn't about to let my rejection go unpunished. One night, she showed up at my room. She flew into a rage and showed me her vampire self. She explained that she'd already made Christian the undead, and if I didn't willingly let her make me a vampire as well, she'd destroy my family."

Jane made a noise in her throat and reached for his hand, holding his fingers, stroking them.

"Even after seeing what she was, I thought I could refuse her. I thought I was stronger than her evil. The next day, Elizabeth fell ill. She had always been a delicate girl, and I initially wanted to believe that she just had some normal sickness. But as the days passed, it became apparent that she had more than a mere cold. I called in doctor after doctor, but they had no answers. Their best guess was consumption, and nothing could be done."

"But it wasn't consumption, was it?"

Rhys shook his head. The image of Elizabeth, small and frail in her bed, was as clear as if it had happened only yesterday. "Lilah came to me again, and she told me she was the one draining Elizabeth's life, and if I didn't cross over, she would kill her."

"So you agreed."

He nodded. "The next night, when I woke in my new vampire state, I went to Elizabeth. She was still in bed, her skin so pale it matched the whiteness of the sheets around her. I touched her, and her skin was icy. I knew then, she was gone. But I couldn't accept it. I couldn't accept that I had given up my soul, and Lilah had killed Elizabeth anyway."

Jane slipped her arms around him. He closed his eyes and pressed his cheek against the top of her head.

"Since she made me, I'd never be powerful enough to kill her. Not in a fight. So I started going to her, pretending that I was enamored with her. She was vain and so conceited, she believed me. And I began to bite her—draining her over and over. Until she literally went mad. It was the best I could do to punish her. But it punished Christian, too."

Jane rubbed his back, comforting him. Telling him with gentle caresses that it was okay. Or that it would be okay.

"You couldn't let Elizabeth's death go unpunished," she stated.

"But I hurt Christian."

Jane shook her head. "No. Lilah hurt him. You tried to protect him."

His chest tightened. She understood. She believed. And for the first time, he almost felt peace when he thought about his family.

"I love you," he told her.

She kissed him. "I love you, too." She moved her mouth to his neck, nibbling the skin just below his jawline.

She peeked up at him, giving him an impish grin. "Did I mention that I have these amazing new teeth?"

He smiled, amazed by how quickly she could make him feel content, happy.

"Really?"

She nodded. "Now lie back and let *me* bite *you*."

As he fell back against the pillows, and he waited for her to taste him, he decided undeath didn't get any better than this.

Epilogue

Jane lounged on the sofa with Rhys, his head in her lap. She lazily stroked his hair, letting the silky strands slip through her fingers. They both watched the flames dance over the logs of the fire.

"Do you think we will ever see Christian again?" she asked suddenly. Sebastian had told them about Christian's reaction to his attack on Jane, and they all agreed that he'd been changed by it. That he'd somehow broken free of Lilah's wicked bonds.

She felt the small shake of Rhys's head against her legs. "I don't know. I hope so. Lilah controlled him for so long, and he did a lot of horrible things at her bidding. That's going to take time to deal with."

"Poor Christian."

Rhys lifted his head to look at her. "I can't believe you can forgive him so easily."

Jane shrugged. "He regretted what he did."

"Almost too late."

"He needs our help—if he'll ever allow it."

Rhys smiled up at her, amused affection lighting his

amber eyes. "You may very well be the only Good Samaritan vampire in existence."

Jane stuck her tongue out at him. "And you are such an ogre yourself."

"I try."

Jane smiled. Rhys liked to pretend he was the same aloof, bitter vampire she'd first met, but in truth, he was honorable and good. And she liked to think, with some help from her, he was now happy and able to deal with the past.

Certainly, he laughed and teased more. She'd even caught him smiling occasionally for no apparent reason.

But she could hardly rib him about that, when she caught herself doing the very same thing. Life as a vampire wasn't nearly as unpleasant as movies and folklore had led the world to believe. Dr. Fowler's book was a much more accurate depiction of vampirism.

Her senses were keener, her thoughts clearer, and her ability to feel pleasure more powerful, although Rhys would likely take full credit for the last change.

Other than the blood thing, vampirism was really quite wonderful. And even the need for blood was less icky than she would have guessed. She and Rhys dined from blood banks. And while Sebastian found the idea disgusting, he did agree that it was better than the lowlifes Rhys used to feed on. Although, he did insist on calling their blood "gag in a bag."

Sebastian was a wanton biter.

Jane only had fangs for Rhys.

"What are you smiling about?" Rhys asked.

Jane's smile broadened. "I'm just thinking about how happy I am."

"Good."

"Are you happy?"

He sat up and turned to face her, his eyes intense. "Janie, you've given me something I thought I'd lost forever. My soul." He picked up her hand and kissed the palm.

Jane sighed; she'd never tire of his touch.

He hooked an arm around her waist and lifted her onto his lap. She curled her arms around his neck, sinking into his unhurried kiss.

They'd given each other more than either of them ever expected to have, Jane realized. They'd given each other lives. Lives filled with love.

A cough sounded from the vicinity of the door, but neither broke their kiss. A cough rang out again, this time louder, and even though Jane realized they should stop, she was powerless under the mastery of Rhys's skillful lips.

"Hello?" Sebastian called.

Finally, they broke off the kiss and looked at him.

"I have some good news for you."

They both waited for Sebastian to continue. "You will be pleased to know the banns were finally called, and the vicar is here."

He stood back, and Dr. No, or whoever he was, strolled into the room.

Both Jane and Rhys gave the two men dubious looks.

"It turns out, David, who isn't really a doctor, does have the ability to marry you two," Sebastian informed them.

"Yep, all legal and everything. Got ordained over the Internet," David stated proudly. "Wanna get hitched?"

Jane and Rhys looked at each other and laughed. Sebastian joined in. Only David/Dr. No seemed confused by their mirth.

But later that night, after Jane and Rhys had made love, and he held her in his arms, he slipped a small gold band on her finger.

"My mother's ring," she said, surprised.

He nodded. "I found them back in the alley."

He held out her father's ring to her.

She took it and slipped the large band onto his finger.

"To R—Yours forever. J.," she said, reciting the inscription on the ring. The initials that stood for her father, Robert, and her mother, Julia. But that now stood for Rhys and Jane.

"Forever," Rhys agreed, and kissed her.

If you enjoyed this Kathy Love book,
you won't want to miss any of her books
on the other Young family members,
available from Brava!
Turn the page for a titillating taste . . .

FANGS BUT NO FANGS

There's Nothing Uglier Than a Vampire Singing "Feelings"

If I hadn't seen it for myself, I'd swear it couldn't be true: my brother, Christian, living in a trailer park in some backwater town, working at a karaoke bar. We're talking about Christian, the cultured, the refined, the snobby—the guy who'd probably sniff the plasma packets and send 'em back in a huff if the blood type wasn't the right vintage. But after centuries of living in the undead fast lane, he's made up his mind that this is exactly where he needs to spend the rest of eternity, atoning for his many, many, sins. It's a self-imposed purgatory complete with lawn ornaments and blaring country music.

But sometimes things just don't work out like you think they will. Sometimes your hell can turn into your heaven. And thanks to Christian's chatty neighbor and boss, Jolee, things seem to be getting a whole lot nicer in Shady Fork Mobile Estates. Not that either of them has the first idea how to have a normal relationship—we are talking about a woman who's only dated deadbeats, and a guy who's only dated the dead. Nobody's perfect.

Still, it's a start for Mr. Rebel Vamp Without a Cause. And fortunately he still has me, Rhys Young, and our younger brother, Sebastian, to help him. We plan to show Christian that everyone deserves a second chance, and winning his beer-slinging, country-singing beauty is a great beginning.

She hadn't hurt him, but something about this woman was addling his brain. What the hell was he thinking finding her attractive? He didn't find mortals attractive. Ever.

She regarded him closely, and he wondered for a moment if he was vamping out in some way. Had his irises widened, making his eyes totally black? Or had his skin pulled taut over his bones? Was a fang hanging out of the corner of his mouth?

Not that she looked frightened. She actually looked . . . concerned?

He was, too. His reactions were not normal.

She dabbed at his arm again, her touch even gentler. Little raspy caresses of the towel, which felt . . . nice. Yes, he was definitely acting, or rather reacting, strangely.

He took in another deep breath to steady himself. A rich, spicy scent like warm honey and cinnamon filled his nostrils. Her scent. His body reacted, his muscles tensing, his fingers twitching. What the hell?

Were his vampy powers coming back? He'd truly believed he had them under control, practically ineffectual. But his acute sense of smell was working fine. Although the scent he smelled wasn't the rusty, salty scent of blood. The heat and spices were just her.

But what caught him more off guard than her scent was his reaction to it. He was aroused. And he'd never been aroused by a mortal unless it was caused by the hunger.

"There," she said, shifting away from him. "All clean."

He immediately stepped back, hoping distance would calm him. This was just too strange.

I ONLY HAVE FANGS FOR YOU

Bite Me

One thing you have to know about my brother Sebastian: he loves being a vampire. After all, what's not to love? He's eternally twenty-five. He's single, and frankly, he's a chick magnet. Yeah, undeath is good. The only thing he's serious about is his nightclub, Carfax Abbey. It's the sort of dark, happening spot where vampires can really let their fangs down. You know, hiding in the shadows, feeding, giving pleasure to unsuspecting mortals, being all cool and vampirey. Whatever. My brother Rhys and I have tried to get Sebastian to clean up his bad-boy ways like we did, but then he went and called us "fang-whipped." Okay, Bite Boy, chew on this . . .

The ultimate righteous reformer, Wilhelmina Weiss, is on a mission to shut down Carfax Abbey. She doesn't approve of my bro's biting ways. It seems the spirited, sexy-without-knowing-it vampire is working undercover as a cocktail waitress in his bar while waging a secret war to bring him down. Sebastian's A-positive he can convince Miss Goody-Vampire-Two-Fangs that nothing beats the ecstasy of a good vampire bite. She's certain she can resist him for as long as it takes to reform him. I gotta tell you, the suspense would kill me—if I weren't already undead.

Now, Mr. "Has anyone ever told you you've got a beautiful neck?" is in way over his. He's finally met a girl who may not be his type, but she's way more than his match. Not that he's (cough) fang-whipped (cough) or anything. No, not my baby bro. One thing's for sure, I've never seen Sebastian so completely at someone's mercy in my life. And frankly, I'm enjoying every minute of it . . .

"Why do you have such a low opinion of me?" She didn't answer or look at him, instead she moved down another step. He stepped onto the same one, their bodies forced to face each other in the narrow stairwell. But he made sure not to touch her.

"Tell me," he demanded with more force than he intended, mainly because she still stared down at the steps instead of at him, and her reluctance to even look at him irritated him.

This time he kept his voice calmer as he pointed out, "You've only worked at Carfax Abbey for a couple weeks. What have I done in that time to give you this opinion of me?"

Still she didn't answer. More fear encircled them. Something about that fear bothered him. It was different, sharper, more desperate than any fear he'd felt before. Why?

"Better yet, why don't you tell me why you are so frightened of me?"

Her head snapped up, and she glared at him. "I'm not frightened of you."

He studied her for a minute, then sighed. "You know that's not true."

She straightened to her full height, which only brought her up to his chin, but her eyes focused on a point over his right shoulder.

"Mina—" he started, and her eyes snapped to his, narrowed and angry. Somehow he found that glare more bearable than the panic he'd seen there earlier.

"That's not my name," she stated.

He frowned, so they were back to this. "Your name is Wilhelmina, I know. But frankly, you don't look like a Wilhelmina to me. You look like a Mina. However, I'll gladly remember to call you by your full name if that will give you a higher opinion of me."

Her eyes searched his for a moment, then looked away again. "It won't."

He sighed. "No, I didn't think so."

They stood there for a moment, he watched her and she watched a point on the floor.

"Why are you so scared of me?" he asked softly.

She shifted away as if she planned to move down a step and then bolt. He couldn't let that happen, not before he understood what had brought on this outburst.

"Mi—Wilhelmina, talk to me." He placed a hand on the wall, blocking her escape down the stairs.

She glared at him with more anger and more of that uncomfortable fear.

"You can bully your mortal conquests," she said, her voice low. "But you can't bully me."

Sebastian sighed. "My earlier behavior to the contrary, I don't want to bully you. Or anyone."

"You can't seduce me, either," she informed him.

"I don't . . ." Seduce her? Was that what all this was about?

"Do you want me to seduce you?" he asked with a curious smile. Maybe that was the cause for her crazy outburst. She *was* jealous.

She laughed, the sound abrupt and harsh. "Hardly. I just told you that I *didn't* want you to seduce me."

"No," he said slowly. "You told me I *can't*. That sounds like a challenge."

Irritation flared from her, blotting out some of the fear. "Believe me, I'm *so* not interested."

He raised an eyebrow at her disdain. "Then why do you care about me being with that blonde?"

"That blonde?" she said. "Is hair color the way you identify all your women? It's got to be a confusing system, as so many of them are bound to have the same names."

He studied her for a minute, noting that just a faint flush colored her very pale cheeks

"Are you sure you don't want me to seduce you?" he asked again, because as far as he could tell, there was no other reason for her to care about the identification system for his women.

She growled in irritation, the sound raspy and appealing in a way it shouldn't have been.

Sebastian blinked. He needed to stay focused. This woman thought he was a jerk; that shouldn't be a draw for him.

"Why did you say those things?" he asked. "What have I done to make you think I'm so terrible?"

Her jaw set again, and her midnight eyes locked with his. "Are you going to deny that you're narcissistic?"

He frowned. "Yes. I'm confident maybe, but no, I'm not a narcissist."

MY SISTER IS A WEREWOLF

Bad Moon Rising

Elizabeth Young's brothers think they have it rough as vampires? Ha! Two words for them: unwanted hair. What werewolf Elizabeth craves is a normal life with a husband, kids, and less shaving. Unfortunately the vaccine she's researched isn't working yet. Worse, she's in heat—and soon every dangerous wolf pack from miles around will be at her door. To buy time, she needs to have sex, and often, with the first human male she can find . . .

Veterinarian Jensen Adler just meant to drown his sorrows, until a stunning, leather-clad brunette made him an offer he couldn't refuse. Now he's caught up in something really weird, definitely dangerous, and okay, extremely hot. So his new girlfriend's hiding something (and she's a little freaky about the moon), but Jensen knows true love when he feels it, and this time, he's not giving up . . . no matter how hairy things get.

"You saw me watching you." Her words were a statement, but he felt the need to respond.

"Yes."

"You liked it." Her fingers grazed his cheek, his jaw, the side of his neck.

He thought to deny it, to put a stop to this right now. But the words wouldn't come.

"I wanted you from the moment I saw you," she murmured, her voice low, husky. And so sexy.

He'd wanted her, too—he couldn't refute it. He looked into her pale eyes, a blue so light they were the color of the moonstones. Her dark hair swirled around her face, adding to the feminine beauty of her features. High cheekbones, a pointed chin. And her lips. So pink and wide that they should have overpowered her delicate features. Instead they looked unbearably sexy, utterly kissable.

Before he realized what he intended to do, his mouth was on hers, tasting her with a greed he couldn't restrain. She responded in kind, her mouth opening to let him in, their tongues tangling. The kiss grew into a frenzy. He wanted to devour her, each brush of their lips, each sweep of their tongues firing his need more, until he couldn't remember wanting anything more than this woman.

Romantic Suspense from
Lisa Jackson

See How She Dies
0-8217-7605-3 $6.99US/$9.99CAN

The Morning After
0-8217-7295-3 $6.99US/$9.99CAN

The Night Before
0-8217-6936-7 $6.99US/$9.99CAN

Cold Blooded
0-8217-6934-0 $6.99US/$9.99CAN

Hot Blooded
0-8217-6841-7 $6.99US/$8.99CAN

If She Only Knew
0-8217-6708-9 $6.50US/$8.50CAN

Unspoken
0-8217-6402-0 $6.50US/$8.50CAN

Twice Kissed
0-8217-6038-6 $5.99US/$6.99CAN

Whispers
0-8217-7603-7 $6.99US/$9.99CAN

Wishes
0-8217-6309-1 $5.99US/$6.99CAN

Deep Freeze
0-8217-7296-1 $7.99US/$10.99CAN

Final Scream
0-8217-7712-2 $7.99US/$10.99CAN

Fatal Burn
0-8217-7577-4 $7.99US/$10.99CAN

Shiver
0-8217-7578-2 $7.99US/$10.99CAN

Available Wherever Books Are Sold!
Visit our website at **www.kensingtonbooks.com**

Thrilling Suspense from
Beverly Barton

Available Wherever Books Are Sold!

Visit our website at **www.kensingtonbooks.com**